THE DISAPPEARANCE OF
ADÈLE BEDEAU

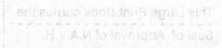

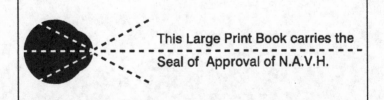

This Large Print Book carries the
Seal of Approval of N.A.V.H.

THE DISAPPEARANCE OF ADÈLE BEDEAU

A HISTORICAL THRILLER BY RAYMOND BRUNET

Translated and with an afterword by

GRAEME MACRAE BURNET

THORNDIKE PRESS
A part of Gale, a Cengage Company

Farmington Hills, Mich • San Francisco • New York • Waterville, Maine
Meriden, Conn • Mason, Ohio • Chicago

**LIBRARY OF CONGRESS CIP DATA ON FILE.
CATALOGUING IN PUBLICATION FOR THIS BOOK
IS AVAILABLE FROM THE LIBRARY OF CONGRESS**

ISBN-13: 978-1-4328-5158-3 (hardcover)

Published in 2018 by arrangement with Skyhorse Publishing, Inc.

Printed in Mexico
1 2 3 4 5 6 7 22 21 20 19 18

CONTENTS

ONE

It was an evening like any other at the Restaurant de la Cloche. Behind the counter, the proprietor, Pasteur, had poured himself a *pastis,* an indication that no more meals would be served and that any further service would be provided by his wife, Marie, and the waitress, Adèle. It was nine o'clock.

Manfred Baumann was at his usual place by the bar. Lemerre, Petit and Cloutier sat around the table by the door, the day's newspapers folded in a pile between them. On their table was a carafe of red wine, three tumblers, two packets of cigarettes, an ashtray and Lemerre's reading glasses. They would share three carafes before the night was out. Pasteur opened his newspaper on the counter and leaned over it on his elbows. He was developing a bald patch, which he attempted to disguise by combing back his hair. Marie busied herself sorting cutlery.

7

Adèle served coffee to the two remaining diners and began wiping the waxcloths of the other tables, pushing the crumbs onto the floor that she would later sweep. Manfred observed her. His place was not exactly at the bar, but at the hatch through which food was brought from the kitchen. He continually had to adjust his position to allow the staff to pass, but nobody ever thought to ask him to move. From his post he could survey the restaurant and strangers often mistook him for the proprietor.

Adèle was wearing a short black skirt and a white blouse. Around her waist was a little apron with a pocket in which she kept a notebook for taking orders and the cloth she used for wiping tables. She was a dark, heavy-set girl with a wide behind and large, weighty breasts. She had full lips, an olive complexion and brown eyes, which she habitually kept trained on the floor. Her features were too heavy to be described as pretty, but there was an earthy magnetism about her, a magnetism no doubt amplified by the drabness of the surroundings.

As she leant over the unoccupied tables, Manfred turned towards the counter and, in the mirror above the bar, watched her skirt inch up her thighs. She was wearing tan tights with white ankle socks and black pumps. The three men at the table by the door also observed her; undoubtedly, Manfred imagined, harbouring similar thoughts to his own.

Adèle was nineteen years old and had been working at the Restaurant de la Cloche for five or six months. She was a sullen girl, reluctant to engage in conversation with the regulars, yet Manfred was sure she enjoyed their attention. She kept her blouse loosely fastened, so that it was often possible to see the lace edging of her brassiere. If she did not wish them to stare, why dress in such a provocative manner?

All the same, when she turned towards the bar, Manfred averted his eyes.

Pasteur was staring at an article in the middle pages of *L'Alsace*. There was a crisis in Lebanon.

'Bloody Arabs,' said Manfred.

Pasteur gave a little snort through his nose to acknowledge the remark. He was not one to engage in controversial discussions over the bar. His duties were limited to pouring drinks and issuing bills. He regarded waiting tables as beneath his dignity. Such chores, along with the dispensing of pleasantries, were left to Marie and Adèle or whoever else was working. Manfred, for his part, had no particular opinion on the situation in the Middle East. He had made the remark only because he had thought it was the sort of thing Pasteur might have said, or which would at least have met with his approval. Manfred was quite happy with Pasteur's unwillingness to engage in chit-chat. When he did pass a remark now and again, it tended to fall flat and it was a relief not to feel obliged to make conversation.

At the table by the door, Lemerre, a barber whose shop was not far from the restaurant, was holding forth on the subject of the milking cycle of dairy cows. He was explaining at some length how the yield could be increased merely by milking the cattle at shorter intervals. Cloutier, who had been brought up on a farm, attempted to interject that any gains made by such a measure were lost in the long term by shortening the milk-bearing life of the cows. Lemerre shook his head vigorously and made a gesture with his hand to quieten his companion.

'A common misconception,' he said, before continuing with his lecture. Cloutier stared at the table and fidgeted with the stem of his glass. Lemerre was a corpulent man in his early fifties. He was wearing a burgundy V-neck sweater over a black polo neck. His trousers were hiked halfway up his belly and secured with a thin leather belt. His hair, which Manfred assumed he dyed, was jet black and combed back from his forehead, revealing a pronounced widow's peak. Petit and Cloutier were both married, but they rarely made reference to their wives and when they did so it was always in the same deprecating terms. Lemerre had never married. 'I don't believe in keeping animals in the house,' was his customary explanation.

From outside, the Restaurant de la Cloche of Saint-Louis was an unremarkable place. The pale yellow render on the exterior walls was stained and chipped. The sign on the wall above the windows was unenticing, but the restaurant's central location made promotion redundant. The door to the restaurant was on a corner adjacent to a car park in which the town's weekly market was held. On the wall next to the door was a blackboard on which the day's specials were written, and above this a small balcony with an ornate wrought iron balustrade. The balcony belonged to the apartment in which Pasteur and his wife lived. Inside, the restaurant was surprisingly spacious. The decor was unpretentious. Two wide pillars divided the room, informally separating the dining area on the right of the door from the tables by the window where locals dropped in during the day for a quick glass, or spent the evening drinking and exchanging views on the contents of the day's newspapers. The dining area was furnished with fifteen or so rickety wooden tables covered with brightly coloured waxcloths and set with cutlery and tumblers. On the wall behind the counter, partially obscured by a glass shelf of liqueur bottles, was a large mirror advertising Alsace beer, its art deco lettering chipped and barely legible in places. This mirror created the illusion that the restaurant was bigger than it was. It also gave the place an air of faded grandeur. Marie often grumbled that it looked shabby, but Pasteur insisted that it gave the place charm. 'We're not running a Paris bistro,' was his habitual response to any suggestion of upgrading. On the wall to the right of the counter were the doors to the toilets, flanked by two hulking dark wood dressers used to store cutlery, glasses and crockery. The dressers had been there as long as anyone could remember. Certainly they predated Pasteur's ownership of the establishment.

Manfred Baumann was thirty-six years old. He was dressed tonight, as he was every night, in a black suit and white shirt with a tie loosened at the neck. His dark hair was neatly cut and parted to one side. He was a good-looking man, but his eyes shifted nervously as if he was trying to avoid eye contact. Consequently, people often felt ill at ease in his company and this served to reinforce his own awkwardness. Once a month, on Wednesday afternoon when the bank where he worked was closed, Manfred went to Lemerre's shop to have his hair cut. Without fail Lemerre asked him what he would like done and Manfred would reply, 'The usual'. As he cut Manfred's hair, Lemerre engaged in small talk about the weather or uncontroversial subjects from the day's papers and when Manfred left, he would bid him goodbye with the phrase 'Until Thursday'.

Yet not three hours later, Lemerre would be sitting at his table with Petit and Cloutier and Manfred would be standing at his place at the counter of the Restaurant de la Cloche. They would acknowledge each other, but no more so than if they were strangers happening to make eye contact. On Thursdays, however, Manfred was invited to join the three men in the weekly game of bridge. Manfred did not particularly enjoy playing cards and the atmosphere was invariably strained. It seemed to Manfred that his presence at their table made the others uncomfortable, yet to turn down their invitation would be interpreted as a snub. The tradition had begun three years previously after the death of Le Fevre. The Thursday after the funeral the three friends were short of a man to make up their four and asked Manfred to join them. He was aware that he was simply filling the dead man's shoes, and Lemerre's customary farewell of 'Until Thursday' made it clear that he was not welcome to join them on other evenings.

Manfred ordered his final glass of wine of the evening. A bottle was kept behind the bar for him and Pasteur drained the remaining contents into a fresh glass and placed it on the counter. Manfred always drank the whole bottle, but he ordered by the glass. This arrangement meant that he paid twice as much for his drinks than if he simply ordered the bottle, but out of habit he never did. Once, he had calculated how much he would save over the course of the year if he were to change his practice. It had been a sizeable amount, but he stuck to his routine. He told himself that it was coarse to stand alone at the bar with a bottle. It would suggest that he came in with the intention of getting drunk, not that that would concern the other patrons of the restaurant. Manfred also felt that this habit might account for Lemerre and his friends' reserved attitude towards him, as if by ordering by the glass he was setting himself above the three men who drank carafes. It gave the impression that he thought he was better than them. This was in fact true.

Pasteur never remarked on Manfred's drinking habits. Why should he? It was no skin off his nose if Manfred wanted to pay twice as much as necessary for his wine.

As the clock ticked towards ten o'clock, Adèle became more animated in her movements. She swept around the tables with something approaching gusto, and even exchanged some sort of joke with the men by the door. Lemerre made a remark, which must have been lewd, because Adèle playfully wagged an admonishing finger at him, before turning on her heel and sashaying back towards the bar. Manfred had never seen her behave in this flirtatious fashion before, but she still lowered her eyes as he stepped back to allow her to pass through the hatch. She disappeared into the back and returned a few minutes later. She was wearing the same skirt as before, but had changed into black tights and high heels, and was now wearing a denim jacket over a tight black top. She had applied mascara

15

and lipstick. She bid Pasteur goodnight. He glanced up at the clock and nodded a grudging farewell. Adèle appeared unaware of the impact of her transformation on the remaining patrons of the bar. She glanced neither left nor right as she made her exit.

Manfred drained the remains of his wine and put the money on the pewter salver upon which Pasteur had placed his bill a few moments before. Manfred always made sure he had the precise amount in his pocket. If he paid with a large note, it meant waiting for Pasteur to rummage in his pocketbook for change, and then having to ostentatiously leave a tip.

Manfred put on his raincoat, which had been hanging on the hat-stand next to the door to the WC, and left with a curt nod to Lemerre and his cronies. It was the beginning of September and the first autumnal chill was in the air. The streets of Saint-Louis were deserted. As he turned the corner into Rue de Mulhouse, he spotted Adèle a hundred metres or so ahead. She was walking slowly and Manfred found himself catching up with her. He could hear the clacking of her heels on the pavement. Manfred slowed his pace — he could hardly stride past her without making some kind of greeting and this would lead to them falling into inevitably awkward conversation. Perhaps Adèle would think he had followed her. Or perhaps her flirtatious display in the restaurant had actually been for his benefit and she had deliberately walked in this direction to contrive a meeting.

No matter how much he slowed his pace, Manfred continued to gain ground. The closer he got, the slower Adèle seemed to become. At one point, she stopped and, steadying herself on a lamppost, adjusted the ankle-strap of her shoe. Manfred was now barely twenty metres behind her. He bent down and pretended to tie his shoelace. He hunched his head over his knee, hoping that Adèle would not spot him. He listened to the clack of her heels on the pavement grow fainter. When he looked up she was no longer in sight. She must have turned off or entered a building.

Manfred resumed his normal brisk pace. Then, as he approached the little park in front of the Protestant temple, he saw Adèle standing by the low wall that separated the park from the pavement. She was smoking a cigarette and appeared to be waiting for someone. By the time Manfred spotted her it was too late to take evasive action. He contemplated crossing the street, in which case a brief wave would constitute adequate acknowledgement of his passing, but Adèle had already seen him and was watching him approach. Manfred was not drunk, but, under her scrutiny, he suddenly felt a little unsteady on his feet. It crossed his mind that she might be waiting for him, but he immediately dismissed the thought.

'Good evening, Adèle,' he said when he was a few metres away. He stopped, not because he wanted to, but because it would have seemed rude to walk straight past as if she was a mere waitress unworthy of a few pleasantries.

'Good evening, Manfred,' she replied.

Until that moment Manfred was not even aware that she knew his first name. And for her to use it suggested some familiarity between them. In the restaurant, she had only ever addressed him as Monsieur Baumann. Had he even detected a flirtatious tone in her voice?

'It's chilly,' Manfred said, because he could think of nothing else.

'Yes,' said Adèle. With her free hand she pulled her jacket closed over her chest, either to attest to Manfred's remark or to conceal her cleavage.

There was a pause. 'Of course, it's always cooler at night when the sky is clear,' Manfred continued. 'The clouds act as insulation. They trap the heat, just like a blanket on a bed.'

Adèle looked at him for a moment and then nodded slowly. She blew a smoke ring. Manfred regretted mentioning bed. He could feel the colour rising to his cheeks.

'Are you waiting for someone?' he asked when it became apparent that she was not going to add anything. It was none of his business what she was doing, but again he could think of nothing else to say. And what if she replied that, no, she wasn't waiting for anyone. What would he do then? Invite her to his apartment or to one of the bars in town that stayed open late and about which he knew nothing?

Before she had the chance to answer, and to Manfred's relief, a young man pulled up on a scooter. He nodded curtly in Manfred's direction. Manfred acknowledged him and bid goodnight to Adèle.

'Good night, monsieur,' she replied.

As he walked off, Manfred stole a glance over his shoulder in time to see Adèle throw her leg over the seat of the scooter. He imagined the young man asking who he was. *Some guy from the restaurant,* would be her likely response.

Manfred lived ten minutes' walk away, on the top floor of a four-storey 1960s apart-

19

ment block set back from Rue de Mulhouse. The apartment consisted of a small kitchen, a bedroom, a living room that Manfred rarely used, and a small shower room. The kitchen overlooked a small leafy park surrounded by other similar apartment blocks. There were benches for the residents and a children's play park. There was a small balcony outside the kitchen window, which caught the sunlight in early evening, but Manfred rarely sat out for fear that the other residents might think he had an unhealthy interest in the play park below. People often thought ill of single men in their thirties, especially those who chose to keep themselves to themselves. Manfred kept his apartment scrupulously clean and tidy.

Once home, Manfred poured himself a nightcap from the bottle on the kitchen counter and knocked it back. He poured himself a second and took it with him to bed. He lifted the book from his bedside table, but did not open it. His encounter with Adèle had left him unsettled, excited even. It was not just she had used his first name, so much as the fact that when her companion arrived, she had reverted to 'monsieur', as if concerned to give the impression that there was nothing between them. Manfred had never thought there *was* anything between them, but she could easily have bid goodnight without using either form of address. It was a deliberate act to conceal the intimate moment they had shared from her boyfriend.

Manfred recalled the sight of Adèle tottering on the pavement in front of him, adjusting the ankle-strap of her shoe. He masturbated with greater vigour than usual and fell asleep without mopping up his emission.

TWO

Saint-Louis is a town of around twenty thousand people nestling at the very edge of the Alsace, separated from Germany and Switzerland by the width of the Rhine. It is a place of little note and aside from a handful of the picturesque oak-beamed houses characteristic of the region, there is little to detain visitors. Like most border towns, it is a place of transit. People pass through on their way elsewhere, and the town is so lacking in points of interest it is as if the townsfolk have resigned themselves to this. The brighter young people of Saint-Louis up and leave for college, most likely never to return.

The town centre, inasmuch as Saint-Louis can be said to have a centre, is a miscellany of unattractive post-war buildings peppered with a few more traditional dwellings that have survived the passage of time and town-planning. The signs above the shops are faded and the window displays are uninviting, as if the proprietors have abandoned the idea of attracting passing trade. The word that most often springs into the minds of those passing through, if they notice the town at all, is nondescript. Saint-Louis is nondescript.

Yet for three hundred years the town has sustained a population. It is a population somewhat less educated, less well-off and more inclined to the political right than the majority of their countrymen, but this mediocre tribe still requires, now and then, a new pair of shoes or an outfit of clothing, they need their hair cut, their teeth attended to and their ailments cured. They must withdraw and borrow money. They require places to eat, drink, gossip, or simply postpone returning home. Their streets must be cleaned, refuse collected, law and order must be kept. Their houses require the attention of plumbers, electricians, joiners, and decorators. Their children must be schooled, the aged nursed, and the dead buried.

In short, the people of Saint-Louis are exactly like people elsewhere, in towns equally drab or markedly more glamorous. And like the inhabitants of other places, the townsfolk of Saint-Louis feel a certain chauvinistic pride in their municipality, even as they retain an awareness of its mediocrity. Some dream of an escape, or live with the regret that they did not get out when they had the chance. The majority, though, go about their business with little or no thought to their surroundings.

Manfred Baumann was born on the Swiss side of the border to a Swiss father and a French mother. Gottwald Baumann was a brewery worker from Basel. He was a short, exceptionally swarthy man with a glint in his eye. Manfred's mother, Anaïs Paliard, was a high-spirited girl cursed with a sickly constitution, from a well-to-do Saint-Louis family of lawyers. Manfred spent the first six years of his life in Basel. He remembered little of these years, yet Swiss-German remained the language with which he felt most at home. He had hardly spoken it since his early childhood, but hearing it still transported him to those hazy early years. Manfred had only two memories of his father from this period of his life. The first was of the rancid smell that emanated from him when he returned from an evening at some bar, coupled with the bristle of his stubbled chin as he leaned over to kiss him goodnight.

The second was Manfred's fondest memory of his father. For reasons he could not remember (perhaps it was his birthday), Gottwald took Manfred to visit the brewery where he worked. Manfred could recall the heady aroma of yeast and the thunder of empty barrels being rolled across cobbles. The other brewery workers were, at least in Manfred's memory, short, swarthy, barrel-chested men, just like his father, who walked with their legs apart and their arms swinging outwards. As Gottwald led Manfred through the yard, the men spotted their workmate and shouted, *'Grüezi Gottli.'*

'You know what that means?' Gottwald had asked. 'Little God. Not bad, eh? *Little God.'* Manfred gripped tight on his father's hand and looked forward to the day when he too would work in the brewery.

When Manfred was six years old, the Restaurant de la Cloche came up for sale and Anaïs's father purchased it for his daughter and her husband to run. The restaurant's town centre location guaranteed a steady stream of trade from nearby shopkeepers and office workers, so, although evening meals were served, the bulk of its business was done during the day. M. Paliard must have thought that he was setting up his son-in-law in a failsafe venture, but he had reckoned without his son-in-law's brewery worker manners and rudimentary grasp of the French language. Gottwald's surly demeanour succeeded in alienating the establishment's clientele. He lacked the graceful manner and authority of the successful *patron*. As the business slid into decline, Gottwald spent every night on the wrong side of the bar, noisily decrying the stuck-up French who had taken their trade elsewhere.

After his father's death, the business was sold, but Manfred and his mother continued to live in the apartment above the restaurant until her delicate health obliged them to move back to the family home on the northern outskirts of the town. Manfred missed living above the bar; the smell of cooking and the sound of the day's debate drifting through the open window as he and his mother ate their evening meal. The bar was the hub of the town. At the family home, Manfred was isolated. To his grandparents, he was less a source of pride than a reminder of their daughter's lapse. Manfred inherited his father's graceless demeanour and his mother's sickly constitution, both of which mitigated against falling into friendship with the ease of other boys. When they had lived above the bar, older men greeted him cheerfully when he returned home from school as if he was one of them. At week-ends, he would run errands for the regulars, earning a few centimes for his trouble. In the evenings, he would sit at the window above the bar listening to the ebb and flow of conversation, mentally contributing his own sage remarks. At the Paliard house there were no voices to listen to, and Man-fred would sit in his room listening to the slow ticking of the grandfather clock that stood on the landing halfway up the stairs.

Throughout his schooldays Manfred was known as 'Swiss' and the nickname had stuck. He loathed it. Lemerre still used it when inviting Manfred to join the Thursday card game. 'You joining us, Swiss?' he yelled across the bar. Manfred wished his mother had reverted to her maiden name but, despite her husband's shortcomings, she remained devoted to his memory. After Manfred and his mother were obliged to leave the Restaurant de la Cloche, Anaïs would often call him to her bedside. Man-fred disliked the smell of his mother's room. It was like a hospital. The dressing table was arrayed with brown bottles of pills. Towards the end, the doctor visited on an almost daily basis, a privilege afforded to families of the Paliard's standing. When Manfred entered the room, Anaïs would smile wearily and hold out her arm. Often she was too weak to raise her shoulders from the pillows that supported her. Manfred sat on the edge of the bed holding his mother's hand.

Anaïs kept a photograph of Gottwald by her bedside. He was standing next to a motor car parked in a lay-by on a twisting road high in the Swiss mountains. The car was a Mercedes that Anaïs's father had lent them for their honeymoon. Gottwald stood in his shirtsleeves, hands on his hips, chest puffed out, his thick dark hair slicked back in the style of the day, a study in virility.

Anaïs liked to tell Manfred the story of how she and his father had met. Gottwald had crossed the border for the Bastille Day celebrations. There was a fête in the square next to the Restaurant de la Cloche. It was an unusually hot day, even for July. Anaïs was seventeen. She and a friend wandered round the stalls sampling the wares on offer. They had drunk two or three glasses of rough cider, which had gone straight to their heads. Anaïs's friend, Elisabeth, spotted Gottwald. He was standing at a stall, drinking a glass of beer, and blatantly appraising the girls who walked by. Elisabeth insisted that they go over and talk to him. Anaïs was reluctant. She had no experience with men, but Elisabeth was already on her way. She stood shyly at her friend's shoulder as she introduced them. Gottwald kissed their hands and said, *'Enchanté, mesdemoiselles,'* in a heavy accent that made them both giggle. Soon they were strolling through the crowds together, Elisabeth gaily telling Gottwald all about herself. She was a striking, self-confident girl who, Anaïs suspected, had already had her share of men. Anaïs studied Gottwald closely. He was not handsome in the conventional way — he was too short for that — but there was something in his demeanour and in his twinkling black eyes that fascinated her. It was clear that Gottwald did not understand half of what Elisabeth was saying, but he kept his eyes intensely fixed on her. Anaïs found herself wishing that her friend would stop wittering so that Gottwald could turn his gaze on her.

They paused at a stall and Gottwald bought them each another cider. Elisabeth had to excuse herself for a moment. As soon as she was gone, Gottwald looked Anaïs straight in the eye and said, 'I'm glad she's gone. She talks too much, but I'd like to see you again.'

Anaïs felt a quickening in her throat. The idea that this swarthy foreigner preferred her to her more beautiful, charming friend

29

was intoxicating. Before she knew it, she had agreed to meet Gottwald the following day. Nothing was said when Elisabeth returned.

That next day Gottwald and Anaïs went for a walk in the woods. It was cool beneath the foliage. They didn't talk much. Anaïs had no idea what to say to a man, but before the afternoon was out, Gottwald kissed her. She had her back to a tree and felt overwhelmed by the weight and powerful odour of the man. She almost fainted with passion, she told Manfred. The relationship continued in secret — Gottwald was not the sort of man Anaïs would dream of introducing to her father — until it became impossible to conceal. That was when Gottwald asked her to marry him.

Anaïs finally died when Manfred was fifteen. She had not left the house for two years and had grown as thin and papery as an old woman. Manfred's grandfather came to talk to him one evening shortly after the funeral. At a certain age, he explained, a man had to make his own way in the world. Two years later, after Manfred had failed his *baccalauréat,* his grandfather summoned him to his study. This was a room on the first floor of the house which Manfred was normally forbidden to enter. The walls were

lined from floor to ceiling with legal volumes
and in the centre of the floor was a large
antique desk. There was a fireplace, but
M. Paliard did not approve of unnecessary
heating and even in the depths of winter he
refused, as an example to the other members
of the household, to light a fire, preferring
to sit over his papers bundled in a hat and
scarf in a fug of frosted breath and pipe
smoke. Manfred was summoned to the
study only to discuss matters of grave im-
port.

Upon entering, Manfred remained standing in the centre of the room for a good five
minutes while his grandfather reached the
end of the document he was reading. This
did not trouble Manfred. It was a matter of
indifference to him how his grandfather
treated him. M. Paliard removed his reading glasses and indicated with a gesture of
his hand that Manfred should sit. He had a
long, craggy face, with narrow pale blue
eyes set under a heavy forehead. He was
almost completely bald and had a wiry grey
beard. Manfred had difficulty recalling an
occasion on which he had seen him smile.

'I have spoken to an associate of mine, a
Monsieur Jeantet,' he began without preamble. 'Jeantet is the manager of Société Générale on Rue de Mulhouse. He has agreed

to take you on, which, under the circumstances, is most charitable of him. You begin on Monday and will be paid after two weeks. I suggest you begin looking for an apartment right away. I will loan you the first month's rent and deposit.'

At the end of his little speech, M. Paliard did something he had never done before. He rose from his seat and poured two small glasses of sherry from a decanter sitting on a silver tray in the window recess. Manfred had never noticed the decanter there before and wondered if his grandfather had had it brought in specially for the occasion. Not only had Manfred never been invited to share a drink with his grandfather, he had never seen him pour a drink for himself. Normally the maid would be summoned for such tasks. Nevertheless, M. Paliard not only poured the drinks, but handed Manfred's to him, before resuming his seat. The two men (for the gesture was clearly intended to mark Manfred's passing into manhood) sipped their sherry in silence. Ten minutes later, M. Paliard stood up to, somewhat awkwardly, indicate that the audience was over.

The following day, Manfred's grandmother took him to Mulhouse to be fitted for a suit. As the tailor fussed around with his measuring tape, Mme Paliard insisted, to Manfred's embarrassment, that the suit should leave some room for growth. Nevertheless, Manfred took some pleasure in the experience. Wearing a suit bestowed gravitas. The image that looked back at him from the tailor's mirror was not the gauche schoolboy he so despised. Afterwards they went for lunch in a smart bistro. Mme Paliard chatted cheerfully through the meal about what a splendid opportunity his new job was. Manfred knew that in reality she was disappointed in him, but he said nothing to contradict her. They shared a bottle of wine, something they would never have done if Manfred's grandfather had been present, and at the end of the meal Mme Paliard burst into tears and told Manfred that he must still come to the house for his meals whenever he wished and that his room would always be there for him. Manfred was fond of his grandmother and pitied her being left alone with his grandfather. He thanked her and promised to visit regularly.

When Manfred arrived at the bank on Monday morning, M. Jeantet immediately ushered him into his office. He was a round man with a red face and mutton chop whiskers. He wore an old-fashioned herringbone suit over a moth-eaten green cardigan. M. Jeantet cultivated an air of genial bonhomie. He greeted his clients with a vigorous handshake and much backslapping and fussed over them like long-lost friends. He habitually patted the female members of staff on the behind and enjoyed making saucy insinuations about their appearance or how they spent their weekends. This he did without discrimination of age or beauty, no doubt to avoid offending anyone he left out. At first Manfred was surprised at the good humour with which his new colleagues tolerated this behaviour, but he soon realised that behind his back they had any number of unflattering nicknames for the boss. It was difficult to believe that Manfred's grandfather regarded this man as an 'associate'.

Jeantet guided Manfred into his office by the elbow and towards two leather armchairs, uttering a series of proclamations about how delighted he was to have such a bright young man on board.

'Sit down, my boy, sit down,' he exhorted. 'That's a fine suit you're wearing. A little loose if I may say, but that's the way you young chaps are wearing them these days. I'm old-fashioned myself, or so my wife tells me. But I say quality never goes out of style, eh? What do you say? Ha ha.'

'Certainly,' said Manfred.

'Now, this occasion calls for a drink, don't you think?' And despite the fact that it was not yet nine o'clock the bank manager reached for a decanter on the table between them. He poured out two generous measures and toasted to a long and fruitful relationship. Manfred sipped his drink, feeling that he was being initiated into an archaic society of sherry drinkers.

'It's important to cement relationships,' Jeantet went on. 'That's something you'll learn. I've got much to teach you — running a bank isn't about money, no, not at all. It's about people.' He paused and gave Manfred a meaningful look to underline the point.

Then quite suddenly, as if a cloud had crossed his face, Jeantet put down his glass and sat back in his armchair, clasping his hands across his belly. Manfred too put down his glass.

'Now,' he said in an altogether more sombre tone, 'your grandfather — a fine man — has told me that you have failed your *baccalauréat*. That is not something to be applauded and normally I would not consider taking on a member of staff whom I did not consider to be up to scratch in the old brain department.' Here he tapped the side of his forehead. 'However, your grandfather has assured me that you are a bright young man, and I am prepared to take him at his word. I trust you will repay the faith I am showing in you.'

He nodded seriously and then, to indicate that he had said his piece, once again took up his glass.

'Academic qualifications are all very well, but what matters in life is hard work and a keen eye for human behaviour. I myself am an avid observer of the human animal. I'm not going to lie, you've landed on your feet with me. Observe and learn, and you'll go far.'

He leaned in over the table and indicated that Manfred should do the same, before continuing in a stage whisper. 'Between you and me, I plan to retire in a few years. Those mangy old bags out there,' he jabbed his thumb towards the door, 'haven't got two brain cells between them. That's monkey work out there. All they're interested in is gossiping and picking up their pay cheque at the end of the month. But a bright young man in a good suit like yourself, if you play your cards right, you could be sitting in my place in just a few years. Now, what do you think of that, my boy?'

Manfred resisted the temptation to tell him that he would rather throw himself into the Rhine than spend one minute more than necessary working in the Saint-Louis branch of Société Générale.

'I'm very grateful for the opportunity,' he said.

That same day Manfred made inquiries about the apartment above the Restaurant de la Cloche, but it was occupied by the new proprietor and his wife. He then, as a temporary measure, took the apartment off Rue de Mulhouse.

THREE

Thursday was market day. At half past twelve the Restaurant de la Cloche was thronging with people. Manfred recognised most of the customers and acknowledged those who spotted him with a nod or a silently mouthed 'good day'. That was the extent of his interaction with his fellow regulars. Among those who lunched daily at La Cloche, there was, like railway commuters, a tacit understanding of the boundaries of communication. Manfred took his place at the table in the corner that Marie had reserved for him. The menu rotated on a weekly basis and offered a choice of two starters, two main courses and a special followed by dessert or coffee. In almost twenty years the daily menus had never varied. Thursday's special was *pot-au-feu*. Approximately once a month, Manfred made a joke to Pasteur about changing the menu. 'Do you see a suggestion box around here?'

the proprietor invariably responded.

Adèle appeared at Manfred's table to take his order. He felt inexplicably excited to see her.

'Hello, Adèle.' He attempted to make eye contact with her, seeking some acknowledgement of what had passed between them the previous night.

'Monsieur,' Adèle replied blankly. She did not raise her eyes from her notebook and she recited his Thursday order (onion soup, *pot-au-feu, crème brulée*) before he had the chance to say anything else. Manfred was tempted to suddenly change his order just to get her attention, but as she turned away with an air of great ennui, he was glad he hadn't. Such an act would only bring Pasteur to the table demanding to know what had brought about such a change of heart. Manfred imagined himself shouting, 'I just felt like a change!' before overturning his table and storming out of the restaurant, batting other customers' glasses of wine against the walls as he went.

He opened his copy of *L'Alsace* to the financial pages and gazed blankly at the columns of share prices. Adèle returned with his soup. She continued to betray no sign of the intimacy that had passed between them. Perhaps when she returned with his main course, he should casually enquire whether she had had a pleasant evening. He could even ask about the young man. What could be wrong with that? He had seen them together after all. Wasn't it perfectly natural to acknowledge the fact? Manfred had already finished the glass of wine that was included in the set menu. The soup was watery and under-seasoned.

Customers arrived and left continually. When it was busy, the Restaurant de la Cloche ran like a well-oiled machine. Marie often paused at a regular's table to exchange a few words, but her eyes were continually scanning the room for empty plates and customers wishing to pay their bills. These were despatched with a minimum of fuss by Pasteur from his station behind the counter. Tables were cleared and reset with military efficiency. There was a constant clatter from the kitchen and the calling of orders as they were delivered to the hatch. Customers spoke in loud voices with their mouths full, conscious that they were not expected to linger over their lunch. Most elected not to have coffee. If they did, it was brought with their dessert. Adèle attended to the other customers with the same sullen demeanour she displayed towards Manfred. She moved slowly and heavily like a cow on its way to milking, but, in her way, she was every bit as efficient as the bustling Marie.

Adèle collected his soup bowl on her way past, balancing the plates from another table on one arm. This was hardly the time to engage her in small talk. But as she turned away, Manfred spoke up. 'Actually, Adèle, if it's not too much trouble, I'd like to change my order. I'll have the *choucroute garnie.*'

This would get her attention! Adèle turned back and said, 'Certainly, monsieur.' Her face remained blank. Manfred had to admire her nonchalance as she turned towards the kitchen.

'And, Adèle,' he said, raising his voice a little to make himself heard above the din, 'Another glass of wine.'

He had to hand it to her, she displayed not a flicker of emotion, but as he watched her push through the swing doors to the kitchen, he could imagine the commotion as she announced that Manfred Baumann had changed his order. And he was having a second glass of wine! He sat back in his chair and surveyed the other patrons of the restaurant. They were oblivious to the momentous events taking place.

Manfred awaited the proprietor's arrival at his table to enquire if the *pot-au-feu* was no longer to his liking. But Pasteur did not come over. He remained behind the bar decanting wine into carafes, acting as if nothing unusual had occurred. He did not so much as glance in Manfred's direction.

Adèle arrived with his *choucroute*. 'Bon appétit,' she said.

The pork was fatty and overcooked. The *choucroute* too sharp. He missed the braised meats of which Marie was so proud. The *pot-au-feu* was Manfred's favourite dish of the week, but that was not the point. He cleaned his plate. He would look very foolish if, having changed his order, he did not appear to have enjoyed his selection. He drained his second glass of wine and sat back with a feeling of great satisfaction.

At the bank, Manfred felt the effect of the extra glass of wine. He caught himself dozing off at his desk and buzzed his secretary to bring him coffee. He saw a farmer named Distain about extending the grace period of a loan. Manfred half-listened for fifteen minutes as the hoary farmer droned on about pressure from the supermarkets, the inequities of common market regulations and the threat to the French way of life. Glancing at his file, Manfred could see that the farm had been losing money for a decade. He granted Distain a repayment holiday of three years, the maximum possible. Distain could barely contain himself. For a terrible moment Manfred thought that the man was going to weep tears of gratitude. As he ushered him out of his office, Manfred had to physically wrench his hand from his grip.

Manfred dreaded Thursday nights. He arrived at the Restaurant de la Cloche at the usual time and took his place at the counter. He ordered his first glass of wine and downed it swiftly. Lemerre and Cloutier were at their table. Petit was late. In the mirror behind the counter Manfred saw Lemerre take out the cards and absentmindedly shuffle them. Petit arrived, took off his jacket and hung it over the back of his chair. Lemerre and Cloutier were already two-thirds through the first carafe of the evening. The three men talked in low voices for some minutes, before Lemerre (it was always Lemerre) shouted across the bar, 'Swiss, are you making up our four tonight?'

Manfred always waited to be summoned in this way. There was no reason why he should not join the men at their table when he arrived, but he never did. Instead, because he keenly felt the absurdity of the charade being enacted, when Lemerre called him over, he adopted an expression of surprise, as if the fact that this was the evening of the card game had slipped his mind.

Manfred obediently took his glass to the table and sat down. The three friends invariably sat in the same seats, obliging Manfred to take what he thought of as the dead man's chair. There could be no discussion of who would partner whom, since any change would necessitate swapping places. Thus Manfred played with Cloutier, and Lemerre played with Petit. Cloutier was a rotten player, unable to read Manfred's bids and timid in his play. Lemerre and Petit engaged in a system of ill-concealed cheats: scratching their noses, coughing and tapping the table. So transparent was their primitive code that it worked in Manfred's favour. They might as well have laid their cards on the table for him to see. Despite the fact that Cloutier played like a half-wit, they invariably won. Once, Lemerre had even accused Manfred of cheating. More often Lemerre and Petit simply shook their heads at their opponents' good fortune.

Adèle brought a fresh carafe of wine and a glass for Manfred. As she bent over the table Manfred stole a glance at her cleavage and thought of the young man he had seen the previous night.

On Thursdays, four carafes were drunk.

Manfred ensured that his consumption of wine kept pace with the others so that he could be accused neither of drinking more than his share nor of lagging behind. At the end of the evening Manfred's contribution to the tab would be pocketed by Lemerre. The three men settled their bill on a weekly basis. Manfred could certainly have made a similar arrangement with Pasteur and bring an end to the embarrassing tipping ritual, but he had never requested a tab and to do so after so many years would seem odd. 'Why,' Pasteur would surely ask, 'have you never asked for one before?' Manfred would have difficulty answering such a question. He could hardly claim that it never crossed his mind. He thought about it on a daily basis.

Lemerre drew up the score sheet on the back of an envelope. Since the death of Le Fevre, Lemerre had become the de facto leader of the group. He smelt of a mixture of hair products and sweat. His jowly face wore a permanent expression of scorn and he could often be heard loudly decrying immigrants, Jews (whom he blamed for the majority of the world's problems) and, a favourite bugbear, homosexuals. 'Your lot,' he liked to tell Manfred, 'have the right idea, Swiss. Keep the Turks and Jews out.' His tirades were delivered in a vaguely effeminate manner, accompanied by elaborate hand gestures, which seemed to suggest that he was sprinkling gems of wisdom among his acolytes. The effect was both comic and menacing. On occasion, Manfred had allowed himself to be goaded into debate with Lemerre, which only led to being denounced as a communist queer. Now he left it to Pasteur to intervene when Lemerre's diatribes got out of hand.

The cards were cut and dealt. Lemerre and Petit engaged in an elaborate exchange of coughs and table-taps from which Manfred inferred that they were both weak in spades. He was long-suited in spades and deduced that Cloutier must hold at least a couple of face cards of that suit. He ignored his partner's opening gambit of two hearts and leapt straight to six spades.

'Where you getting a call like that from?' said Lemerre.

Manfred shrugged. He took all thirteen tricks with ease.

'Didn't have the bottle to go the whole hog?' Lemerre goaded. 'A faint heart never won a fair lady, eh?'

The game continued in the same vein. Manfred even threw a hand now and again, giving Lemerre the opportunity to gloat about his mastery of the game.

On the rare occasions Cloutier had the lead, Manfred watched Adèle go about her business. Her demeanour was less sullen than usual. She exchanged a few pleasantries with diners. Her posture was more upright, as if a sack of coals had been lifted from her back. Clearly, thought Manfred, she was in love with the young man on the scooter. He did not feel pleased for her, only a certain loathing for the young man, indeed for all young men who could woo a girl with a scooter and a few vulgar compliments. Adèle came over to the table with the final carafe of the evening.

Without thinking, Manfred blurted out, 'You look nice tonight, Adèle.'

The three companions stopped dead. Petit's hand, about to lay a card, was suspended in the air. The three looked at each other, waiting for their cue from Lemerre. He merely burst into raucous laughter, immediately echoed by his two cohorts. Manfred blushed deeply and looked at the table.

'You watch yourself there, my girl,' Lemerre spluttered through his laughter. 'Quite the lady's man, our Swiss.'

Adèle appeared unfazed. She directed a thin smile in Manfred's direction and returned to the counter with the empty carafe.

At the end of the evening, Manfred bid the other players goodnight and left the restaurant. He was relieved that Adèle was still sweeping up when the game had come to an end and the last carafe had been drunk. He was quite certain that she would be meeting the young man again at the little park outside the Protestant temple. Sure enough, he was there, leaning on the seat of his scooter, smoking a cigarette.

This time Manfred got a better look at him. He could not have been more than eighteen or nineteen. He had fair, wispy hair and his complexion was fresh, as if he had yet to start shaving. As Manfred drew closer, he wondered if the youth would recognise him from the previous night. If he did, he gave no sign of having done so. He neither made eye contact nor averted his gaze. He had blue eyes and thin lips. Manfred felt a strange sense of relief that he did not look like the kind of young man who picked up and discarded girls readily.

As Manfred passed by, the young man drew on his cigarette. He held it awkwardly between the tip of his thumb and index finger. Smoking was as yet an affectation. Manfred imagined he must be as awkward in bed, if he had got that far. It pleased him that Adèle was not involving herself with some worldly Romeo. He continued past the little park towards his apartment. Then he stopped and turned around. When he considered this later, he could not explain what had made him do it. He had not thought about it in advance, nor could he remember making any decision. It was a momentary impulse to which he submitted.

At the end of the little park was an apartment building set back from the pavement. Manfred ducked towards the doorway of the apartments and concealed himself behind the shrubbery. The young man was facing in the direction from which Adèle would approach. There was no danger of him spotting Manfred and, even if he turned round, he was well hidden. The youth finished his cigarette and looked at his watch. A few minutes passed. Manfred began to wonder what he was doing there, but he had waited this long, it would be foolish to leave now. In any case, were he to do so, he might make a noise and give himself away.

Adèle appeared, walking slowly along the pavement. The young man raised his hand in greeting and Adèle waved back but did not quicken her pace. Manfred wondered

49

why he did not meet her outside the bar. They must have had some reason to not wish to be seen together. Perhaps their parents did not approve of their liaisons. Manfred, though, could not imagine Adèle living with her parents. If asked, he would have guessed that she was an orphan or that she had run away from home. There was something in her self-containment that suggested she was alone in the world.

They greeted each other with a more passionate kiss than the previous evening. They remained in a close embrace for some time. The young man put his right hand on Adèle's behind. She gripped the back of his neck and arched her groin into his thigh. Manfred could feel himself becoming aroused. When they parted, the young man offered Adèle a cigarette, which she accepted. They climbed onto the scooter. They made a wide turn in the road and rode off, Adèle's arms around the youth's waist. And that was that. That was what Manfred had furtively loitered to see. He hurried off, suddenly afraid that someone might have seen him spying on the couple. But it was late and the streets of Saint-Louis were deserted.

FOUR

Manfred did not waver from his usual Friday selection, *andouillette* with mustard sauce and mashed potato. Adèle had not turned up for work. Manfred felt a pang of disappointment. He realised he had been looking forward to seeing her. Pasteur was in a foul mood as Adèle's absence obliged him to wait tables. He took orders brusquely, tapping his pencil on his note-pad as he waited for diners to reach a decision. Manfred did not ask him where Adèle was. Nor did he ask for his empty water jug to be filled. Pasteur's ill temper upset the ambience of the restaurant. Customers were not given to lingering over their lunch at any time, but today they ate more quickly than usual. While one normally had to raise one's voice to be heard over the din of clattering plates and animated chatter, the atmosphere was now subdued. Manfred ate his pear tart and paid his bill hurriedly. He was left with fifteen minutes to kill before he had to go back to the bank. He could think of nothing to do, so went back anyway. No one commented on his early return.

In the evening Adèle was still absent. The restaurant was quiet and Pasteur was back in his usual place behind the counter. His foul mood seemed to have subsided. When he was on his second glass, Manfred asked him where Adèle was. He tried to keep his tone casual.

Pasteur shrugged. 'She didn't turn up at lunch and she didn't turn up this evening.'

'Is she ill?'

'Your guess is as good as mine, pal,' said Pasteur.

Manfred ignored his curt tone.

'She hasn't called?'

Pasteur looked up impatiently from his paper. He had said all he wished to on the subject. When Marie emerged from the kitchen, Manfred contemplated asking her, but he thought better of it. People might wonder about this sudden interest in the waitress. If Pasteur was not concerned, why should he be? Why indeed was he so interested? In the months that Adèle had worked at the restaurant he had rarely given her a second thought, other than lustful ones. He had never once wondered where she lived, what she did in her spare time or what, if anything, went on in her head.

Later on, after Marie had taken the final carafe of the evening to Lemerre's table, she paused behind the counter to wipe down the surfaces. This was Pasteur's job, but he plainly thought he had done enough menial work for the day.

'Busy day, Marie?' Manfred said.

'A busy day, yes, Monsieur Baumann,' she replied, before disappearing into the kitchen. Manfred nursed his final glass of wine a little longer than usual. Marie emerged from the kitchen a few minutes later, but she did not linger by the counter. She set the tables for the following day's service before retiring to the apartment upstairs. Manfred paid his bill and left.

Around three o'clock the following afternoon Manfred was sitting at the table in his kitchen reading a detective novel. There was a knock at the door. He started. No one ever called on him and anyone wishing to do so would have to use the buzzer in the street to gain access to the building. He sat stock-still for a few moments. It was probably some pollster or evangelist whom another resident had allowed in. Manfred held his breath and strained his ear for the sound of departing footsteps. Then there was a second sharp knock. It was an insistent, impatient rap — one that suggested the person on the other side of the door knew he was inside. Manfred pushed his chair back silently and padded along the passage. He listened for a moment and then put his eye to the peephole.

A man with closely cropped grey hair and narrow grey eyes was looking directly at the door. Manfred recognised him. He was a policeman. When Manfred opened the door, he held up his ID, which he must have been holding in his hand in readiness. 'Inspector Gorski, Saint-Louis police.'

'Yes,' said Manfred.

Gorski was a stocky man of average height in his mid- or late-forties. He was wearing a slate grey suit, dark blue shirt and a tie of a similar colour. He had a light raincoat folded over his left arm. He showed no sign of recognising Manfred. Manfred held out his hand and then let it fall to his side. Was one supposed to shake hands with a policeman?

'Might I have a word, Monsieur Baumann?'

There was no reason to be alarmed that the detective knew his name. It was inscribed on the small silver plaque on the door.

'Of course.'

There was a pause. Manfred waited for the policeman to say something else before he realised that he was waiting to be invited inside. He stood back from the door. Gorski thanked him and stepped into the narrow passage that led to the kitchen. Gorski was obliged to squeeze past Manfred, before Manfred in turn squeezed past him to show him into the kitchen. For a number of years Manfred had employed a cleaner, but he had never liked having someone else poking around the apartment. It made him feel uncomfortable and there was, in any case, little for her to do as he was quite fastidious. He washed up as soon as he had finished eating and firmly adhered to the credo of keeping everything in its place. The old woman used to vacuum the already immaculate rooms and take care of his laundry and ironing, a chore Manfred disliked. But it embarrassed him to think of her stripping his bed and washing and folding away his underwear. Manfred had been relieved when she died (he could not have possibly dismissed her), and in the four years since then few people had set foot in his apartment. These days Manfred did his laundry in the scullery in the basement of the building on Sunday afternoons. It was not enjoyable, but it served to occupy a part of the weekend he otherwise struggled to fill.

The two men stood face to face in the kitchen. Manfred felt that the detective was scrutinising him. If there was a flicker of recognition in his grey eyes, he would most likely ascribe it to the fact that in a town like Saint-Louis the inhabitants crossed paths a great deal. Indeed, though he generally kept to the opposite pavement, Manfred walked past the police station on his way to and from the Restaurant de la Cloche every day. It would, in fact, be odd if the detective had never seen him.

Manfred felt like he was in a scene from a film. Next the cop would say, *You haven't asked me what this is about?* and he would immediately fall under suspicion. But Manfred had missed his opportunity. Whatever he said now would sound stilted and unnatural. Of course, he suspected why Gorski was there. In a sense he had been expecting him. He should have confined himself to a polite *How can I help you?* Or he should have said straight out that he assumed the policeman's visit was something to do with the waitress. Gorski did not appear to notice Manfred's discomfort. He must be accustomed to people behaving awkwardly in the presence of the police. Indeed, to behave

56

in a relaxed manner might suggest that one was used to dealing with the law and was therefore a suspicious character.

Gorski patted the back of the chair that Manfred had been sitting in.

'Do you mind?' he said, sitting down without waiting for an answer.

Manfred asked if he could off the detective a cup of coffee. Gorski declined and Manfred sat down on the opposite side of the table. He would have liked to occupy himself with the business of making coffee. Gorski had done nothing to put him at his ease. He picked up the book Manfred had been reading and examined it. Manfred smiled apologetically. He contemplated telling the policeman that he was well versed in more elevating literature, but he did not do so. Perhaps the policeman read only detective novels, or read nothing at all and would think him snobbish. In any case, what was wrong with passing a Saturday afternoon with a popular novel?

Gorski laid the book carefully back on the table.

'This shouldn't take long,' he said, but he did not appear to be in any hurry.

Manfred clasped his hands and set them on the table in front of him in an attempt to stop fidgeting. He did not feel he was making a good impression.

Gorski suddenly pushed his chair back and stood up. This instantly made Manfred feel that he was about to be interrogated, but he could hardly now jump to his feet to put himself on an even footing with the policeman.

'I'm investigating the disappearance of Adèle Bedeau,' said Gorski.

'Disappearance?' said Manfred. He was pleased with the way it came out — as if he was genuinely surprised. It was better, Manfred decided, that he had not mentioned Adèle before this point. Just because a girl did not appear for work and failed to inform her employers of the reason for her absence, it did not mean that something untoward had happened.

Gorski shrugged. 'Perhaps "disappearance" is too strong a word. A couple of days ago she was around and now she isn't. Nobody knows where she is. So, to all intents and purposes, she has disappeared.'

Manfred nodded.

'I take it that you know Mlle Bedeau?'

'Yes,' said Manfred. It would be stupid to deny it. 'She's a waitress at the restaurant where I eat lunch.'

'And that is the extent of your relationship?'

'I'm not sure I would say we had a relationship. Until just now I didn't even know her second name.'

He felt a little more relaxed. Gorski did not give the impression that he was going to unduly press him. The detective sat down.

'She is a waitress and you are a customer. Nothing more?'

'Yes.'

'You've never seen her outside the restaurant?'

'You mean in a social sense?'

'In any sense.'

Manfred shook his head slowly, as if giving the matter some thought.

Gorski gave no indication of disbelieving him.

'Mlle Bedeau hasn't been seen since she left work on Thursday evening. You haven't seen her since then?'

It was on Thursday that he had spied on Adèle and the young man in the little park. Manfred had no wish to become embroiled in a police investigation, but perhaps what he had seen was of significance. What if the youth on the scooter was a suspect in Adèle's disappearance? What if he was the only one who had seen them together? But only a moment before, he'd told Gorski he had never seen Adèle outside the restaurant.

59

It was not advisable to contradict himself.

'No,' he said. 'No, I haven't.'

Gorski nodded curtly, as if this was precisely what he had expected Manfred to say. Did he already know that Manfred had seen Adèle on the night in question?

He stood up abruptly. 'I won't detain you any further, monsieur. Thank you for your time.' He handed Manfred a card and told him to call if he thought of anything.

Having seen Gorski out with the same awkwardness in the narrow passage, Manfred returned to his chair at the kitchen table. How stupid it had been to lie. The policeman had disconcerted him. It would have been a simple matter to tell him what he had seen on Thursday evening, to have described the young man and in which direction they rode off. He need not have mentioned how he had loitered at the edge of the park. Now he had withheld evidence from the investigation. What was more, when his omission came to light, as it inevitably would, he would be sure to fall under suspicion.

Later Manfred sat with his forehead against the window of the train to Strasbourg. It was done now. Short of calling the number on Gorski's card and pretending that he had suddenly remembered what he had seen, there was nothing he could do to remedy the situation. And in any case, if the situation arose again, would he not behave in exactly the same way? What benefit would there have been in divulging what he had seen? More questions would certainly have followed. He would become involved in the investigation and Manfred did not like to be involved in anything. And where, after all, did the truth end? Should he have confessed his silly crush on Adèle, a crush based on nothing more than the girl concealing their familiarity from her friend? Should he have told Gorski how he surreptitiously watched Adèle go about her chores in the restaurant, hoping, like a schoolboy, for a glimpse of her brassiere?

Before heading to Chez Simone, Manfred went to a large brasserie near the station. The waiter recognised him and acknowledged him with an upward movement of his head. Manfred ordered a mushroom omelette with *frites* and a half-bottle of wine, as he always did. A group of students, three boys and two girls, sat around a nearby table by the window, scarves knotted fashionably around their necks. Manfred opened his book on the table, but he did not read it. He observed the students with the detachment of an anthropologist. They were entirely oblivious to his presence. Manfred was not close enough to hear the subject of their discussion, but it was obvious that the boys were competing to impress their female companions with witty or learned remarks. At a certain point, a third girl joined the group and an elaborate round of handshakes and kisses was exchanged. The new arrival was exceptionally pretty, and the boys now unashamedly directed their attentions towards her. The two other girls engaged in a separate conversation. Manfred felt like he was witnessing a ruthless evolutionary ritual.

He paid his bill. He had to pass the students' table on the way to the door and, as he did so, he slowed his pace and inhaled the scent of the newcomer. None of the students so much as glanced at him.

Manfred always had a couple of drinks at Simone's before engaging on the actual business of his visit. When it was free, he took the seat at a table in the corner and sat watching the other customers. The place was lit only by the lights illuminating the bottles behind the bar and by the candles on the tables. Madame Simone sat on a high stool at the end of the bar with a glass of wine, a cigarette constantly burning in her hand. The smoke made languid coils in the lights behind the bar before dispersing into the general fug. She was close to fifty years old and dressed in a black wraparound dress fastened beneath her breasts. She had a pronounced nose, a wide red mouth and darting, twinkling eyes, thickly painted with mascara. She always greeted Manfred with great warmth, called him darling and kissed him on both cheeks. She greeted all her patrons in this way, but Manfred was always touched by her welcome. Simone never dispensed drinks. Such duties were performed by whichever of the girls were in the bar at the time. In all his visits, Manfred had never seen Simone take a sip of her drink. It was a prop to create the illusion that one was not in a public establishment, but a personal guest, sharing a drink with the hostess. Now and again Simone joined a group of men at their table and gracefully passed a few minutes with them.

Chez Simone was located in a basement in an alley off Rue des Lentilles. There was no sign outside. It was not a brothel, at least Manfred did not think of it as such. It was perfectly acceptable to come in, drink a glass of wine (Simone did not serve beer), and leave. Girls did not approach you and ask you to buy them drinks, but such a thing could easily be arranged with a word or a look to Simone. When the time came,

Manfred caught Simone's eye, and she indicated with a brief nod that everything was in place.

Through the door to the right of the bar were three rooms. They were furnished like real bedrooms, complete with bookcases and dressing tables, each set out with feminine articles. As Manfred went through to the back, Simone informed him which room he should use. The girl was new, or at least Manfred had not seen her before. She was petite and blonde, perhaps eighteen or nineteen years old. Manfred was standing, as he always did when the girl entered, with his back to the far wall. He smiled a greeting without parting his lips.

'Good evening, monsieur,' said the girl. She had an eastern European accent. Manfred decided she was Hungarian. He had once read that the girls in Budapest were the most beautiful in Europe. But he did not ask her name or where she was from. Despite the fact that Manfred had been visiting Simone's for many years, he never ceased to find the transaction embarrassing. Even with the girls he saw regularly, the awkwardness never disappeared. He wondered if they ridiculed him behind his back or made excuses to Madame Simone not to service him. The girl was standing by the door, unsure what to do.

'Has Madame Simone . . . ?' Manfred wanted to say 'briefed you', but he let the sentence trail off in the hope that he need not say more.

'Yes, monsieur, I think so,' she said. She was pretty and did not seem discomfited by the situation. She moved towards the bed in the centre of the room and lay on her back without undressing. She parted her legs.

'Keep your legs together,' Manfred said. It came out a little curtly, which he regretted, but he did not like to talk more than necessary. It mortified him to have to give instructions.

'Yes, monsieur,' she said.

'Put your arms by your sides.'

The girl complied. Manfred tried not to think about the fact that this was only one in a series of indignities which she would endure over the course of the night. He climbed fully clothed on top of the girl and began to rub himself against her body. He kept his hands on her shoulders and stared into her eyes. Her face betrayed no particular emotion, boredom perhaps. To Manfred's relief, she did not simulate pleasure, as some of the other girls did. Theatrical moaning or exhortations ruined the experience for him, but he never had the nerve to ask them to be quiet. After a few minutes it was over and Manfred rolled off the girl and sat on the edge of the bed facing the wall. He fished in his wallet for a banknote and passed it to her without looking round. This was by way of a tip, as he had already paid Simone for her services. Manfred had no idea if his tip was generous or even if the other patrons left tips. He did not want to appear tight-fisted, nor did he wish to be overgenerous, as if he was trying to compensate the girls for the unpleasantness of the experience. In reality, he believed that however strange his behaviour was, it could hardly be anything other than easy money for the girls. So, he tipped the same amount he paid Simone for his half hour, a sum he understood was split between Simone and the girl in question. He never varied his tip, even if the girl had irritated him in some way, or if, like tonight, the encounter had been close to pleasurable. He would not wish one girl to think that he was less satisfied with her services. Mainly, he did not wish the girls to think ill of him.

'Thank you,' said the girl, taking the note.

'Thank you,' said Manfred, glancing over his shoulder. The girl took this as an indication that the transaction was over and left the room. The whole episode had lasted little more than ten minutes. Manfred stood up, undid his trousers and mopped up his emission with a handkerchief he had brought for the purpose. Then he sat down on the bed for a few minutes, breathing slowly and evenly.

He returned to the bar. Simone asked if everything had been to his satisfaction.

'Yes. Thank you,' Manfred replied, as he did every week.

He resumed his seat in the corner and ordered a final glass of wine. These were Manfred's favourite moments of the week. Now that the act was over, he felt quite relaxed. The blonde girl emerged from the back. She spotted Manfred in the corner and smiled at him as if what had passed between them was entirely normal. Manfred liked her. She had been nice. Half an hour later, he left to catch the last train back to Saint-Louis.

FIVE

Manfred had been watching his grandfather struggle to fill his pipe for fully ten minutes. The old man's hands shook violently these days, but Manfred knew any offer of assistance would be gruffly spurned. They were sitting on the patio overlooking the garden, awaiting the summons for Sunday lunch. After a few more minutes Bertrand Paliard succeeded in lighting the pipe. A momentary expression of satisfaction passed across his face as he took his first draw, but this was swiftly overtaken by a fierce fit of coughing. His nurse, who had been standing in attendance by the French windows, took a couple of steps towards him. There was an oxygen mask to hand, but she merely stood by as he struggled for breath. She did not approve of him smoking. The tobacco had a warm nutty aroma, a smell which always reminded Manfred of his miserable teenage years.

After his mother died, Manfred felt like a lodger in the Paliard house. In his early teens he had grown quickly. He was ill at ease with his newfound height and the unwelcome attention it attracted. Consequently he developed a stoop. His grandfather nicknamed him Nosferatu on account of the way he crept around the house, keeping close to the walls. At school he kept himself to himself. He was not picked on. He had on one or two occasions proved capable of standing up for himself so, despite his physical and social awkwardness, bullying was reserved for softer targets. He was aware, too, that the death of both his parents cast a kind of barrier around him. It made him unapproachable both to those kids who wanted to ridicule him and to those, if any, who might have wished to befriend him.

Manfred began to long for companionship, for a pal to discuss the merits of the girls at school, or to sit with into the small hours in his room listening to records and discussing their favourite authors. This pal would invite him over and he would be welcomed into a surrogate family, in which the mother cooked lavish Sunday spreads and the father took the boys on Sunday fishing or hiking trips. There were candidates for such friendship at school. Manfred could spot the other awkward cases at a hundred metres, by the way they hovered on the fringes of the crowd, by the books they slyly fished out of their satchels at break, by their ability to disappear into the background. But Manfred was incapable of breaching the silent understanding he had — or thought he had — with his fellow maladroits.

As for a girlfriend, it was not for the want of carnal thoughts that Manfred did not countenance the possibility of so much as a friendship with a girl. He could barely utter a word to a member of the opposite sex without his face breaking into a deep crimson blush. So he avoided girls altogether. Still, they occupied most of his waking thoughts. He observed them surreptitiously at school, and walked, unnoticed, a few metres behind them on the way home, listening to their laughter, noting the minutiae of how they dressed, admiring the smooth curve of their suntanned legs. He entertained elaborate sexual fantasies, but he also daydreamed of being introduced to a girl's parents. He would behave in a polite and respectful manner and be regarded as a nice young man with good prospects. Most of all Manfred longed to walk through the woods hand in hand with a girl who would call him Mani, just as his mother had.

During the summer holiday before his *baccalauréat* year, Manfred was more isolated than ever. In term-time, there was at least an illusion of being among people, of a routine to get him out of bed and out of his grandparents' house. Manfred spent entire days in his room with the shutters closed, lying on his bed staring at the ceiling. His grandparents seemed to care little how he passed his time. He read voraciously, devouring Camus and Sartre and wallowing in the horrors of de Sade. The darker the work, the more he relished it. Sometimes he wrote passages in a notebook, but he invariably tore out the pages and destroyed what he had written, frustrated at the triteness of his efforts. If his grandmother suggested that he accompany her to Strasbourg for the day or asked him to carry out a chore in the garden, Manfred would most likely comply, but with such a sullen demeanour that she soon gave up and left him to his own devices. Meals in the household were generally eaten in silence.

Manfred began to take the nickname his grandfather gave him to heart. He convinced himself he was most at home in the dark. He stole around the house as quietly as possible, keeping to the cool shadows of the old house, taking pleasure in startling the maids. He entertained fantasies of stealing into girls' rooms and sinking his teeth into their necks as they slept. They would awake in an erotic reverie, addicted, like him, to a life in the shadows.

Manfred's grandfather stared into the middle distance. His pale blue eyes were watery from his coughing fit. He looked terribly sad. His pipe had gone out. The garden was overgrown. When he retired from practice fifteen years previously, he had got rid of the gardener, insisting that he could take care of the grounds himself, but ill health had rendered this impossible. Ivy had spread its tentacles across the pale yellow brick wall at the back of the garden. The wooden door that led to the woods was now inaccessible. The jamb was rotten and the pale blue paint had mostly flaked off, leaving the wood exposed to the elements.

Manfred offered to relight his grandfather's pipe and, to his surprise, he handed it to him. Manfred ignored the filthy look from the nurse, got it going and handed it back to him. M. Paliard nodded a curt thank you, but did not put it to his lips. Manfred had always loathed the old man, just as the old man loathed him. Now he seemed to be clinging onto life only out of spite. Even his pipe no longer seemed to provide him with any pleasure. But there was no question of discontinuing the ritual of Sunday lunch. Such a thing would upset his grandmother.

The maid appeared at the patio door and, to Manfred's relief, announced that lunch would be served. He left the nurse to manoeuvre his grandfather and his medical apparatus into the dining room. Manfred had never got used to sitting there at the table, waited on by maids. His grandmother complained constantly about the difficulty of finding suitable staff. The current maid was Spanish. During lunch Mme Paliard constantly corrected her, addressing her in exaggeratedly childish French and then talking to Manfred about her as if she wasn't there. Manfred kept his eyes on the food that was placed in front of him and nursed a glass of mineral water. He craved a glass of wine, but alcohol was not served at lunchtime in the Paliard household. Bertrand did not approve of drinking during the day, as he did not approve of many things. Despite this, Mme Paliard chattered breezily through lunch. Manfred suspected that she tippled in the kitchen. He did his best to contribute to the conversation, if only to prevent the meal being passed in silence. As soon as the dessert plates were cleared, he took his leave.

Later that afternoon, Manfred took his sack of washing down to the laundry room in the basement of his building. Someone had left a blouse in one of the dryers. He held it up in front of him. It was pale blue and translucent. The fabric had a pleasing grain between his fingers. It felt expensive. He could smell conditioner, lavender perhaps, a scent an older woman might favour. Manfred felt a strong desire to bury his face in the garment and inhale the aroma, but resisted for fear that its owner might come in and catch him doing so. Instead he folded the garment neatly and placed it on top of the machine.

Manfred transferred his clothes from the washing machine and set the dryer to the highest temperature. He sat down on the wooden chair next to the door and opened his book, but he was unable to concentrate. Perhaps he should go up to his apartment and fetch a hanger for the blouse. Its owner might appreciate such a gesture. But Manfred did not like to leave his clothes in the basement. It was not that he thought someone would steal them, rather that if a cycle finished, another resident might need to unload the machine, and Manfred did not like the idea of a stranger going through his clothing. It was for this reason that Manfred did his washing on Sunday afternoons when the laundry room was always deserted. Other residents presumably had better things to do with their weekends and did their washing at times more traditionally set aside for drudgery. Even so, Manfred always made sure his underwear was in a presentable condition, in case he had to unload the machine in the presence of another person.

Manfred decided against fetching a hanger. It was not as if he had carelessly discarded the blouse. He had folded it neatly and if its owner came to retrieve it while he was upstairs, he would not get credit for this act of kindness. The woman might even admire the skill with which he had folded the blouse. Manfred craned his head into the stairwell that led to the laundry room. No one was coming. He got up and folded the blouse more carefully, gently smoothing it with the palms of his hands. Then he re-took his seat and picked up his book, the same detective novel he had been reading when Gorski called.

The spin cycle ended. Manfred removed his clothes from the machine and folded them into his laundry sack. There was not room to dry clothes in his apartment and he disliked the slovenly appearance of clothes hanging on radiators. He wondered if he should wait for the woman to return to retrieve her blouse, but perhaps she had not yet noticed it was missing. Manfred decided that he would take the blouse to his apartment and leave a note on the dryer saying that he had done so. He was pleased with this plan. He bundled the remaining clothes into his sack without folding them, laid the blouse on top and, not wishing to meet the woman coming out of the lift, took the back stairs to his apartment. Manfred found a piece of paper and pencil and sat down at the kitchen table to compose the note. He must make it sound casual. There was no need for an elaborate explanation. Rather he should make it sound as if his decision to take the blouse to his apartment had been made without thinking, as if it was the most natural thing in the world. After three or four false starts, he settled for the most neutral wording he could think of: *Blouse found in dryer. Please contact Apartment 4F.* Then he signed it, *Manfred Baumann.*

Manfred took the stairs back to the basement. The light was on in the basement stairwell. He could hear someone moving around in the scullery. There was a woman bending over the dryer. She was wearing jeans, a faded blue T-shirt and baseball boots. She had yellow blonde hair, tied in a ponytail. She did not hear Manfred approach.

'Excuse me,' he said softly.

She jumped and turned round.

'I'm sorry,' said Manfred, 'I didn't mean to startle you.'

'Too late,' said the woman. She was slim, in her late thirties or early forties. She had pronounced cheekbones and a pale complexion. Her eyes were grey and a little lined. Manfred had never seen her before. She returned her attention to the washing machines, opening the doors and whirring the cylinders.

'Are you looking for your blouse?' Manfred asked.

'My blouse, yes,' she said.

'I've got it,' said Manfred. 'I found it in the dryer.' He handed her the note as if to corroborate his story. 'I didn't want to leave it down here, in case someone went off with it. It looked expensive.'

The woman looked at him suspiciously and then read the note.

'Thanks,' she said in a tone wholly lacking in gratitude.

Manfred stood for a moment, not sure what to say.

'Shall I fetch it for you?'

He wanted the woman to say that she would accompany him. There was something attractive about her.

'That would be good,' said the woman, 'thank you.' She smiled. 'Sorry, it was nice of you to . . .' She glanced at the note, before adding, 'Manfred.'

Manfred's heart was pounding in his chest. 'Or you could come with me?' He jabbed his thumb towards the stairwell.

The woman shrugged and followed him. Manfred told himself to say something, no matter how banal. If he didn't say something quickly, the entire journey to his apartment would be passed in painful silence.

'Have you lived here long?' he said.

'Sorry?' said the woman. She was a few steps behind him and the stairwell echoed with their footsteps.

'Have you been in the building long?' Manfred repeated. 'I haven't seen you before.'

They reached the metal door at the top of the basement stairs. Manfred held it open and the woman went through. She pressed the button for the lift and the door opened immediately. They got in and Manfred pressed the button for the fourth floor. The lift was small and the woman stood at Manfred's shoulder. They were almost touching. The lift clattered into action. The woman smelt of the same scent that he had detected on the blouse. It wasn't lavender, it was something less floral, more earthy.

'I was saying I haven't seen you before,' Manfred said. He kept his eyes on the numbers above the door.

'I've been here a few months,' said the woman. 'Since February.'

'I see,' said Manfred. It was a stupid thing to say. *I see.* What was that supposed to mean? It sounded like he was interrogating her, as if he intended to use this piece of information to contradict her at a later date. When the lift reached the fourth floor, Manfred got out first so that the woman would not have to squeeze past him. They walked along the corridor in silence.

'Here we are,' he said, when they reached the door.

'4F,' said the woman, proffering the note she was still holding.

'Would you like to come inside?'

The woman stepped into the passage and waited as Manfred went into the kitchen to fetch the blouse. He returned and handed it to her.

'You folded it. Thank you,' said the woman. She seemed surprised and not displeased.

'I would have ironed it if I'd had time,' said Manfred.

The woman smiled kindly as she might to a child who had done well. She was quite beautiful.

'Thanks again,' she said and turned to go.

Manfred audibly drew breath. 'Can I offer you a coffee?' he said. 'Or a cup of tea?' He did not know why he had added the offer of tea. Manfred did not drink tea and did not keep any in the apartment. The woman pursed her lips and looked at him for a moment, as if she was evaluating him.

'I'd better not,' she said. 'Another time perhaps.'

'Of course,' said Manfred. The woman stepped into the corridor.

Manfred closed the door gently behind her and exhaled slowly. He felt he had acquitted himself well. He went into the kitchen and started sorting through his laundry. The woman had appeared to actually consider accepting his invitation. *I'd better not.* The phrase suggested that she would have liked to accept, but she was unable to. Perhaps she was married and thought it would be improper to accept his invitation, that they would be engaging in something illicit. Or perhaps she had merely meant that she did not have time. In any case, she had not flatly refused. She had implied, clearly implied, that it was beyond her control and given a different set of circumstances, she would have accepted. And then, as if things were not already clear enough, she had added, *Another time perhaps.* Manfred had not detected any note of sarcasm in her voice. Of course it was difficult to imagine how 'another time' might come about, but even so he felt quite elated by the exchange. He should have asked her name. And he should buy some tea.

Manfred fetched the ironing board from the kitchen cupboard, plugged in the iron and sat down at the table, waiting for it to warm.

SIX

When Manfred arrived at the bank on Monday morning, the staff were talking animatedly about the disappearance of Adèle Bedeau. Mlle Givskov, the senior teller, was voicing the opinion that girls these days were asking for trouble the way they ran around. If this girl had got herself into trouble, she probably only had herself to blame. Mlle Givskov had been taken on by M. Jeantet a year or so after Manfred joined the branch. Her presence made Manfred uneasy and he kept his distance from her. Manfred bid the staff good morning and hurried past into his office. A few minutes later Carolyn brought in his coffee. She was a nice girl, nineteen years old, rather plain and slow, but with a cheerful disposition. Manfred liked her. She never seemed to be trying to impress him as some other new members of staff did.

'Terrible, isn't it,' she said, 'this business

with the girl.'

'I'm sure it'll turn out to be nothing,' said Manfred, a little brusquely. He had no wish to be drawn into a discussion of the matter.

Carolyn placed his coffee on the desk. Manfred looked up from the papers he had been studying. She looked a little crestfallen. He had no wish to snub her. She was sensitive to such things. Once, she had burst into tears when Manfred had pointed out a minor error in a transaction.

'She's only been gone a couple of days,' he said. 'She's probably just gone off with some boy.'

Carolyn appeared to take Manfred's theory very seriously. 'There was no mention of any boyfriend in the paper,' she said.

'People don't always advertise such things.' He immediately regretted the remark. It made him sound like someone who routinely engaged in deception or at least expected others to do so. Because Manfred did not socialise with his staff or talk about himself, he was aware that his personal life was the subject of conjecture. He had overheard some of the girls speculate that he was homosexual. Sometimes when he came out of his office, the room fell silent. At the annual Christmas lunch, people jockeyed to avoid sitting next to him. It was the same at the biannual gatherings of local branch managers. When the time came to mingle informally, Manfred found himself on the margins, unable to break into any of the groups that congregated around the room.

'Did you know her?' Carolyn asked.

'By sight,' said Manfred. 'I have lunch in the restaurant where she worked.' It was about as revealing a statement as he had ever made to her. He realised he should not have used the past tense. It implied he had some knowledge that she would not be returning to work.

'What is she like?' asked Carolyn, anxious to have some inside information to share with her workmates. 'She looks very pretty in the picture in the paper.'

'Are we going to be doing any work today or are the wheels of the banking industry going to grind to a halt because some girl has disappeared for five minutes?'

Carolyn looked hurt. 'Sorry, Monsieur Baumann,' she said and left the room. Manfred had told her that she could call him by his five name when they were alone in his office, but she never did.

At lunch Manfred had the special, as he always did on Mondays. He was anxious to stick to his routine from now on. There would be no repeat of his erratic actions of the previous week — the second glass of wine, the changing of his order, his ridiculous comment about Adèle's appearance. From now on he must avoid attracting attention to himself. He must not give people cause to think that he had been behaving oddly.

A new waitress was working the tables by the window. She was small and skinny and kept her short hair neatly secured in a clasp. She moved hurriedly between the tables and kitchen, and looked constantly as if she was about to drop the plates she was carrying or upset some glasses. Manfred did his best to avert his eyes from her.

Marie arrived at his table and took his order. She looked a little tired.

'Terrible business,' she said.

'I'm sure it'll turn out to be nothing,' said Manfred.

Marie frowned. 'That cop doesn't seem to think so,' she said. 'Seems that someone saw Adèle with a man on a motorbike the night she disappeared.'

Manfred pursed his lips and nodded slowly. He didn't know what to say. 'Do they know who he is, this man?' he said eventually.

'That cop has been in here asking

questions,' she said. 'He seemed to think it was significant.'

'I daresay,' said Manfred.

He ate his soup in silence, absentmindedly turning the pages of his newspaper. He shouldn't have mentioned a boyfriend to Carolyn. It made it seem as if he had foreknowledge of the development, which of course he had. He should learn to keep his mouth shut. The atmosphere in the restaurant was subdued. Pasteur lurked behind his counter. Manfred wondered if he was surreptitiously watching him, keeping an eye on him to see if he was acting strangely. Gorski must have spoken to everyone at the restaurant. The thought made him uneasy.

Marie brought his *Potée Marocaine*. He had finished his wine, but he resisted the desire to order another, instead pouring himself a glass of water from the carafe on the table. The *Potée Marocaine* consisted of a pile of couscous, a *merguez* sausage, a chicken leg and piece of indeterminate meat, served with a dish of sharp sauce. Manfred saw Pasteur nod a greeting towards the door. He looked over his shoulder and saw that Gorski had come in. He walked over to the bar and shook hands with Pasteur over the counter. There seemed to be some kind of understanding between them. Marie hovered by the hatch as the two men engaged in a brief conversation. Gorski turned, Manfred thought, to leave, but instead threaded his way through the tables to where he was sitting. It was clear he had known that Manfred would be here.

He stood with his hands on the back of the chair opposite Manfred and smiled a humourless greeting.

'Mind if I join you?' he said.

Manfred spread his palm towards the empty chair to indicate that he did not object. He could hardly refuse. Gorski took off his raincoat and folded it across his lap as he took his seat. This suggested, to Manfred's relief, that he did not intend to stay long, or at least that it was not his intention to order lunch. Manfred looked past Gorski's shoulder towards the counter. Marie had disappeared into the kitchen and Pasteur was conspicuously polishing glasses, even though for the previous fifteen minutes or so he had been standing around doing next to nothing.

'Don't let me interrupt your lunch,' Gorski said.

Manfred had laid down his cutlery. He disliked dining in company. Gorski made no pretence of being surprised to find

Manfred here, that it was somehow seren-
dipitous.

'Something was puzzling me,' he began, 'I
was hoping that you might be able to clear
it up.'

Manfred nodded.

'Something in connection with the disappearance of Adèle Bedeau.'

'Yes?' said Manfred.

'It seems that on the night of her disappearance, Mlle Bedeau was seen riding
through town on the back of a scooter with
a young man.'

Manfred looked at his food.

'It's significant because this is the last time
anyone saw her. It seems that she left the
restaurant, met this young man and rode
off with him. Obviously, it's important to
ascertain exactly what her movements were
on that night.'

'I understand,' said Manfred. His lunch
was getting cold.

'Of course there's nothing unusual about
a girl meeting a young man, but one detail
puzzles me. She was spotted riding past the
restaurant coming from the direction of Rue
de Mulhouse. It struck me as odd that if
she was going to meet this young man, why
did he not wait for her outside the restaurant? Why would she have walked some

distance in the opposite direction, meet the fellow and then ride off in the direction from which she had just come?'

Manfred did not say anything. It did not appear that Gorski was inviting him to speculate on the matter.

'Coupled with the fact that this young man, who is the last person to be seen with Mlle Bedeau, has not come forward, it suggests to me that there must have been some reason for keeping their liaison secret.'

'I can assure you, Inspector,' Manfred said, 'that I do not own a scooter and do not even know how to ride one.'

Gorski gave a little snort through his nose, as if acknowledging the punchline of a weak joke.

'That's not at all what I'm getting at.' He offered Manfred a thin smile. 'I'm simply asking those people who were in the vicinity to cast their mind back to the night in question and think about whether they may have seen anything significant.'

'I didn't see anything,' Manfred said a little too quickly.

Gorski raised a finger to silence him.

'On the night in question, you were in here in the restaurant playing cards with Messrs Lemerre, Petit and Cloutier. At the end of the game, you left, at about half past

89

ten, I believe.'

Manfred shrugged. 'I couldn't say exactly.'

Gorski ignored his comment. 'Did you go home directly?'

'Yes,' said Manfred. He could see all too clearly where this was leading.

'And your route home took you along Rue de Mulhouse past the little park at the Protestant temple?'

'Yes.'

'Well, I'm sure you can see what I'm going to ask you: Adèle left the restaurant only a few minutes after you and must have walked in the same direction to meet this young man. Just think carefully for a moment. Is it possible that you saw anyone, a young man, who might have been waiting for a rendezvous?'

Manfred took his time. He had known as soon as he had seen Gorski what his answer to such a question would be. He shook his head slowly. 'No, I'm sorry,' he said, 'I didn't see anyone.'

Gorski pursed his lips and nodded thoughtfully.

'I'm sorry I can't be of more help,' said Manfred. 'Perhaps they met in a café or at the boy's apartment.'

He assumed that the ordeal was over and Gorski would conclude proceedings with an apology for interrupting his lunch.

'You know,' he said, his tone suddenly more conversational, 'I've been a policeman for twenty-three years. In my experience, when people say that they wish they could be of more help, they very often can be.' He flashed Manfred his humourless smile. Manfred felt himself swallow. He told himself to hold Gorski's gaze. After a few seconds, he looked down at his food. If he had nothing to hide, he would interpret Gorski's remark as nothing more than a world-weary generalisation.

Gorski did not budge from his seat.

'On the previous night,' he continued, ignoring Manfred's statement, 'you were also here. You drank a bottle of wine at the counter and left around ten o'clock.'

'I couldn't say what time it was, but yes, that's correct.'

'You're quite a regular here, aren't you?' said Gorski.

Manfred shrugged. It wasn't a crime, was it? 'I suppose you could say that.'

'A creature of habit?'

Manfred stared at Gorski, not sure what expression to adopt. Was he going to bring up the fact that on the day Adèle had last been seen, Manfred had, in a complete reversal of his normal routine, ordered the

91

choucroute instead of the *pot-au-feu* and had a second glass of wine? Perhaps he had been told of the little compliment he had paid Adèle during the card game. Taken together, these actions could easily form a picture of a character who, around the time of the waitress's disappearance, had been behaving strangely. Why else would the detective have mentioned that he had been described in this way? Manfred felt his cheeks begin to colour.

'I don't know if I'd say that,' he said.

'Well, everyone I've spoken to,' he made a vague gesture with his hand, 'has described you in the same way, as a creature of habit.'

Manfred could not help glancing around the room. He intensely disliked the idea that Gorski had been asking about him, asking *everyone* about him. He wondered what else they had said.

'Is there something wrong with that?' he said.

Gorski pursed his lips and shook his head slowly. 'Not at all.' He leaned forward as if something had just occurred to him. 'Let me ask you one question: did you notice anything unusual in the restaurant on Wednesday night?'

Manfred gave this some thought, or at least attempted to give the impression that he was giving it some thought. He decided that this would be a good time to take a mouthful of food and did so. When he had swallowed, he shook his head.

'Nothing I can think of,' he said.

Gorski looked a little disappointed.

'Really?' he said. 'It seems to me that in a place like this,' he made a gesture with his hand to indicate that he meant the restaurant, 'not a great deal happens. One night is pretty much like any other. Accordingly, when anything out of the ordinary does occur, no matter how banal it might seem to an outsider, it does not go unnoticed by the regulars of the establishment.'

Manfred found Gorski's manner of expressing himself quite irritating. He took the last sip of his wine. He would have liked to order a second glass but, after having done so the previous day, this would then be taken as a new habit and he would then be obliged to take two glasses of wine at lunch every day.

'I've asked everyone the same question and received the same response. On the night in question, Adèle had asked M. Pasteur if she could leave a little early. Before she left she changed her clothes and put on some make-up.'

'You could hardly expect me to notice

something as trivial as that,' said Manfred.

'Lemerre, Petit and Cloutier, whom I questioned separately, all noticed it and mentioned it unprompted,' said Gorski.

'Perhaps only one of them noticed and drew it to the attention of the others.' Manfred felt this was a rather clever remark. Gorski tipped his head as if to acknowledge that this was a possibility. Manfred felt that he had won a small victory.

'They sit by the door. They're hardly likely to fail to notice a provocatively dressed woman,' he added.

'I didn't say that Adèle was provocatively dressed. I merely said that she had changed her clothes.'

Manfred stalled. He would do better to keep his mouth shut.

Gorski allowed his previous remark to hang in the air for a few moments.

'You're right, of course,' he continued. 'From their vantage point, they could hardly have failed to notice that Adèle had changed. But you, I think I am correct in saying, were standing at the counter adjacent to the hatch from which Adèle emerged. Following your own logic it seems even more unlikely that you would not have noticed this transformation.'

'Well, I didn't,' said Manfred.

Gorski clasped his hands in front of his face and tapped his forefingers together. Manfred had the impression that his ordeal was almost over.

'You left the restaurant very shortly after Adèle, the precise time is unimportant.' He adopted a puzzled tone, as if he was merely thinking out loud. 'Did you see in which direction she walked?'

'As I said before, I didn't see her.'

'And as you walked home did you see any young men, who might be waiting for . . .' he picked his word carefully, 'for a tryst?'

'No.' He was allowing his irritation to show.

'And if I were to ask you to accompany me to the station and sign a statement to that effect, that is what you would say?'

'Yes,' said Manfred. His course had been set since the first time he had spoken to Gorski. He could hardly change tack now.

'Very well.' Gorski slid his chair back noisily. 'My apologies for interrupting your lunch.'

Manfred's wine glass was empty, but he dared not order another. He did not wish to appear as if his encounter with Gorski had disconcerted him. Pasteur continued to polish glasses behind the bar. He did not look in Manfred's direction. Marie had her hand on the shoulder of the new waitress and was directing her to clear a recently vacated table.

SEVEN

Gorski regretted bringing his raincoat. It was a warm, sunny day with no prospect of rain. He paused in the doorway of the Restaurant de la Cloche and lit a cigarette, his coat draped over the crook of his left arm. He walked along Rue de Huningue until he reached the intersection. The police station was located a few minutes' walk along Rue de Mulhouse, but Gorski had no desire to return there. Instead he crossed the street and continued along Avenue Charles de Gaulle. Most of the shops were closed for lunch and the streets were quiet. Gorski liked this part of the day. It was as if the town paused to draw breath for a moment, not that the pace of life in Saint-Louis demanded such a lull. Even so, Gorski strode along purposefully, as if to give the appearance that he was on his way to an important appointment.

He turned into a narrow side street where,

a little further on, there was an inconspicuous bar called Le Pot. The name of the bar was painted in brown Germanic lettering above the door. A dark red *Bar/Tabac* sign was fixed to the wall with a rusting metal bracket. At night the sign was lit up, but during the day it would be quite possible to pass along Rue des Vosges without noticing there was a bar there at all. There were no windows save for two narrow oblongs of glass above eye level, which were for the purposes of ventilation only. The door was glass, but it was so plastered with posters advertising lottery tickets and various brands of cigarettes that it was impossible to see inside. The proprietor was aware that his bar was not particularly inviting, but the fact that, once inside, one could not be seen from the street, constituted a large part of its appeal.

Inside, the bar consisted of one small square room. The walls were painted with a dark mustard wash and decorated with faded prints depicting scenes from Old Alsace. Around two walls was a maroon banquette, the vinyl of which was cracked and worn. In one or two places, foam stuffing spilled out. In front of the banquette, five metal tables were bolted to the floor. In addition, four wooden tables were arranged in the centre of the room.

Gorski took a seat on the banquette and indicated to the proprietor with a little mime that he would take a *pression*. The bar occupied the wall opposite the door. On the right of this was the *tabac* area from which cigarettes, smoking paraphernalia, and lottery tickets were sold. These two areas of the bar were separated by the wooden flap through which the proprietor accessed the bar. There were three beer taps, offering *biere d'Alsace,* a German *weißbier,* and a dark ale. On the left of the bar was a stainless steel water bath, used to heat the hotdogs which were the only food served in Le Pot. The boiler was never turned off and it was from this that the bar got its characteristic aroma. The proprietor kept the lighting low, so that it was usually hard to tell whether it was day or night. In the late afternoon, however, if the sun was shining, two shafts of light penetrated the high windows and panned across the bar like the beams of a slow searchlight.

There were three other customers in the bar. A man in a shabby suit sat on the banquette beneath the high windows reading a newspaper, a glass of white wine on the table in front of him. He looked vaguely familiar. This was a common occurrence for

Gorski. His work brought him into fleeting contact with a great number of people and in a small town like Saint-Louis it was inevitable that he ran into them again. His predecessor, Ribéry, had been blessed with total recall of the names and faces of people he met, but Gorski possessed no such a talent. Still, it bothered him that he could not remember who the man was.

Two men in workmen's overalls stood at the bar. One of them looked at Gorski as he settled himself at his table. He probably recognised him. The previous day he had held a press conference at which he had given out the description of the young man seen on the scooter with Adèle. Gorski had been at pains to stress that the young man was sought only as a witness, but the papers had naturally chosen to cast the development in the most lurid light. Gorski's picture had appeared next to the story in *L'Alsace* and in several other papers. He nodded a greeting in the direction of the man at the bar, who immediately looked away.

The proprietor brought his beer. He was a short, swarthy man with the build of an ex-boxer. He had small beady eyes and a slack, unattractive mouth. Gorski had overheard regulars address him as Yves, but he never greeted him by name. Similarly, although he must have recognised him, the proprietor did not show any sign of knowing Gorski. That was his way. Some bars fostered an atmosphere of conviviality. Le Pot was not one of them. If you made a remark to the proprietor, he would pass the time of day, but otherwise customers were left to themselves.

As Yves set his beer in front of him, Gorski asked him for a hotdog. Before he made his way back to the bar, he made a tour of the tables, wiping each of them down in the same unhurried manner. Gorski sipped his beer. It was pleasingly cold and crisp. His hotdog arrived on a paper plate. The meat was pink and flabby and disintegrated unpleasantly as soon as he put it in his mouth. He thought of Manfred Baumann tucking into his *pot-au-feu* or whatever it was he had been eating.

His talk with Baumann had gone pretty much as he had anticipated. If he was lying, he was hardly likely to admit to the fact unless confronted with irrefutable evidence to the contrary. Gorski was used to being lied to. People lied as a matter of course and even when their lies were shown to be implausible, they were stubborn. Gorski understood the mechanism well. If, for example, his wife was to later ask him how he had spent his afternoon, he would, of course, omit any mention of his visit to this bar. What interested him was not so much the fact that someone lied, but how they behaved when they did so. Often people would reach for their cigarettes or become suddenly distracted by some irrelevant activity. They became incapable of maintaining eye contact. Women toyed with their hair. Men fingered their beards or moustaches. Gorski liked to question people in their everyday surroundings. Once a person had been dragged to the police station they were already disoriented and it became harder to discern whether their behaviour should be attributed to their unfamiliar surroundings or to the fact that they were trying to hide something. Gorski recalled that when he had visited Baumann at his apartment, he had, despite being initially reluctant to invite him inside, off ed him coffee. It was a typical gesture — at once overcompensating for his previous hostility and attempting to postpone the start of the interview. Even at that point, when he had no way of knowing what Gorski's visit was about, Baumann had behaved in a way that suggested he was uncomfortable.

Often, when confronted with their lies,

people feigned indignation. How many times Gorski had heard the phrases *This is outrageous!* and *How dare you!* or been idly threatened with legal action. He took such outbursts, if not as a sign of guilt, at least as an indication that the person in question had something to hide. Something perhaps completely unrelated to the object of his enquiry, but *something* nonetheless. Manfred Baumann had not done this. He was, Gorski suspected, too meek an individual for such a course of action. Neither had his demeanour betrayed much of his inner thoughts. He struck Gorski as the type who, for whatever reason, was accustomed to keeping a lid on things. He was repressed.

On the other hand, the possibility that Baumann had not seen anything could not be entirely dismissed. People were unobservant, especially when going about their daily routines. They walked or drove to and from work, sat in the same offices and cafés every day without giving the least thought to their surroundings. Often, when questioned, people were unable to describe the furniture or decor of places they visited regularly. Still, Manfred Baumann intrigued him. Whether he was lying or not, there was something in his manner that piqued Gorski's curiosity. He was at once evasive and obsequious, as if he wanted to be liked or at least approved of.

Nevertheless, it was a measure of how poorly the case was progressing that Gorski was spending so much time thinking about Baumann, who had, in all likelihood, nothing whatsoever to do with the girl's disappearance. The case was of the worst sort. It was not even clear whether a crime had been committed. Yet the disappearance of a young woman always garnered press attention and the police were obliged to investigate, or at least be seen to investigate. Had it been a middle-aged man who had disappeared, someone like Manfred Baumann, for example, the case would not even make the 'In Brief' section of *L'Alsace*.

Thus far, Gorski had been unable to form more than a rudimentary picture of the young woman whose disappearance he was investigating. Adèle Bedeau's mother had died some years before and her birth certificate recorded no father's name. Mme Pasteur was fond of her and plainly harboured maternal feelings towards the girl, but Adèle had revealed little to her employer. She was a good worker, punctual and polite, but little more. It did not seem to matter to her whether she was scrubbing the kitchen floor, chopping onions, or waiting tables.

She carried out whatever task she was allotted with the same world-weary air. Marie Pasteur described her as diligent. It seemed to Gorski that she was resigned. She simply didn't care what she did. Her relations with her employers and the patrons of the Restaurant de la Cloche were cordial enough, but she did not ask questions, talk about herself, or joke around with the other employees. She was entirely self-contained. And outside work, Gorski had discovered little more. The tiny furnished apartment she rented in a building on Rue de Jura could barely have revealed less. She paid her rent on time, and her neighbours had little to say about her.

Gorski had gone through her rooms feeling, as he always did on such occasions, like an intruder. The apartment consisted of a single bed-sitting room with an adjoining kitchenette and a tiny shower room. It was early on Saturday afternoon when Gorski had gained access. There was no concierge in the building and the landlady, whose name he had forgotten, leaned on the door jamb, her arms folded under her large bosom, a bored expression on her face. She was a squat woman with dyed hair and thick plastic-framed glasses. The venetian blind was lowered and Gorski had the impression that it was seldom raised. The air was stale. Gorski felt uncomfortable under the landlady's gaze. He disliked being scrutinised going about his work, especially so when it involved going through the personal effects of a young female.

He went into the kitchen and opened the doors of the cabinets. There were a few mismatched items of crockery, glasses, some tinned food. The fridge was empty, save for some fruit yoghurts in plastic containers, a pat of butter and a jar of strawberry preserve. On the worktop there was a packet of loose tea and a wooden board with a half-eaten loaf in a brown paper bag from a nearby bakery. Gorski picked up the bag of tea and smelt it. There was a single cup and a side plate with a few crumbs, unwashed in the sink. Gorski did not read much into the lack of comestibles. Most likely Adèle took most of her meals at the Restaurant de la Cloche. He flicked open his notebook and found the name of the landlady, before stepping back into the sitting room.

The room was furnished with a sofa-bed that had been neatly stored away, an ugly glass-topped coffee table, a small chest of drawers and an old-fashioned wardrobe, too large for the room, which Gorski imagined was a hand-me-down from the landlady's house.

'There's no need for you to stay, Mme Huber,' he said.

The landlady did not appear to understand that he wished her to leave.

'When will I be able to move her things out?' she said. 'I can't afford to let the place go unlet.'

The girl had been gone for a matter of thirty-six hours. Gorski stared at her.

'There's no reason to believe that your tenant will not return,' he said. 'However, for the time being, the apartment is under police jurisdiction.'

He deliberately avoided using the term 'crime scene'. People tended to get overexcited when they heard this phrase. And in any case, the apartment was not technically the scene of any crime.

Mme Huber looked at him sceptically. 'What about the rent?'

'I assume you've been paid till the end of the month.'

She nodded grudgingly.

'That's three weeks away,' said Gorski. 'Let's assume for the time being that the matter will be sorted out by then.'

The woman shrugged. Gorski asked her for the key and she handed it over without a word, before allowing him to usher her out of the apartment. When she was gone, he sat down on the sofa and lit a cigarette. He looked around the room for some sign of Adèle Bedeau. There were no pictures on the wall, no photographs on the bedside table, no books or magazines. Adèle had lived there for almost a year and seemingly done nothing to make the space more homey. Aside from the mismatched furniture, he might have been in a hotel room. Gorski got up and went to the window. He raised the blind to reveal an aspect of wasteland and the back of the breaker's yard on Rue de la Paix.

Gorski made a cursory examination of the wardrobe and chest of drawers. He had no wish to fumble through the girl's underwear or other garments and, even alone, he felt embarrassed doing so. There was nothing to suggest a hasty departure, nothing that suggested the *absence* of things. It was something his mentor, Ribéry, had taught him — not just to look at what was there, but to look for things that should have been there but weren't. Adèle's toothbrush was in the bathroom, along with other bottles and potions Gorski was familiar with from his own wife and daughter. On top of the wardrobe was a battered suitcase. Gorski lifted it down and placed it on the coffee table. It was dusty. It was the sort of place where a girl might keep her private bits and pieces. He flicked open the brass clasps. The case was empty. Adèle, it seemed, was a girl with no secrets. He put the suitcase back in its place. In the bedside table drawer, he found a half-finished tab of contraceptive pills. That was something. The last pill that had been taken was Thursday's, suggesting that she had not returned home since then. Of course, it was possible Adèle was the absent-minded type, but if she had chosen to disappear, she had certainly not done so in a premeditated manner.

Afterwards, Gorski knocked on the doors of the neighbouring apartments. No one had ever done more than greet Adèle in passing. They had never seen her bring anyone back to the apartment or heard voices from inside.

'Is she in some sort of trouble?' a grey-haired woman, two doors along the landing, had asked.

People often asked this, their glee poorly disguised as concern. Gorski had no doubt the old woman would be quite delighted to be told that her neighbour had been brutally raped and done to death.

Gorski's train of thought was interrupted

by Yves taking a fresh glass of wine to the man in the shabby suit. The workmen who had been standing by the bar had gone, but he had not even noticed them leave. Perhaps it was not so unlikely that Manfred Baumann had seen nothing on the night of Adèle's disappearance.

As Yves placed the glass on the man's table, he looked up from his newspaper and caught Gorski's eye. He pretended that it had not happened and immediately lowered his gaze. Gorski remembered him. He was a schoolteacher who had left the profession after a male pupil made some unsavoury allegations. Gorski had conducted a cursory investigation, but the pupil's claims had proved malicious. Nevertheless, as happens in such cases, a cloud hangs over the accused and the man resigned his position. Gorski would have liked to convey with a cordial look that he did not regard him as guilty, but the former teacher had not given him the opportunity to do so. Most likely, the man did not wish to be reminded of an unpleasant episode in his past.

Gorski ordered a second beer. Yves brought it over and wordlessly removed his paper plate and napkin. The man finished his drink and left without looking in Gorski's direction. Now that the bar was empty,

Gorski felt vaguely ridiculous. The proprietor studiedly busied himself polishing glasses and wiping down the surfaces behind the bar. There was a telephone on the wall next to the door to the WC. Gorski thought of phoning the station to check on the progress of the investigation, but it would be impossible to do so without being overheard. There was nothing else for it but to return to the station. He drank his beer, paid at the counter, and left.

He passed the rest of the afternoon in his office, typing a report on the investigation for the examining magistrate. Why, even in this official document, did he feel the need to present matters in a positive light? The men he had despatched to question residents in the area about further sightings of Adèle or the young man on the scooter had not turned up anything. It was frustrating. Having dismissed the idea that the waitress had disappeared of her own accord, Gorski was left with three further possibilities: she had met with an accident, committed suicide, or she had been murdered. The first of these could also be dismissed. Nobody answering Adèle's description had been admitted to a hospital in the vicinity of Saint-Louis, and if she had met with a fatal accident, her body would have been discovered by this time. Suicide could not be entirely dismissed. Had she thrown herself into the Rhine — the preferred method of suicide in the area — it was possible that her body would not be recovered for days or even weeks. However, nothing in her behaviour leading up to her disappearance suggested that she intended to do away with herself. Which left homicide, but without a body there could be no murder investigation. It was all speculation and Gorski did not like speculation. He liked to proceed with solid, logical steps built on concrete evidence. In his twenty or so years as a detective, he had trained himself to extend the same attention to whatever scraps of information were connected to a case, no matter how insignificant they might appear. His credo was to eliminate intuition, what his colleagues liked to call 'hunches'. And for the time being there was only one lead, the boy on a scooter. Until the young man was identified or Adèle's body was discovered, there was little chance of progressing the investigation. Already, Gorski had the familiar sinking feeling in his stomach that the case was going cold.

At half past six he went home, resisting the temptation to stop off in a bar on the way. At seven o'clock, Gorski's wife, Céline, placed a dish of baked fish and potatoes on the table. Gorski uncorked the bottle of wine they had opened the previous evening and poured each of them a glass. His daughter, Clémence, was seated at the table, a paperback flattened on her dinner plate. She was sixteen and had inherited her mother's fine features and chestnut hair. She had retained a boyish figure, something Gorski found unaccountably reassuring. Clémence closed her book and pushed her glass forward. Gorski poured the remains of the wine into it.

Céline dished out the food. There was barely enough to go around. She was not much of a cook. Gorski sometimes wondered if her frugal helpings accounted for Clémence's lack of physical development. Céline herself was half a head taller than Gorski, willowy, with small breasts and slim hips. It was a miracle she had ever borne a child and, after Clémence, she had sworn it was not an experience she intended to repeat.

Gorski rarely spoke about his work with Céline, and especially not over the dinner table, but the disappearance of Adèle Bedeau was big news. Clémence was fascinated, but Gorski had nothing new to tell her. 'Without a body, it's all in limbo,' he said.

He took a mouthful of fish. It was tasteless. Céline refused to have salt in the kitchen, maintaining that it was nothing more than a road to high blood pressure.

Clémence looked disappointed. 'But you still think she was murdered?'

Gorski shrugged. 'People disappear all the time.'

He picked a fishbone from between his teeth and placed it on the edge of his plate.

'*I* think she was murdered,' said Clémence. She ignored a look from her mother.

'What about the motive?' he asked.

'A crime of passion, of course. Most murders are committed by a person known to the victim.'

'That's true,' said Gorski. He enjoyed playing along with Clémence's theories. 'But if that were the case, where's the body? It's unlikely that a murder committed in the heat of the moment could be covered up.'

'I think it was the fat butcher on Avenue de Bâle. He killed her, chopped her up and put her in his sausages.'

Céline finally intervened. 'Can't we discuss something more suitable for the dinner table?'

Gorski and Clémence exchanged a conspiratorial look. The rest of the meal was passed in silence.

Céline ran a fashion boutique in town. The shop had never done better than break even. The stock was too upmarket for Saint-Louis, but Céline insisted that the women of the town needed to be educated. In spring and autumn she held a reception to present her latest collection, as she liked to call it. She hired models, served champagne and canapés and invited what great-and-good Saint-Louis had to offer. Céline insisted that Gorski attend these gatherings. She encouraged the ladies to bring their husbands, since, she maintained, it would be they who would be opening their chequebooks at the end of the evening. Gorski spent these evenings with the other reluctant husbands, loitering close to the table where the drinks were served. These occasions were less about the success of Céline's business than establishing 'the Gorskis' as part of the Good Society of the town. Céline made no attempt to conceal her belief that her husband's job was an impediment to such status. When they were first married, she had encouraged him to give up the police to study law. After his promotion to inspector, her aspiration switched to mov-

ing to a proper town, perhaps even Paris —
somewhere her business could thrive and
where she could mix in what she called
'sympathetic society'. But, Gorski explained,
it wasn't easy for a provincial cop to get a
move to a big city. Once, he had put in for
a transfer to Strasbourg, but when it was
turned down he did not pursue it. Gorski
sympathised with his wife's desire to move
to somewhere less dreary than Saint-Louis,
but over the years he had convinced himself
that it was not viable. It was not that he had
grown fonder of Saint-Louis. The truth was
that he was privately convinced that he had
found his level.

EIGHT

During the summer after the death of his mother, Manfred's principle activity was to walk in the woods behind the Paliard house. He had never enjoyed hot weather and even on the warmest days it remained tolerably cool on the forest floor.

One day, Manfred was lying on his back in a small clearing, his head resting on a soft mound of moss at the base of a tree. His shirt lay in a crumpled heap by his side. His eyes were closed but he was not asleep. He was listening to the papery rustle of the leaves in the breeze. It sounded like a distant stream. He breathed evenly and deliberately. The ground was bone dry and scattered with twigs that smelled like kindling. Manfred imagined a fire raging across the forest floor like a tidal wave. He pictured his body engulfed by flames and turned to blackened cinders which would float high on currents of air above the treetops.

Manfred opened his eyes suddenly. A girl was standing a few feet from where he lay. He had not heard her approach.

'How long have you been there?' he said.

'A while,' said the girl.

She was wearing a yellow cotton dress printed with orange flowers. She had leather sandals on her feet. Her hair was blonde and secured with a yellow bandana. She had large blue eyes, which she kept fixed on Manfred. She did not appear in the least embarrassed. She had a boyish figure and stick-thin arms. She was perhaps fifteen years old, although her childish outfit suggested she might be younger.

'Who are you?' Manfred asked, as if he was a landowner discovering a trespasser.

The girl shrugged and smiled a little. 'No one,' she said. 'Just a girl. Who are you?'

Manfred was impressed by the girl's reply. He could think of no better response.

'Just a boy,' he said. But he had a sudden urge to tell her everything about himself, how his father had run the Restaurant de la Cloche, how his mother had died, how he now lived with his grandparents, how he sometimes stared at his bedroom ceiling for a whole day without noticing the time pass.

The girl sat down next to Manfred, smoothing her dress underneath her as she did so. She sat with her arms around her knees, not saying anything. She was the most beautiful girl Manfred had ever seen. Right there and then he wanted to marry her and be with her every moment of his life until he died. He was suddenly embarrassed by his skinny, naked torso. He untangled his shirt and put it on.

The girl just sat there. Manfred couldn't think of anything to say that wouldn't sound stilted or phoney. The hem of the girl's dress fluttered slightly in the breeze. Downy blonde hair grew down the nape of her neck. Eventually she turned her head and looked at him.

'Not much of a talker, are you?'

Manfred felt himself blushing. If he didn't say something now, she would get up and leave and he would never see her again.

'I . . .' He hoped that if he started a sentence, something would tumble out, the way that when he recited a poem under his breath, the words just came. But nothing followed. He started again.

'Do you live near here?' It was so banal he wished he'd kept quiet. 'I've never seen you before,' he added by way of explanation.

'My parents have rented a house on the other side of the woods,' she said.

'You're on holiday?'

'I suppose,' said the girl.

Manfred knew that he should now ask where she was from. But he didn't want to know. All that mattered was that they were both here at this place at this moment. He didn't want to think of her in some far-off town or city where he didn't live, going to a school he didn't attend, talking to boys that weren't him.

'And you?' said the girl.

'Me?'

'Do you live round here?'

'I live with my grandparents on the outskirts of Saint-Louis,' he said.

'With your grandparents?'

'My parents are dead.' He had said it to gain the girl's sympathy, so that even if she didn't like him she might take pity on him. Perhaps she would take his hand.

'How thrilling,' she said, 'to be alone and make your own way in the world.'

'I'm not alone,' said Manfred. 'I'm with you.'

The girl got up and said she had to go. Her parents would be expecting her. She was not wearing a watch. Manfred felt his stomach tingle.

'Will I see you again?' he said.

The girl widened her eyes a little and made a little popping sound with her lips.

'Will you come here again tomorrow?' he asked.

'Maybe,' she said. 'It depends on my parents.'

'I'll be here,' said Manfred.

Then she disappeared into the forest.

Manfred returned to the clearing where he had met the girl for the next three days. He arrived ever earlier, the second and third days bringing himself a supply of water and fruit to get him through the day. He also brought books and a rug from the cupboard under the stairs. He selected the books carefully. The girl was clearly no dummy, so any pulp or *policiers* were out of the question. Camus, Sartre, Hemingway were clearly too mannish to make a positive impression on a frail girl in a yellow dress. Over-familiar classics would make Manfred seem a tyro — he should surely have read such key works already. In the end he chose two novels by Zola from his grandfather's bookshelf. He had previously, without having read a word, dismissed Zola as incurably dull and reactionary — all that stuff about fate flew in the face of his beloved existentialists — but from the very first pages of Zola's preface to *Thérèse Raquin,* Manfred was enthralled. One day, he too would write a book that would scandalise society and be wilfully misunderstood, only for history to prove him right. He would fearlessly expose hypocrisy, cant and sentimentality. And through his years of vilification, the girl in the yellow dress would be by his side.

Zola's description of his characters, trapped by temperament and lacking free will, felt like a release to Manfred. A burden was lifted from his shoulders. He too was a prisoner of the forces that had shaped him: the awkward, unsociable nature that made everyone ill at ease in his company; his dismal situation as an imposter in his grandparents' house; his uncertainty at what path to take when he left school. He was no longer in control of his own destiny. What, after all, had led him to meet the girl in the yellow dress? Not free will, but fate.

She appeared on the fourth day, as Manfred knew she would.

'Hello,' she said as she stepped into the little clearing.

'Hello,' said Manfred. On the rug he had laid out a brown paper bag of cherries and the flask of apple juice he had brought in his satchel. Manfred lay on his side, his head propped on his hand, his book open in front of him. The girl sat down as she had before, her arms clasped around her knees, her back to Manfred. She was wearing the same dress as before.

'How long have you been here?' she asked.

'All day,' said Manfred.

'Were you waiting for me?'

'Yes,' he said. He liked the fact that the girl did not look at him when she spoke.

'What if I hadn't come?'

'I'd have come back tomorrow,' he said.

'That's nice.'

'I wanted to see you again.'

'I wanted to see you too,' said the girl.

'It's strange, don't you think, that we met the way we did,' said Manfred. 'I mean, if I hadn't been in this clearing at the exact moment that you came by, if you had taken a different turning, if you hadn't been on holiday here, if I had been born somewhere else . . .'

The girl did not look round, but she shrugged her shoulders.

'You might as well say that whenever two people meet it's strange. Our meeting is no stranger than any other meeting between two people who don't know each other.'

'But we didn't plan to meet, did we?' said Manfred.

'How could two strangers plan to meet?' said the girl. 'If they had intended to meet, they wouldn't be strangers.'

Manfred was silent for a moment.

'What I mean is,' Manfred went on, feeling like he was leaping off a cliff without knowing how deep the water below was, 'that neither of us has exerted any will of our own. And yet, because of this happenstance, something — maybe everything — has changed.'

The girl looked over her shoulder at Manfred for the first time. 'Yes,' she said, 'I feel it too.'

That evening Manfred chatted merrily with his grandparents over the evening meal. He could see them exchanging bemused glances as he solicitously asked if they had had a pleasant day. The fug that normally surrounded him had lifted. Everything was light. Afterwards he helped clear away the dishes and joined his grandfather in his workshop and helped him bevel the edges of a chest of drawers he was making.

In bed that night, the dark, gloomy world of Zola no longer held any appeal. The desperate animal lust of Thérèse Raquin and her lover no longer attracted him. He lay instead in a reverie in which the girl was the protagonist and he her unworthy suitor. Unlike the dark fantasies he entertained about other girls, he had no lustful thoughts about the girl in the yellow dress. His love (he had no reservation about using this word) for her was on an altogether more elevated plain. When they parted, she had kissed him lightly on the cheek and they had clasped each other's fingers for a few seconds.

The following days were the happiest of Manfred's life. Even as he was experiencing them, he felt that it was not possible to be happier — for him or for anyone. He knew too that the girl felt the same. They had invented love. Until the moment the girl had stepped into the clearing, love had existed only as a word, an abstract concept that no other person had actually experienced.

They met every day. Manfred brought the rug to sit on and stuffed his satchel with bread, pâté, and fruit from his grandparents' larder. They ate lunch, feeling less like teenagers than a contented aging couple. Juliette came from Troyes. Her father was a lawyer who expected her to follow him into the profession. He was a taciturn man of iron will. Her mother was a docile woman whom Juliette had never once seen stand up to her father. She was a mere extension of her husband, who spent her days lunching with other such wives, shopping or having her hair done. But she was always home in time to dress for the evening meal.

Juliette despised her. She had no interest in law, but she felt unable to resist her father's strictures. She was not blessed with a rebellious nature. These illicit meetings with Manfred were the greatest transgressions of her life. She envied Manfred's freedom and wished her own parents dead.

Yet despite her view of herself as meek and compliant, Manfred found Juliette quite unique and possessed of a self-confidence he envied. She was not at all like the superficial, giggling girls he observed at school, with their twin manias for clothes and the very stupidest boys. Juliette had a sense of herself that did not require the affirmation of others. She was beautiful without ever giving the impression of thinking twice about her appearance.

Manfred encouraged her to stand up to her father, to follow her own course in life, whatever that might be. Juliette reminded Manfred of the speech he had delivered on the subject of Zola's preface to *Thérèse Raquin*. If he really believed what he had said, weren't we all like rats on a wheel scurrying in a predetermined direction, unable to change course? But Manfred was full of plans for the two of them. They would elope to Paris, or further afield, to Amsterdam, London, or New York. Manfred would write a great novel, an epic series, like Zola's *Rougon-Macquart* cycle, and they would be feted among the artists and writers of Europe. Years later, Juliette's father would appear unexpectedly at their door. He would break down, admitting that his dictatorial ways had driven his daughter from the family and that it was only now in old age that he realised this. He would be proud that his daughter had made her own way in the world. Then Manfred and his father-in-law would sit up into the small hours, drinking whisky and reflecting on the paths their lives had taken.

Juliette smiled indulgently at Manfred's fantasy. 'You haven't met my father,' she said. 'In any case, would I not then just be following your dream instead of my father's?'

On the final day of Juliette's holiday, the lovers met in the clearing as usual. Manfred felt melancholy. The thought of not seeing his beloved for days or weeks was too much to bear. He could not, knowing now that there was an alternative, return to his old life of torpor.

Juliette had brought two bottles of rough cider from the cellar of the cottage.

'If my father finds out, he'll kill me,' she laughed.

Manfred was disturbed that she could be so light-hearted on this black day, but he determined not to spoil their last hours together by reverting to his gloomy ways. They popped the stone stopper of the first bottle and passed it back and forth. They talked animatedly of how they would write to each other every day, sending their letters *poste restante* under outrageous pseudonyms. At weekends Manfred would travel to Troyes and sleep rough in the railway station just for the chance to snatch a few minutes with his beloved. They would smuggle notes to each other with dramatic entreaties: *Do not fail me! I am forever yours! My love, I am pining for you!*

Yet Manfred was preoccupied. Thus far their relationship had been consummated by no more than goodbye kisses and holding hands. As they sat side by side now on the blanket, Juliette held Manfred's fingers gently between her hands. But with the prospect of days or weeks without seeing one another, Manfred felt that they must mark the time they had spent together in some way. They must give their bodies to each other as a statement that they now belonged together and that their lives would from that moment be intertwined. As Manfred had contemplated this the previous evening, he had not thought of it as a sexual act (the practicalities of such a thing terrified him), but rather, although he considered himself an atheist, as something spiritual. He could think of no other way to describe it.

As they sat, blithely wittering about their future together, Manfred's stomach was churning. He had no idea how to initiate such a thing. Thus, he had decided that he would trust to fate — if it happened, it was because it was meant to happen. If it didn't, so be it. He also placed his faith in the fact that ever since he had met Juliette, their thoughts and feelings had wholly coincided. Was it not almost certain therefore that she had lain alone on her bed the previous night having entirely the same thoughts as he had? Was it, moreover, not inevitable that she had shared the same thoughts? Perhaps she had brought the cider along with the intention of easing their passage into adulthood.

They finished the first bottle. Manfred felt it go to his head. He broke off a chunk of bread and chewed on it to alleviate the mild nausea he felt. Juliette, seemingly oblivious to the effects, flipped open the stopper of the second bottle and handed it to Manfred. A little sun filtered down to the forest floor. The soft blonde hairs on Juliette's arm shone as she passed the bottle to him. She let out a small hiccup and covered her mouth with her free hand, giggling a little. This display of tipsiness reassured Manfred.

The time came for Juliette to leave. Manfred was gripped by fear. It was now or never. He grasped Juliette's wrist gently and said her name. She moved her face towards his as if she had been waiting for this invitation. Their mouths met, clumsily at first. Juliette manoeuvred her body so that her face was perpendicular to his. She pushed the tip of her tongue between Manfred's lips. Her hand clasped his neck. Manfred's mind soared off into the trees. He had no idea that such intensity was possible. Soon they were lying next to each other. Manfred's left hand rested on Juliette's hip. Did he dare to slide it down and feel the curve of her buttock under her dress? He did so, his fingertips alive to the grain of the cotton.

Emboldened, Manfred drew his lips down to her neck. Juliette held his head tightly there, her breath quickening. Manfred ran his tongue to the junction of her neck and shoulder. With her free hand, Juliette unbuttoned the top buttons of her dress, took Manfred's hand in hers and pressed it onto her breast. Manfred cupped the soft flesh in his palm. Her nipple was firm m between his fingers.

Manfred had not counted on such a rapid progress. He had only the sketchiest idea of what was expected of him. The thought of disappointing Juliette appalled him, but they were on the brink of something momentous. There was no choice but to go through with it. Juliette moaned softly as he caressed her breast. Her eyes were closed. Manfred manoeuvred himself on top of her and continued to kiss her on the neck. Then as quickly as it had begun, Juliette gripped his wrist and said, 'Let's not. Not now.'

Manfred simultaneously felt a wave of relief and a feeling that it was too late to stop, as if he was the driver of a locomotive spotting a car on a level crossing only a few metres ahead.

'Yes, of course,' he heard himself saying, but as he said it he ground his groin against her. He recalled how his mother had described her feeling of being overpowered by her father as he kissed her against a tree in this same forest all these years before. He had his hands on Juliette's neck. He could not now prevent himself from coming and as he did so he raised himself to see Juliette's face. Her eyes were bulging. Her body convulsed beneath him, heightening his passion. Then they both went limp. Manfred felt suddenly ashamed. He rolled off and lay next to Juliette waiting for his breathing to settle, staring at the branches of the trees shimmering above them.

He took Juliette's hand in his.

'I'm sorry,' he said, 'I couldn't stop myself.'

She didn't reply. Manfred raised himself onto his elbow. Juliette's head lay slackly to one side. Her mouth and eyes were open. She was not breathing.

Manfred stared at her blankly for a few long moments. Then he nudged her arm. She didn't react. He placed his hand on her heart. It was not beating. Manfred leapt to his feet, his hand over his mouth. He felt himself gasping for breath then he threw up, turning his head away from the rug. He retched until there was nothing more in his stomach. He sat there on his knees for a long time, or what seemed like a long time. Perhaps it was no more than a minute. What he remembered most was the horrible look of disbelief and betrayal frozen on Juliette's face.

Manfred got up from his knees. He surveyed the surrounding trees. Nobody had seen them and there had been nothing to hear. If Juliette had only cried out, he would have stopped. He had not been aware of what he was doing. Manfred realised that what he was about to do was dreadful, but he braced himself to go through with it. He cleared the two bottles off the rug and put them in his satchel. Then he picked up the apple cores they had left on the ground, the end of a baguette, the wax paper wrapper of the pâté and the knife they had used to spread it. Next he grasped the corner of the rug and tugged it hard. Juliette's body rolled slowly off it into an ungainly heap. Her face was pressed against the ground and her dress was rumpled around her waist. Manfred pulled it down over her buttocks. Tears were streaming down his face, but he surveyed the clearing for any other debris. He scuffed the thin pool of his vomit into the earth and slowly backed out, unable to take his eyes off the wreckage of Juliette's body. Then he turned and ran through the trees.

NINE

The woman was standing by the bank of metal mailboxes in the foyer, leafing through her post. Manfred was leaving for work as he always did at 8.15. She was wearing a grey business suit and the blouse he had found in the laundry room. Manfred felt pleased by this, as if it was a gift he had given her and she was wearing it to please him. Manfred normally collected his mail in the evening when he returned from work, but he stopped and unlocked his box. There was never anything of interest in there and there was no wastepaper basket in the lobby to discard junk mail, which meant either stuffing it into his briefcase and disposing of it at work or carrying it in his hand to the litter bin in the street. The woman looked up from her mail and said good morning. She did not seem displeased to see him. She smiled. There were laughter lines around her eyes.

'Oh, good morning,' Manfred said, trying to appear as if he had only just noticed her.

'How are you?' she said.

'Well,' said Manfred. 'And you?'

The woman shrugged, widened her eyes slightly, as if the answer to Manfred's question was self-evident. Manfred reached into his box and retrieved a handful of pamphlets. There was a pet product catalogue along with leaflets advertising offers at local supermarkets.

'The usual,' he said.

The woman proffered her own bundle in a show of solidarity. 'I can't believe they think anyone actually looks at this stuff,' she said.

'Actually,' said Manfred, 'studies have shown that direct mailings are by far the most effective form of advertising. In comparison, television or radio commercials are rather inefficient. Mail-outs can be much more easily directed at the target market. They're cheap and can be easily adapted to local communities.'

The woman raised her eyebrows, rolled her eyes slightly. 'Quite the smooth talker, aren't you, Manfred Baumann?' Manfred could feel his cheeks colouring. Despite the woman's sardonic tone, he was pleased that she remembered his name.

'I wouldn't say that,' he said.

'Actually, I owe you an apology,' she said. 'I was very rude when we met before and didn't introduce myself.' She held out her hand. 'Alice Tarrou.'

Manfred stuffed his mail back into his box and took her hand. 'Manfred Baumann,' he said.

'Yes,' she said, 'I know.'

They moved towards the entrance of the building. Manfred held the door open for her. Alice indicated that she was walking in the opposite direction from town. Without thinking, Manfred accompanied her. It was sunny and there was the characteristic freshness in the air of the time of year. The grass verge that separated the apartment block from the main road glistened with dew. Manfred commented that it was a pleasant morning and Alice agreed. They walked in silence for a few steps. The heels of Alice's shoes clacked on the pavement. Manfred glanced up at the windows above them. Anyone who happened to see them together might assume that they were husband and wife, or at least that they had spent the night together. It was quite thrilling. He pictured them sitting at the table in his kitchen; Alice, hair dishevelled, bundled in his robe eating a croissant, a pot of coffee bubbling on the hob. Manfred stole a look at her out of the corner of his eye.

'You're wearing the blouse,' he commented.

'So I am,' said Alice. She glanced at him.

Manfred wondered if he should pay her a compliment. He was not in the habit of making personal comments to women.

'It's nice,' he said.

Alice smiled. 'Thank you.'

They had reached the end of the block. Alice turned left and doubled back around the building. Manfred followed her.

'Is your car round here?' Alice asked.

'No,' said Manfred. 'I don't drive.' He had never seen any reason to learn.

'Gosh,' she said.

She asked where he worked and Manfred told her. Alice looked puzzled. He was walking in the opposite direction from the bank.

'I have a meeting in Strasbourg this morning,' he said. 'I'm taking the train.'

Alice nodded. 'Ah,' she said. Manfred was pleased. The idea that he had a meeting in Strasbourg seemed to have impressed her. Then he was gripped by a fear that she would say that she too was on her way to Strasbourg and would off him a lift. What plausible reason would there be to refuse? He would have to say that he was car-sick and preferred to take the train. That would make him appear feeble, however. Car-sickness was not the sort of thing a man who travelled to Strasbourg for business meetings would suffer from. In any case, what if Alice offered him a lift on another occasion, perhaps to drive to a country inn on Sunday afternoon? He would have to pretend that there was some medication he could take in advance in order to facilitate such a trip. It was in fact true that Manfred did not enjoy travelling by car. He suspected it brought on the migraines from which he suffered periodically.

Alice came to a halt next to a small silver sports car. It had a roof that could be taken down. She fished in her bag for the key.

'You don't seem like a bank manager,' she said. Manfred was not sure what she was suggesting by this, but imagined she did not mean it negatively. People usually thought of bank managers as officious, older men, old-fashioned in their appearance.

'Thank you,' he said.

Alice laughed. 'You're welcome.'

She unlocked the driver's-side door and tossed her bag on to the passenger seat. She climbed into the car and put the key in the ignition. She did not offer him a lift. Man-fred stood on the pavement, unable to think how to end the encounter. Alice closed the door and wound the window down.

'We should have that coffee some time,' she said.

'Assuredly,' he said, immediately regretting his ridiculous choice of word.

'How about tomorrow?'

'Tomorrow?' Manfred repeated.

'Why not?' said Alice. 'Are you busy?'

Manfred shook his head. He wondered if he would be missed at the Restaurant de la Cloche.

'Why don't we make it dinner?' said Alice. She suggested a restaurant. 'Seven?' she said.

Manfred nodded dumbly. She fired the engine and drove off. Manfred waved. Then he continued through the car park, past the children's play park and exited on the opposite side, in the direction of the railway station. He looked at his watch. It was 8.25. He had spent less than ten minutes in Alice's company. He walked purposefully into the station. He could not risk the possibility of Alice seeing him on Rue de Mulhouse. He liked to arrive early at the bank, but what of it if he was a few minutes late? Mlle Givskov had keys and was authorised to open the premises. He would still arrive by the time the bank opened to the public at nine o'clock. He headed through the underpass to the platform where the trains for Strasbourg departed. He contemplated buying a ticket, but decided against it. Anyone observing him would assume that he had a weekly ticket or was making a return journey. In any case, it was possible to buy a ticket from the conductor on the train.

There were around twenty people on the platform. Most of them stood hunched over *L'Alsace*, a briefcase at their feet. Manfred did not recognise anyone and nobody so much as glanced in his direction. He placed his own briefcase at his feet and stood with his back to the red brick wall of the waiting room. A train pulled in. Nobody got off. The commuters boarded in an unhurried fashion. Manfred remained against the wall. A whistle blew from the end of the platform and the train pulled away. Manfred picked up his briefcase and took the stairs back down to the underpass. Anyone seeing him leave the platform would assume he had disembarked from the train that had just left. He felt quite pleased with himself. He took the back way along Avenue de la Marne to the bank and arrived just as Mlle Givskov was opening up.

The morning passed swiftly. There was no

further talk among the staff of the missing girl, at least not within Manfred's hearing. Manfred greeted Carolyn cheerfully when she brought in his mid-morning coffee and successfully engaged in small talk. The girl seemed pleased to have the opportunity to pass a few amiable moments with her boss. Manfred ploughed through a backlog of loan reviews and applications. Decisions he had been putting off for days now seemed straightforward. If a person defaulted on their loan, it was their responsibility, not his. The bank could not be expected to throw money away willy-nilly.

By twelve o'clock Manfred had cleared so much work he decided to take his lunch early. If he bumped into Alice, it was perfectly plausible that he could have had his meeting in Strasbourg and returned by this time. The air was clear and Saint-Louis seemed to have shaken off some of its drabness. Manfred passed the little park at the Protestant Temple. Two old women were sitting on a bench with bags of shopping at their feet. They did not look up as Manfred passed. As he had some time on his hands, he decided to take a walk to the Rhine before he had lunch. He walked briskly, working up a light sweat on his brow. These last few months he had noticed a thickening around his midriff. If he weren't careful, he would end up like Lemerre. As he strode along he twice thought he spotted Alice, but on both occasions it was just a woman dressed in a similar fashion. Most likely she did not work in Saint-Louis. Nevertheless, he found himself hoping to bump into her or even spot her driving past in her little sports car.

Manfred half-expected Gorski to be waiting for him at the Restaurant de la Cloche, sitting at his table with his raincoat folded on his lap, nursing a glass of wine. The prospect did not worry him. Yes, he had behaved foolishly, but Gorski had no way of knowing he had lied. If he had any evidence to back up his insinuations, he would have questioned him formally. It would all blow over in a few days.

TEN

Juliette's parents raised the alarm early in the evening when she did not appear for dinner. The night had brought a violent thunderstorm. At first the police were unperturbed. Perhaps the girl had wandered off and sought shelter from the storm. But when she did not turn up in the morning it did not take long for the search party to discover her body. The story was a sensation. Juliette's picture adorned the front pages of every newspaper in the country. Some monster must be at large. Reporters drew parallels with other unsolved murders, but the investigation could establish no connection to any previous cases.

Gorski had been a detective for only two years. His superior, Inspector Ribéry, was on holiday in the Swiss Alps when the story broke and the case landed in the lap of the younger officer. The torrential overnight rain destroyed whatever evidence might have existed at the crime scene. Gorski came in for vicious criticism in the press for failing to raise the alarm sooner. In reality, he had not been informed of the disappearance until the morning after it was reported, as the matter had been dealt with by the duty officer at the station. But Gorski did not think it politic to make this public.

Ribéry returned two days later. He was nearing retirement and had no wish to steal the limelight from his young colleague, especially as his more practised eye could see that, given the lack of evidence or obvious motive (the post-mortem had revealed no evidence of sexual assault), the case was unlikely to come to a rapid or satisfactory conclusion. Instead, he made it clear to Gorski that justice must be seen to be done. Gorski understood what was implied. He was determined, however, that this, his first prominent case, would not be prematurely prosecuted on account of pressure either from his jaded superior or from the press, who bayed daily for fresh developments.

Gorski pored over the crime scene photographs for hours on end. What accounted for the curious position of the body? It appeared that the girl had been strangled standing up and then thrown to the ground. Had she been walking with her assailant prior to the murder, or had she been followed into the woods? Or was it a crime of opportunism, committed by someone already lurking around the clearing? It was not even possible to state with any certainty that the girl had been killed there. Perhaps she had been done to death elsewhere before being dumped in the woods. This struck Gorski as unlikely since no attempt had been made to conceal the body, but it could not be entirely ruled out. Certainly on one score the press were correct: a monster was at large.

Gorski spent long hours sitting in the clearing where the body had been found. The area had been meticulously searched, but not a scrap of evidence had been discovered. Still he sat in the clearing smoking, listening and looking, as if he expected the trees to somehow reveal their secret. It was a lesson for him: detective work had nothing to do with intuition or inspiration. Mostly it was a matter of slavishly following procedure. The rest was luck.

The luck came two weeks after the murder. Police in a neighbouring district picked up a tramp living rough in some woods. The man, Emile Malou, had a previous conviction for sexually assaulting a minor. Gorski drove to Mulhouse to interview him. Malou was cooperative. He insisted he had never been in the woods at Saint-Louis and had never set eyes on Juliette Hurel. He had no alibi for the day in question and made no attempt to concoct one. He simply said he could not remember where he had been. It struck Gorski as the response of an innocent man. And while the tramp's previous conviction had been for the attempted rape of a fourteen-year-old girl, there was, Gorski reminded the examining magistrate, no evidence of sexual assault in this case. There was nothing to connect Malou to the crime.

Then a local widow came forward. She said that she had seen a suspicious-looking character in the vicinity of the woods around the time of the murder. She could not remember the exact day, but she picked out Malou, whose picture had already appeared in the papers, at an identity parade. It was enough for the examining magistrate. Malou was charged and found guilty, but Gorski remained unconvinced. He visited Malou in prison and told him he believed that he had been wrongly convicted. The tramp just shrugged and refused to appeal. He appeared content to spend the remainder of his life in the relative comfort of prison. 'I'm getting too old for living rough,' he told Gorski. 'In here I get a bed and three meals a day.' Nevertheless Gorski vowed to continue the investigation. Notwithstanding the wrong done to Malou, a killer remained at large. For months Gorski spent his weekends walking in the woods, hoping to come across an overlooked clue, but he knew it was futile and in the end he gave up. When Malou died in jail a few years later, Gorski was the only person to attend his perfunctory committal.

Gorski returned to the clearing for the first time in several years. He parked as he always had in the lay-by on the D468, which more or less followed the course of the Rhine north. The white paint on the little wooden gate which led into the woods had mostly flaked off and the jamb was rotten. As he made his way along the path towards the clearing, Gorski tried not to think about what it was that had made him return. He had not told anyone where he was going and, were he to bump into anyone, he would be hard pressed to explain his presence. Instead he concentrated his mind on the pleasant sounds of twigs cracking under his shoes and the papery rustle of the leaves in the breeze.

After the murder, Gorski had returned to the clearing on a regular basis. Later, his visits became less frequent. After the trial, he accepted the plaudits of the press for solving the case and kept his thoughts about the safety of Malou's conviction to himself. If his colleagues harboured similar doubts, they too kept them to themselves. He once confessed his misgivings to Céline, but she had been dismissive. The case was closed — why would he want to re-open old wounds? From the start she had found what she called his 'obsession' with the dead girl distasteful. She complained that he spent more time thinking about a corpse than he did about her.

As the frequency of Gorski's visits to the clearing dwindled, he felt guilty, like a widower who lets his wife's grave become overgrown. At first, his visits were borne of the conviction that something must have been overlooked, that there was some evidence staring him in the face, but after a few months Gorski knew that there were no such clues or, if there had been, they had long since been destroyed. But still he came. He would sit smoking, hoping somehow to gain some insight into the crime. He was embarrassed to admit it, even to himself, but he half hoped to 'see' the crime. He tried to think himself into the mind of the killer. But nothing ever came. Once he had heard a character in a film say that actions left an imprint on a place, just as a fire leaves a tang of charcoal in the air, but he didn't believe such nonsense. His mind would wander to other topics and he would only be roused from his thoughts when he came to the end of his packet of cigarettes. Certainly, one thing was clear: the killer could not have chosen a more peaceful spot for his deed. In all the times Gorski visited the clearing, he never once encountered another human being.

The clearing had changed little since Gorski's last visit. A few years before, storms had brought down a few trees, which were already blanketed in moss. They resembled peacefully sleeping bodies. Gorski sat on one of these fallen trunks and took his cigarettes from the pocket of his jacket. It was chilly beneath the foliage. There was no sign of what had occurred twenty years before. Gorski sat smoking in the clearing. He had no real idea why he had returned, although naturally the disappearance of the waitress had revived his memories of the murder of Juliette Hurel. Was it possible that the two events were connected? Both involved teenage girls and had occurred in the same locale, albeit twenty years apart. It was not unheard of for killers to lie dormant for years, however; nor was it out of the question that there were unsolved murders elsewhere that were the work of the same man. But, in all likelihood, the only connection between the two crimes was Gorski himself. In any case, until Adèle Bedeau's body turned up, Gorski could not even be sure that he was dealing with a homicide. Murder was, at this point, merely the most likely of the scenarios he had turned over and over in his head. Without a body, he had nothing to go on, no time or cause of death, no forensic evidence, no motive. So, in lieu of any tangible leads, he had wandered into these woods in the vague hope of a moment of insight. Gorski shook his head and gave a little laugh through his nose. There was nothing to do but wait. He was no more in control of the destiny of this case than he had been all these years before.

He finished his cigarette and got up. He felt weary and the seat of his trousers was damp from the moss. He trudged back along the path to the side road where he had left his car. As he drove back towards the town he passed the cottage the Hurels had rented. He drove back into Saint-Louis and pulled up outside a grocer's. He went inside and bought some fruit and other items. The woman at the till asked him if he had found the waitress yet.

Gorski shook his head. 'I can't say too much about it,' he said.

The woman gave him a look as if to suggest that Gorski had just taken her into his confidence.

'Mum's the word,' she said with a meaningful nod.

'I appreciate your discretion,' said Gorski.

He asked for two packets of Gitanes and stuffed them into the pocket of his jacket. He decided to walk the ten minutes to Rue des Trois Rois. His father's pawnshop was now a florist's. After his father's death, Gorski had not had the will to have it cleared out and it had lain empty for years. For some reason he was glad it had become a flower shop. The owner, Mme Beck, was a cheerful sort who made a habit of looking in on his mother, who still lived in the maisonette above the premises. The florist often brought Mme Gorski off-cuts from bouquets to spruce up her living room. The apartment was still accessed through the back of the shop and the brass bell which rang when Gorski pushed open the door was one of the few remnants of his father's shop. Mme Beck was busy with a customer when he entered. Gorski gestured towards the stairs behind the counter and made his way up to the apartment. The florist mouthed a greeting and waved him through.

In his childhood, the shop stayed open until seven in the evening, and after school Gorski would sit on a stool doing his home-work on his lap, while his father, in his brown store-coat, a pencil behind his ear, leaned on the counter. In the backroom, Gorski's mother sat at a rickety desk, updat-ing the huge leather-bound ledger in which the transactions were recorded. Her hand-writing was an elegant copperplate. At six o'clock, Madame Gorski went upstairs to prepare the evening meal. At this point it fell to the young Gorski to record any further business in the ledger. He treated this task with great solemnity and would hunch over the great book, tongue peeping from the corner of his mouth, aware that his parents' livelihood depended upon the accuracy of his entries.

The shop was a trove of jewellery, string-less musical instruments, bric-a-brac, furni-ture, military paraphernalia, silverware, books and taxidermy. It was Monsieur Gor-ski's policy to offer a price on every item brought into the shop, no matter how worthless. 'You never know,' he liked to say, 'what a customer may bring in next time.' The shop smelt fusty. The windows were piled so high with goods that little natural light entered the premises and Monsieur Gorski kept the lighting inside dim. 'Respectable people are ashamed of entering a pawnbroker's,' he would say. 'They do not wish to be illuminated when they do so.'

At precisely seven o'clock, Monsieur Gorski would step out from behind the counter and wordlessly turn round the sign that hung on a string on the door. He would then remove his store-coat, hang it on the hook behind the counter, put on his suit jacket and, carefully adjusting the cuffs of his shirt, ascend the stairs for the evening meal. The Gorskis never took a holiday.

Gorski knocked lightly on the door of the apartment. He visited once or twice a week, but his mother always behaved as if it was a tremendous surprise to see him. Sure enough, she greeted him with a delighted 'Georges!' when she opened the door and kissed him warmly on both cheeks.

'I brought you a few things,' Gorski said, setting the brown paper bag of groceries on the counter in the kitchenette.

'Georges! I've told you, you mustn't,' she said.

Mme Gorski was in her eighties, but aside from the arthritis that made it impossible for her to leave the apartment, she was in excellent health. Her mental faculties showed no sign of waning. She refused to countenance any suggestion that she might be happier in a nursing home. Nor would she consider moving in with her son.

'I don't want to be a burden,' she would say. 'In any case, this is my home.'

Gorski never pressed her. The thought of his mother cooped up in the little apartment saddened him, but the idea of his mother and Céline living under one roof was absurd. He had never even broached the subject with his wife.

Mme Gorski chatted merrily to him as he set about preparing a salad and some tinned sardines he had bought. He laid everything out on the table in the living room and they sat down to eat. He poured each of them a small glass of the sweet white wine his mother liked to drink.

Monsieur and Madame Gorski would speak little during the working day. On the rare occasion that a particularly interesting item was brought into the shop, it was only over the evening meal that it would be discussed. It was not businesslike to show enthusiasm or even interest in the presence of customers. Monsieur Gorski had perfected a tone of complete monotony, which he used whether making an offer on a valuable painting or a worthless piece of costume jewellery. After dinner, he would peruse the day's newspaper for half an hour, before leaving the house for the Restaurant de la Cloche, where he would drink two or three glasses of red wine and perhaps take part in a game of cards with some of the other local shopkeepers.

Once a month, Mme Gorski took herself to Mulhouse for the Saturday market. From the age of twelve, the young Gorski was charged with keeping the ledger. Saturday was an important day for the business. Fewer items were brought in — customers preferring to commit this shameful act when the shop was quiet — but Saturday was Selling Day. From six o'clock in the morning, Gorski and his father would sort through the items that had reached their redemption date and display them prominently in the shop. On Saturdays, Monsieur Gorski cast off his tedious tone and spoke lyrically about the craftsmanship, rarity and beauty of the items for sale. He did not press customers to buy, instead allowing his enthusiasm and expertise to lure them into a purchase. He never explained his strategy, but he knew his son was observing everything. Gorski understood he was being subtly instructed in the running of the business and that in due course he was expected to take over.

However, as Gorski reached his teenage years he was drawn in a different direction. He became aware of another side of his father's business. Now and again, policemen came into the shop. These were not uniformed *gendarmes*, but world-weary detectives in crumpled raincoats. They would ask if Monsieur Gorski had recently come into possession of such-and-such an item. He would invariably give such queries careful consideration before shaking his head slowly or calling over his shoulder to his wife: 'Madame Gorski,' — as he always addressed her in the shop — 'Could you bring out the silver necklace that came in on Wednesday?'

If the article turned out to be what the detectives were looking for, Monsieur Gorski would provide the name he had been given by the customer and furnish them with an invariably vague description. The detectives would thank him and leave with the item. Monsieur Gorski never betrayed any emotion after these encounters. He had, after all, been left out of pocket, but Gorski came to realise that he regarded such things as an occupational hazard, or perhaps more accurately as an inevitable business expense.

Gorski began to recognise certain customers, each of whom had their own speciality. He noticed that his father always offered these characters a lower price for their items than he would to other customers, but they never haggled or stormed out with their goods. They merely accepted whatever Monsieur Gorski was prepared to offer. Gorski realised that his father was an intermediary in a dance between the cops and the curiously meek burglars, thieves, and opportunists who made use of his services.

Gorski began to look forward to the visits of the detectives. He admired the dignity with which they conducted their business with his father. Each party knew exactly what was going on, but betrayed none of this in the manner with which they dealt with one other. One cop in particular fascinated Gorski. He was in his fifties and a little more talkative than the others. Before he came to the point of his visit, he would browse for ten minutes or so, commenting on certain items. He appeared to know a little about art and would sometimes embark on a lengthy critique of a landscape or portrait that caught his eye. He appeared to like Monsieur Gorski and it was in the company of Inspector Ribéry that Monsieur

Gorski came closest to letting his sober weekday manner slip. He enjoyed discussing paintings with the detective and would join him in front of a particular picture and contribute his own remarks about the brushstrokes or the way the artist had captured the light. These discussions sometimes became quite animated before the inspector abruptly brought them to a halt and broached the real subject of his visit. Then the two men would resume their professional demeanours as if nothing else had passed between them.

At the age of sixteen, Gorski was expected to leave school and gradually take over the running of the business. Neither his father nor mother had ever asked their son what he planned to do but, as the end of the school year approached, it became clear that it had never occurred to them that he might wish to continue his studies. They were not people to whom education meant a great deal. Comments were passed about how useful it would be to have him around the shop more often.

The knowledge that he meant to disappoint his father weighed heavily on the young man. He brooded for weeks about how to broach the subject. Certainly, it would not come up in the course of conversation. The Gorskis were not a family for chit-chat. In the shop they only spoke about business, and the evening meal was eaten for the most part in silence. The young Gorski began to resent his father for taking him for granted, for not considering that he might have other — loftier, he thought — aspirations. He became surly and uncooperative, in an immature attempt to provoke his father into enquiring what the matter was. But he never did.

In the end, Gorski's hand was forced. One evening, as the plates were being cleared, he made his announcement: 'I mean to become a policeman.'

Monsieur Gorski raised his head from his paper and looked at his son over the rims of his reading glasses. He pursed his lips and nodded slowly, as if he had been expecting this all along.

'An excellent profession,' he said. 'I know many fine policemen.'

He returned his gaze to the newspaper and after half an hour, put on his coat and went, as usual, to the Restaurant de la Cloche.

A week later Gorski was summoned upstairs on his return from school. Inspector Ribéry was seated at the dining table with a small glass of cognac. Monsieur Gorski stood nervously by the window as if it would be impolite to sit in the presence of his social superior. Gorski stood at the table in front of the inspector. He had a large equine face and small beady eyes.

'Your father tells me that you wish to become a policeman.'

'Yes, monsieur,' Gorski replied.

The inspector nodded approval as if he was hearing this information for the first time.

'A detective,' said Gorski, overcoming his shyness, 'I want to be a detective.'

The inspector nodded again. 'You should stay on at school. Come and see me when you're eighteen and we'll see what we can do.'

And that was that. Gorski remained at school. His father no longer had him help out in the shop. Perhaps he no longer saw the point, or perhaps he did not want the future detective training his eye on his more questionable dealings. It was never discussed. Instead, Gorski spent his weekends labouring on the farm of a family acquaintance. He enjoyed being outside, away from the stale atmosphere of the shop. He spent the money he earned on detective novels and books on criminology and psychology. He devoured Simenon, learning, he thought, the subtle arts of detection from the inscrutable Maigret.

When the time came, Gorski presented himself at Ribéry's office. Of course, he would have to serve his time on the beat like any other cop, the inspector explained. The statement puzzled Gorski, as it seemed to suggest that he was not like any other cop. Gorski did indeed spend three years on the beat, but Ribéry often pulled him from the rota and took him to inspect a crime scene or to observe the questioning of a suspect. He realised that he was the inspector's protégé. At first it was thrilling to be called to the scene of a burglary or assault, but he quickly realised that his knowledge of criminology easily outstripped that of the inspector, who, it turned out, was a slow-witted man more interested in his lunch, which he invariably took at the Restaurant de la Cloche, than in pursuing criminals. He also realised that there was little in the way of crime to be solved in a town like Saint-Louis, and the life of a provincial inspector did not unduly impinge on the practice of drinking a carafe of wine over lunch and spending the afternoons drifting from bar to bar, sharing a snifter with the proprietors. Gorski began to see his life unfolding beyond Saint-Louis. Once he made detective, which he did in his mid-twenties, he would move to more exciting pastures — Strasbourg, Marseille or even Paris, somewhere alive with crime, violence and murder.

When he joined the police, Gorski moved into a small apartment near his parents. He dutifully attended Sunday lunch, but conversation was as stilted as ever. Monsieur Gorski never asked his son about his work. Gorski naturally enquired about the pawnshop, but it became apparent that his father's heart was no longer in it. His health was failing and without a son to whom he could pass on the business, what was the point in slaving away? The shop, through which Gorski still entered on his visits, had always been cluttered, but there had been an order to the clutter. Monsieur Gorski could locate an item procured years before in a matter of seconds, but now stock was piled higgledy-piggledy or left unsorted in boxes. Gorski scuttled through the shop as quickly as he could. He had broken the old man.

It was inconceivable that Monsieur Gorski would retire. In the end he simply could not continue. He died of pneumoconiosis, caused, the doctor told him, by years of working in the dusty, ill-ventilated shop. He spent two dismal years sitting in his chair by the window above the premises. It was at this time that Gorski investigated the murder of Juliette Hurel. Not only was this the most sensational thing to have occurred in Saint-Louis for as long as anyone could remember, it was the only case in which Monsieur Gorski ever betrayed an interest. During the years of his father's confinement, Gorski visited more frequently, bringing round a little shopping and sometimes some flowers to spruce up the dreary room.

'You got the bastard yet?' Monsieur Gorski would wheeze as soon as his son was over the threshold.

'Not yet, Dad,' Gorski would reply. He continued to answer this way even after Malou was convicted.

Mme Gorski never asked her son about his work. She made no secret of how proud she was of him, but she would not consider it her place to inquire about the day-to-day business of his job. Naturally she would be aware that he was now investigating the disappearance of Adèle Bedeau. She watched television and read the papers like everyone else, but she did not allude to it. Instead she sustained a monologue about the various people who had looked in on her since his last visit. Gorski, for his part, had no wish to discuss his investigations with his mother. It was relaxing to listen to her stream of gossip about these people he didn't know.

Gorski washed up the crockery and put on his jacket.

'See you soon,' he said.

'Don't you worry about me,' she said.

Gorski let himself out through the shop and walked back to his car. The light was fading and the streets were quiet. Gorski pulled up outside the police station. As he was locking his car, he saw someone raise an arm to him from the opposite side of the street. It was a young man, in his late teens or early twenties. He threw a cigarette onto the pavement and trotted across the road.

'Monsieur Gorski?' he said. He looked nervous. He kept his eyes trained somewhere around Gorski's midriff as if he expected at any moment to receive a blow to the back of the head. Gorski knew immediately that he was the boy on the scooter.

'Yes.'

'I wanted to talk to you,' he said. 'You're investigating Adèle's disappearance.'

'That's right,' said Gorski. 'You know something about it?'

The boy nodded. Gorski lead him up the

steps into the station. Schmitt was at the counter behind the glass partition. He looked up disinterestedly and buzzed the door open. The boy followed Gorski into the corridor. Gorski took him to an interview room and went off to fetch some coffee.

ELEVEN

In the days that followed Juliette's death, Manfred was numb. Sorrow, guilt, and fear vied for his attention. Fortunately his grandparents were accustomed to him spending long hours alone in his room. That first evening he did not join his grandparents for dinner. How could he sit there when his sweetheart lay crumpled and dead in the woods and he, with whom she had only moments before exchanged the most passionate exhortations, had killed her? And yet, even then, there was an instinct of self-preservation that kept him in his room. It would surely be obvious to anyone who set eyes upon him that he was the guilty party.

During the storm that broke that evening, Manfred spent the night rigid on his bed, imagining Juliette's body on its sodden deathbed. He saw the wind whipping up the cotton of her dress, the rain plastering her hair to her forehead. It was all he could do to prevent himself from rushing back out to the woods to cradle her drenched body. But he did not do so. And, at some point, he must have fallen asleep, because when he awoke the next morning, he experienced a brief moment of nothingness before the events of the previous day flooded back into his mind.

The storm had left a heavy smell of wet earth in the air. Manfred went downstairs at ten o'clock. His grandmother was in the garden. In the kitchen, the housekeeper ignored him as he spread a piece of bread with butter. He took one bite, which he was unable to swallow, and put it in the bin. Then he returned to his room. Later, there was a flurry of voices downstairs as news of the murder filtered through the household. Normally, the servants talked only in hushed tones, as if they were in a library. Manfred lay on his bed awaiting the police, but no one came. He realised it had been a mistake not to appear for dinner the previous evening. From now on he must act as if nothing had happened. He must at all times act naturally.

His grandfather looked askance at him when he appeared at the dining table. Manfred did what he always did when someone looked questioningly at him. He cast his eyes down and said nothing. He could hear the servants in the kitchen discussing the murder, but the matter was not mentioned at the dinner table. Instead, the meal was passed with a few banal remarks about the storm and Monsieur Paliard's day at work. It seemed to Manfred a sick joke that his grandparents could behave as if nothing of note had occurred, as if his entire world had not come to an end. It seemed, furthermore, beyond belief that nobody could see that he was the killer. Manfred forced down a few mouthfuls of food before excusing himself at the earliest opportunity. He went upstairs and threw up.

Within two or three days, Manfred accustomed himself to behaving normally. He presented himself at mealtimes, skulked in his room and even forced himself to leave the house during the day, although he did not, of course, go near the woods. He betrayed no particular curiosity about the murder, nor did he pretend that it was of no interest to him. He began to think of himself as an actor preparing for the role of his former self. He drew no satisfaction as each day passed without his arrest. He was indifferent to his fate. But he came to understand why no one could see that he was guilty. All the talk in the papers and among the servants was of a monster, some beast abroad in the woods or further afield who could and, undoubtedly would, strike again. The maids were nervous of leaving the house and women were advised not to walk the streets unaccompanied. Amid this talk, Manfred was just a boy. Nobody was looking for a boy.

In the early evening of the fourth or fifth day, Manfred heard a detective being ushered into the parlour at the front of the house. It was some minutes before Monsieur Paliard made his way to where the policeman was waiting. Manfred's grandfather had a low opinion of the police and he would have made a point of keeping the detective waiting. The murmur of voices reached Manfred in his bedroom. He pictured the detective, in his fifties, wearing a crumpled raincoat over a crumpled suit, neatly parted grey hair, narrow darting eyes. The voices subsided then he heard footsteps and his grandmother calling his name from the bottom of the stairs.

Manfred sat on the edge of his bed. He imagined being led handcuffed down the drive to a waiting police car, a crowd of onlookers greeting his appearance with catcalls. As he drew nearer, their cries would subside and he would hear them stage-whisper, *But he's no more than a boy. Not even a man.*

Manfred stood up and walked slowly down the stairs. He felt relieved that his burden was about to be lifted. He wondered if the detective would accuse him straight off or slyly question him, slowly drawing the truth from him. There was no need for such a strategy. Manfred had no intention of denying anything.

The detective was not as he had imagined. He was young, thirty perhaps, with a modest, unthreatening air. He stood, looking somewhat ill at ease, with his back to the large stone fireplace. There was a tray of coffee things untouched on the table. The parlour was rarely used. It was a large formal room, which even at the height of summer retained a chill.

'Our grandson,' said Monsieur Paliard by way of introduction. His tone was apologetic. Manfred stood with his back to the wall next to the door. The detective did not invite him to sit down.

'I'm investigating the murder of Juliette Hurel,' he began. Manfred was surprised that his cheeks did not colour at the mention of Juliette's name.

'Your grandparents say that you often go

walking in the woods where her body was found.'

'Yes,' said Manfred, 'Sometimes I go there to read.' Revealing this additional information suggested, Manfred thought, that he was willing to cooperate fully.

'I don't suppose you ever came across the girl when you were in the woods?'

Manfred was surprised at the way in which the detective phrased his question. It seemed an invitation to denial, as if he had already made up his mind that the response would be negative. It seemed easier to agree.

'No,' he said.

'I understand you were in the woods the day Juliette was murdered,' the detective went on.

'No,' said Manfred, 'I went walking along the river that day.'

The lie took him by surprise. Up until that moment, he had imagined confessing everything at the first opportunity. But this lie had come from nowhere and at once he saw that it was a good one. Nobody knew where he had been that day, so one quiet place was as good as another.

'Oh,' said the detective as if a little disappointed that his lead had evaporated so quickly. 'And you've never seen anyone suspicious around the woods?'

Again the question phrased in the negative. Perhaps, Manfred thought, the detective had asked these questions so often that he had no expectation of a positive response. There was no significance in him asking Manfred. He was just crossing another potential witness from the list.

'No,' said Manfred. That much was true.

The detective nodded, as if Manfred had confirmed what he had expected him to say. He clasped his hands together to indicate that the interview was over and took his leave, apologising somewhat obsequiously for disturbing his grandparents. Manfred went back to his room and lay on his bed staring at the ceiling. He felt no relief, merely the feeling that the inevitable had been postponed. In a way, he was disappointed. It would have been better to get the thing over and done with.

When Manfred returned to school at the end of the holidays, he withdrew completely from his peers. He had always been on the periphery. His status as an orphan made his classmates wary of him, but it also provided a shield behind which he could hide. However oddly he behaved, people put it down to 'what he had been through'. He had always heard whispers to this effect. Now, however, Manfred's retreat was complete.

While his classmates flirted and arranged dates, he was nothing more than an observer. Nobody seemed to notice. He had always struggled to fit in and if he had now given up trying, it was no real loss to anyone. And while part of Manfred longed to participate, to be part of the crowd, the greater part of him was relieved. He developed a sense of superiority. His peers were mere children. The girls with their giggling and obsession with clothes seemed silly creatures, an entirely different species from Juliette. And the boys, posing with their leather bomber jackets, cigarettes held in the cup of their hand, were despicable. Little did they know that he, Manfred Baumann, had experienced love of the most intense and profound nature and had committed an act that placed him outside the normal boundaries of society.

Manfred followed the trial of the tramp Malou with dispassion. It did not occur to him to come forward and exonerate him, nor did he take any pleasure in his conviction. It had been clear to Manfred since the visit of the detective that he was going to 'get away with it'.

It was around this time that Manfred experienced his first migraine. It came upon him at his school desk without warning, or

173

at least he did not recognise the signs. All he knew was that he found himself clutching at a severe pain in his temples. He was helped to the school sickbay where the nurse insisted that an ambulance be called. Perhaps he was suffering an aneurysm. The medics gave him a cursory examination and, to his relief, refused to take him to hospital.

Manfred did not tell his grandparents about the incident and no questions were asked when he failed to appear for the evening meal. The headaches began to occur every few weeks. Each one lasted a day or two and left him drained of energy for days afterwards. Manfred spent these days in his room with the curtains drawn and the sheet pulled over his head. The slightest noise sent fresh shards shooting through his skull. During the episodes he lost all sense of time. Minutes dragged by as if mired in mud and whole days vanished as if struck from the calendar. Manfred could recall little of what occurred.

Even to the staunchly godless Manfred, it was impossible not to see these attacks as a punishment. But in the absence of a vengeful God, what force governed such things? Even in his pained state such thoughts irritated Manfred; the universe was chaotic and meaningless. Still, it was difficult not to see the killing of Juliette and the onset of the headaches as connected.

It became impossible to conceal what was occurring from his grandparents. Despite his protestations, Manfred's grandmother insisted on making an appointment with the family doctor. Doctor Faubel was a middle-aged man with greasy thinning hair and a shiny complexion. He smiled pleasantly as Manfred sat down. The surgery smelled strongly of dark tobacco.

'So,' he began, 'headaches, I hear.'

'Yes,' said Manfred. He was simultaneously relieved that he did not have to explain why he was here and embarrassed that his grandmother must have already briefed the doctor, as if he was still a child. 'Headaches' did not seem like a legitimate reason to take up a doctor's time, especially headaches that Manfred, despite himself, believed to be a kind of just punishment.

Faubel asked a series of questions about the nature, frequency and duration of the 'painful episodes', as he called them. He appeared to take Manfred's complaint quite seriously.

'On a scale of one to ten, how would you rate the level of pain?' he asked.

Manfred was about to respond, 'Ten,' but that would be ridiculous. He had read of certain techniques of torture that would undoubtedly be more painful. Besides, he did not wish to appear lily-livered or melodramatic.

'Seven,' he said.

'Seven?' the doctor repeated. He emitted a breathy whistle.

'Eight, maybe,' Manfred said.

Faubel asked Manfred to describe what he did during the painful episodes.

'I just lie there with my eyes closed. It's as if I become the pain. There's nothing else to think about.'

'And prior to the onset of these attacks, do you experience any unusual sensations?'

Manfred looked blankly at the doctor.

'Unusual effects of light, perhaps, a kind of flaring? Like an aura?'

Manfred nodded. This was precisely what he experienced. He would not have described it as an aura, as he disliked the word's mystical connotations, but it was as if he was looking at the world through the glass of a rainy window. Colours appeared to slide into one other. Faubel smiled to himself, clearly pleased with the accuracy of his diagnosis. He explained that Manfred was suffering from migraines. It was the first time Manfred had heard this word. The causes of migraines, Faubel went on, were

176

unknown and there was no cure. The only option was to try to manage the condition.

Manfred felt a pang of disappointment. His hopes had been raised by Faubel's insight into his symptoms.

'It's quite common for migraine to rear its head in someone your age. Often the frequency of attack decreases and, in time, it can even disappear completely.'

Faubel instructed Manfred to keep a diary of everything he ate and drank, what exercise he took, his sleep patterns and whether he was feeling anxious or depressed. He was to make another appointment when he had experienced another two painful episodes, at which point they would review his journal and see if they could identify any triggers for the attacks. The most important thing in combating migraine, he said, was to establish a routine and stick to it.

Manfred left the doctor feeling downhearted. As instructed, he kept a journal for the next two weeks, but as he did not experience an attack in this period, he let it lapse and never made the return visit to Doctor Faubel.

As the school year wore on, Manfred's aloofness and indifference to his peers seemed to exert a certain fascination upon some of his female classmates. He had matured into a good-looking young man and his lack of attention to his appearance perhaps struck these girls as possessing a certain charm. One girl, Sonia Givskov, took to hanging around Manfred during lunch hour, sitting in his vicinity and passing remarks about whatever book he was reading. She had a large nose, matronly breasts and thick lips, and wore unfashionable clothes, which Manfred suspected her mother made for her. Before the events of the summer Manfred would have felt her a kindred spirit, but now he felt nothing but contempt for her. She was not Juliette. Yet the more dismissively Manfred behaved towards her, the more she appeared to be in his thrall. He did not have the heart to shoo her away and out of some vague principle he refused to actually avoid her, so they took to sitting together, mostly in silence. Occasionally, Manfred heard mocking remarks about Sonia Givskov now being his girlfriend. But such tittle-tattle meant nothing to him. The idiots around him had no idea who they were dealing with. Nor would he betray Sonia Givskov by contradicting them.

In another way this arrangement with Sonia suited Manfred. Despite the fact that he had no desire to ever be with anyone other than Juliette, the school environment conspired against him. He could not fail to notice the down-covered napes, tanned calves and saucily revealed bra-straps of the girls around him. He initiated a rigorous regime of masturbation, performing the act first thing in the morning and as soon as he returned home from school, whether he felt the urge or not. It had been a lack of control over his sexual desire that had led to the death of Juliette, and he made a pact with himself to curb this malevolent force at all times. The perception that he and Sonia Givskov were an item meant that other girls kept their distance. She acted as a buffer.

Manfred let his schoolwork slide. In his state of numbness, he no longer cared what happened, neither in the here and now of school, nor in the future. He did not deliberately flunk tests. He simply no longer knew or could be bothered recalling the answers. He had never been popular with his teachers. Despite his good marks, he lacked charm. He sat at the back of class, never put his hand up and when called upon answered in monosyllables. He was surly. The only person who appeared to notice Manfred's drive to failure was his French master. M. Becault was in his twenties. He wore an unconvincing ginger beard and dressed in corduroy trousers, cheesecloth shirts and tweed jackets, as if these middle-aged clothes would somehow bestow authority on him. His beard, Manfred observed, disguised a weak chin and slack mouth, but he was otherwise a pleasant-looking man. In the corridor he would form his lips into a thin smile and nod almost deferentially when passing one of his students. Becault committed the cardinal sin of the novice teacher: he wanted to be liked. Consequently, he suffered continual discipline problems. He regularly blushed when texts alluded to the sexual act. Becault had always been Manfred's favourite teacher.

Once or twice in previous years the pair had chatted uneasily for a few minutes after class. Shortly after the death of his mother Manfred had written an essay on *The Outsider*. 'The real shock of *The Outsider*,' he wrote, 'is not Mersault's indifference to his mother's death. Rather it is the animosity of others towards this indifference.' Becault had read these lines back to Manfred and asked him what he meant. Manfred shrugged. He was both flattered by Becault's attention and embarrassed. In truth, he was not sure what he meant and he suspected that Becault was using this as an attempt to get him to 'open up' about his

180

own bereavement. When Manfred failed to articulate anything, the conversation fizzled out. 'Well, it's an excellent essay,' Becault had said, handing it back.

Despite the abortive nature of this conversation, Manfred felt some sort of kinship with Becault. He pictured his teacher as an awkward, disillusioned teenager, always on the outside looking in. For a while he entertained fantasies about meeting Becault in a café to discuss books or other worldly matters. They would smoke and drink coffee together. Sometimes Becault would pause and chat for a few moments in the canteen about whatever Manfred was reading. On account of his weak manner and eccentric appearance, there were rumours that Becault was a homosexual. When he stopped to talk, Manfred was conscious of other students' eyes upon them. Nothing would have pleased Manfred more than to engage in discussion, but it was not politic to do so. Invariably the situation became awkward and Becault would take his leave with a limp comment such as 'Best be getting on,' or 'Mustn't keep you from your lunch.'

A few months into the school year, Becault asked Manfred to stay behind at the end of class. Manfred slouched in his seat at the back of the room. Becault perched on an adjacent desk. He had shaved off his beard during the summer. The flesh around his mouth was pink and flabby.

'You don't seem yourself,' he said.

'I wish I wasn't myself,' said Manfred.

Becault smiled, as if to himself, and exhaled a little laugh through his nose.

'I'm concerned,' he said. He proffered an essay Manfred had written on Gide. 'This is . . .' He let his sentence trail off with a shake of his head. Manfred shrugged.

'You used to be my star pupil.'

'I don't like Gide.'

The teacher seemed encouraged. 'It's not a question of liking Gide,' he said. 'This is nothing more than a rant. You used to write so well. You had insight.'

Manfred stared at the front of the room.

'I just want to help you,' he said.

Manfred said nothing.

Becault pursed his lips. 'How are things at your grandparents'? You're living with your grandparents, aren't you?'

Manfred turned and looked at him. He imagined the little daydream he must nurture of fostering his students, of providing them with pastoral care. Probably he went home at night and struggled over a novel about a homosexual provincial schoolteacher in love with one of his pupils. But he had no idea that he was dealing with the Beast of Saint-Louis. Manfred scraped his chair back across the linoleum floor and got up.

'I don't need the help of some sad faggot,' he said. He gathered up his bag and jacket and left the room. Becault remained on the desk at the back of the room for some time. He left the teaching profession the following term.

TWELVE

By Wednesday morning, Manfred's excitement at the prospect of meeting Alice Tarrou had given way to a kind of dread. It was inconceivable that he could pass an evening in the company of a woman like Alice without embarrassing himself in some way. He spent the day concocting reasons to break the appointment, but could think of nothing credible. In any case, Alice had not given him her telephone number, so, short of loitering in the foyer, he had no means of contacting her. His only option was simply not to turn up at the appointed hour. But even setting aside the discourtesy of such an act, he was bound to run into Alice again at some point, and he imagined that she would not be the type to take such a snub lightly. He had no choice but to go through with it.

Manfred spent his lunch wondering whether he should mention to Pasteur that he would not be in that evening. His absence would be noted and likely become the subject of speculation. He imagined Lemerre holding forth about how he was probably off stalking the waitresses of another bar or how, on account of being mixed up in the disappearance of Adèle, he was now ashamed to show his face. And then the following evening, he would have to endure his jibes about how he was now too good for the Restaurant de la Cloche: 'Got better things to do with yourself, have you, Swiss?' It was better to lay the groundwork beforehand. When he was paying his bill at the counter, Pasteur muttered, 'See you later.'

Manfred grasped the opportunity. 'Actually,' he said, 'I don't think I'll be in tonight.'

He lingered at the counter for a moment, waiting for the proprietor to react. Pasteur counted the coins from the silver salver into the till and then looked up as if to enquire why he was still there. Manfred wondered if he had heard him.

'See you tomorrow, then,' Pasteur said eventually.

Manfred nodded and left. The afternoon passed slowly. He left the bank at five and hurried home. He took a shower and shaved for the second time that day, a white towel wrapped around his waist. Then he examined his face in the bathroom mirror for any stray whiskers and clipped his nasal hair with a pair of scissors he kept in the bathroom cabinet for this purpose. He splashed his face with cold water and patted it dry before applying cologne. Manfred prided himself on his fastidious personal hygiene. On more than one occasion, a girl at Simone's had remarked that he smelled nice. He was not such a bad-looking chap. Was it so implausible that Alice Tarrou would find him attractive?

Manfred returned to his bedroom and dressed. Once a year he bought himself a new suit from the same tailor's in Mulhouse that he had visited with his grandmother as a teenager. M. Boulot invariably greeted him with great warmth and enquired after the wellbeing of his grandparents. In earlier years, he would inform Manfred of the latest trends, but Manfred was not interested and insisted on the same cut and colour as he always had. As a result the rail of suits in Manfred's wardrobe were all but identical, distinguishable only through subtle variations in the fabric. There was no need for Manfred to go on acquiring new suits — he had more than enough to last him a lifetime

— but he continued to make his annual pilgrimage to M. Boulot's out of loyalty. In a similar way, the rack on the back of the wardrobe door consisted almost entirely of black ties of a narrow girth, enlivened by a few of bolder colours. These were gifts from his grandmother, which Manfred would occasionally wear to Sunday lunch in order to please her, but remove immediately after he left the house. Such gaudy accessories made him feel like a ridiculous dandy. He had no wish to attract comments on his dress. Nor did he wish to have to think about what he would wear on such-and-such a day. His only concession to casual dress was to loosen his tie a little and undo the top button of his shirt at the end of the working day.

He sat at the kitchen table. Now, in fresh clothes, he felt a little more relaxed about the impending encounter. What, after all, could really go wrong? It was not yet six o'clock. He planned to arrive early to accustom himself to his surroundings before Alice arrived, but he still had the best part of an hour to kill. He found a notebook and began to write a list of possible topics of conversation. Manfred was not in the habit of asking personal questions, but he was aware that on occasions such as these it was regarded as normal practice. Indeed, were he not to ask Alice some questions about herself, she might think that he was the sort of egoist who only wished to talk about himself, something which could not be further from the truth. He tapped his pencil on the piece of paper and wrote the word *Work*. It was dull, but work was a perfectly acceptable topic. Alice had already asked him what he did for a living. He would merely be reciprocating. Indeed, if he did not ask, Alice might think that he was a chauvinist who thought women were only fit to be housewives. Or whores. He tried to think of ways in which he might phrase a question: *So, Alice, what do you do for a living? What line of work are you in?* As he rehearsed the words in his head, they sounded quite absurd, as if he were interviewing a prospective employee. He crumpled up the paper and threw it on the floor. What was he going to do, take it out of his pocket and consult it at the dinner table? He was sure to make a fool of himself. He should never have agreed to this stupid date in the first place. The more he thought about it, the more he was not even sure if he liked Alice Tarrou. She was off and supercilious. And clearly she was someone who was used to getting her own way. He had foolishly allowed himself to be flattered by her attention, but he had no wish to be drawn into any entanglements. He was quite content with his life the way it was. If he lived the way he did, it was because that was how he wanted to live. He had no desire to change anything. The date had been a mistake. There was no question of cancelling, but he could easily and quite politely make it quite clear that he had no interest in becoming more deeply involved.

Manfred arrived at the restaurant on Avenue de Bâle at ten to seven. He had walked the back way alongside the railway line to avoid being spotted by any of the regulars of La Cloche. The restaurant was housed in a traditional oak-beamed building. Inside, the dining room was low-ceilinged, but surprisingly large. The walls were panelled with dark wood and fitted with brass light fittings, which emitted a yellowish light. A number of oversized pot plants stood like sentries next to the various doors. The tables were covered with starched white cloths and laid with an intimidating array of cutlery and glasses. Only two other tables were occupied. Manfred was shown to a table in the centre of the room. He explained to the waiter that he was expecting someone and asked for a glass of wine.

Manfred recognised a man at one of the other tables. He was in the construction trade and over the years had had occasional business with the bank. He acknowledged Manfred with a little bow of his head. He was with a woman and they were chatting animatedly. The man talked with his mouth full and pointed his knife at his dining companion — for some reason Manfred did not think she was his wife — who did not seem to notice his ill manners. The other table was occupied by a solitary man in a suit; probably, Manfred thought, a salesman passing through town. He had a paperback open on the table in front of him and kept his eyes fixed on the pages. Manfred wished he had asked to be seated elsewhere. He felt like an exhibit in a museum. His wine arrived. He assumed that Alice would be late and downed it in a couple of swallows before ordering a second.

Alice arrived on the stroke of seven o'clock. She was wearing a knee-length grey wool dress, fastened around her waist with a thick brown leather belt. The waiter took her coat and showed her to the table. Manfred stood up and held out his hand.

'Good evening,' he said.

Alice ignored his hand and kissed him on

both cheeks, placing her hands on his upper arms as she did so. Manfred inhaled her perfume. It was dry and earthy like the floor of a forest before a fire. She sat down and ordered a Martini without so much as glancing at the waiter.

'Well,' she said, 'here we are.'

'Yes,' said Manfred. He made himself smile. Alice was wearing pale red lipstick. She pursed her lips and widened her eyes, then glanced around the room. She leaned forward and whispered, 'It's like a morgue in here. Maybe we should go somewhere else.'

'It's fine,' said Manfred. 'We're here now.'

The idea of just getting up and leaving horrified Manfred and, worse, Alice might suggest going to the Restaurant de la Cloche. The waiter arrived with Alice's drink and two menus bound in maroon leatherette. Ordering provided a welcome distraction from the business of making conversation. While they waited for their starters, Alice lit a cigarette with a chunky brass lighter, which emitted a whiff of butane. She turned her head to the side and blew out a slow stream of milky grey smoke.

'So, Manfred Baumann,' she said, 'what have you got to say for yourself?'

Manfred unconsciously put his hand to

his face and slowly massaged the flesh around his mouth. *What did he have to say for himself?* He had nothing at all to say for himself. The carpet in the restaurant was dark brown with a pattern of messy yellow whorls. Manfred felt a little dizzy. He was tempted to excuse himself and make a dash for the door, but he did not do so. Alice leaned forward a little. Her fingers played on the stem of her glass. The second hand of her wristwatch moved slowly around the dial. Her dress was snug around her breasts, which did not appear to be constrained by a brassiere. Manfred raised his eyes to Alice's face. She appeared quite relaxed.

'So,' Manfred began, 'you've only been in your apartment a few months?' It was the only thing he could think of to say. He breathed out as if he had just put down a heavy object.

'That's right,' said Alice.

'Yes,' said Manfred, 'it struck me as odd that I hadn't run into you before.'

There was no reason to make this remark. It made him seem like the sort of busybody who liked to keep tabs on the comings and goings of his neighbours, when nothing could be farther from the truth. He only knew the names of his immediate neighbours because they were written on the little plaques on their doors and he did his best to avoid all contact with them.

'And *I* hadn't run into you before,' said Alice. She widened her eyes as if this was an astonishing coincidence.

Manfred gave a little laugh. Despite everything, the conversation was proceeding quite satisfactorily.

'Do you like it?' he said.

'Architecturally?' she said.

'Living there, I meant. Do you like living there?' said Manfred.

Alice gave a little snort of derision through her nose. Manfred recognised the gesture from before. It gave him a sense of intimacy, as if they were lovers who knew each other's quirks inside out. Still, it was a stupid question. What was there to say about living in a drab apartment building exactly like a thousand other drab apartment buildings elsewhere? Of course, there had been the incident with the dog faeces in the stairwell only a week earlier and there was the ongoing dispute about the need to refurbish the laundry facilities, but, even if she knew about these things, Alice would probably not deem them worthy of comment.

Alice shrugged. 'It was supposed to just be a stopgap. I haven't even unpacked most of my things.'

The starters arrived. Alice had asked for a green salad, even though it was not on the menu. Manfred ordered an expensive bottle of white wine. The waiter poured a little for him to sample before filling their glasses.

Alice, it transpired, had moved into the building following the breakdown of her marriage. She talked almost uninterrupted for the rest of the meal, pausing only to top up her glass or take the occasional mouthful of food. Her husband, Marc, ran a large concrete firm. They met when Alice's stationery company won the contract to supply his firm with letterheads and other goods. Marc was twelve years older and Alice had been flattered by his attention. Shortly after they married, Marc's firm began to supply various large government projects, which entailed a lot of travel. They both had affairs and — Alice shrugged — after a while it became apparent that they were sharing a house, but weren't really married anymore. It was all perfectly amicable. There were no children to complicate matters. 'I'm not the maternal type,' Alice said. They still met for dinner once or twice a month and had even taken to sleeping together now and then. Alice mentioned this last detail without a hint of self-consciousness, but the thought of Alice engaged in the sexual act brought the colour to Manfred's cheeks. He put his glass to his face to disguise the fact.

Manfred found himself building up a healthy loathing for this successful man with his easy way with women. He probably wore ostentatious jewellery and spoke in a loud voice in restaurants. He did not like the idea of Alice continuing to see him and the fact that they persisted in sleeping together was certainly not healthy.

Alice paused and looked at Manfred, as if she had almost forgotten he was there. During her monologue he had confined himself to nodding and the occasional 'I see.' They had ordered a second bottle of wine. Alice had consumed her share, but Manfred felt quite drunk. Alice excused herself and Manfred took the opportunity to pay the bill.

They walked back along Rue de Mulhouse. Alice put her hand in the crook of Manfred's arm. He was not sure if this was a sign of affection or merely to steady herself.

They passed the little park where Adèle had met her friend. Some people were gathered on the pavement outside a shop on a side street. It was not late. Lemerre and his cronies would still be at their table by the door of the Restaurant de la Cloche.

Manfred wondered what Lemerre would have to say if he could see him walking home with a woman on his arm. Something obscene, no doubt. The streets were deserted, as they always were at this time of night. They reached the apartment building. Manfred unlocked the door and they stood in the foyer.

'Well,' he said, 'thank you for a very pleasant evening.'

He had decided that he would take the stairs and allow Alice to take the elevator. It would be less awkward to part here in the foyer.

'How about a nightcap?' said Alice.

'A nightcap?' Manfred repeated.

'Why not?' she said. She prodded him playfully on the arm.

Manfred could think of no plausible reason to refuse.

'Where?' he said.

She shrugged. 'Your place? My place is a mess. Half of my stuff is still in boxes.'

'I don't think that's a good idea,' said Manfred, but she was already leading him to the elevator. Manfred got in and pressed his back against the grooved metal of the tiny box. Alice stood with her shoulder touching his. The smell of her perfume mingled with alcohol and cigarettes.

Alice led the way along the corridor to Manfred's door.

'4F,' she said.

'Perhaps we should go to a bar,' said Manfred. 'I've only got whisky.'

'Whisky's fine,' said Alice, 'I like whisky.'

Manfred unlocked the door and led Alice along the passage to the kitchen. They stood by the table.

'I'll fetch another chair,' said Manfred. He unlocked the door to the balcony where three folding chairs were stored.

'Why don't we sit in the living room?' she said.

Manfred was about to object, but Alice was already on her way. Manfred went into the bedroom to fetch the whisky from the bedside table.

'My apartment is exactly the same layout,' she called. He returned to the kitchen to get glasses. Alice had switched on the lamp next to the sofa and was standing in front of the wall of books, which were arranged more or less alphabetically. Manfred stood in the doorway with the bottle and glasses in his hand.

'That's a lot of books for a bank manager,' said Alice. She appeared impressed. 'Quite the enigma, aren't you, Monsieur Baumann.'

Manfred could not help feeling a thrill when she used his name like this. He had a sudden vision of a future with Alice. They would become lovers. They would maintain their separate apartments, but at weekends they would spend time together, going for country walks or whatever it was that lovers did. Without it ever being mentioned, it would become known at the bank that he had a lover. The whispers about his sexual orientation would come to an end. He would no longer spend every evening drinking at the counter of the Restaurant de la Cloche, exchanging awkward remarks with Pasteur. Lemerre and his cronies would look at him with newfound respect. But he knew, of course, that none of that would happen.

Alice sat on the sofa. She took off her shoes and curled her feet beneath her thighs. Manfred poured out two measures of whisky and handed one to Alice. He sat down on the armchair.

'How long have you been here?' she asked.

'Eighteen years,' he said. 'It was supposed to be a stopgap for me as well.'

She laughed. She rummaged in her bag for her cigarettes and lit one. Manfred got up and fetched an ashtray from the kitchen, relieved to be out of the room for a moment. Alice smiled a thank you when he placed the ashtray on the table in front of her.

'This is nice,' she said. She appeared to find Manfred's discomfort amusing.

The building was completely silent. Alice put her elbow on the arm of the sofa and rested her chin on her hand.

'So what about you, Manfred?' Her dress was stretched tightly around her breasts.

'What about me?'

'Tell me about yourself.'

'There's nothing to tell.'

'Come on,' she said, as if cajoling a tongue-tied child.

Manfred sipped his whisky. He was beginning to feel nauseous. A car passed outside. He averted his eyes from Alice's breasts. He was terrified that Alice was going to attempt to seduce him. He was not so naive as to be unaware of the events that were expected to ensue from a 'nightcap'.

'Have you ever been married?' she asked.

Manfred shook his head. He wished Alice would stop asking questions.

'There must have been someone,' she said playfully. She took a slug of whisky.

Manfred topped up her glass. She smiled, a little apologetically, as if she realised he did not want to talk about himself, or perhaps as if she realised that the whole evening had been a mistake. Manfred suddenly had the impression that she was about to get up and leave.

'I was in love once,' he said.

'Oh,' said Alice. She suddenly perked up.

'It was a long time ago,' said Manfred. 'She was very beautiful.'

'What happened?'

Manfred looked at her.

'She was murdered.'

Alice clasped her bottom lip in her teeth. 'I'm sorry,' she said.

Manfred shook his head. He had a sudden urge to tell her the whole story, to spare her no detail about what had happened that summer. But he said nothing. He swilled the whisky round in his glass. Someone in an adjoining flat turned on a television.

They drank the rest of the whisky in silence. Alice's toenails were painted red. Manfred imagined kneeling at her feet and kissing them. After a while, Alice said she should be going. She put on her shoes.

'We should do this again sometime,' she said. 'Why don't we do something on Sunday?'

Manfred was so relieved that she was leaving that he nodded agreement. At the door, she reached up and clasped the back of

Manfred's neck and kissed him. Manfred kept his hands by his sides and then placed them on her hips. He could feel the grain of the fine wool of her dress with his fingertips. When they parted, she put the back of her fingers to her lips and widened her eyes. Manfred did not know what to say. Alice said she had better go and Manfred watched her disappear along the corridor.

THIRTEEN

It was the evening of Céline's autumn show at the boutique. Gorski had been instructed to be at the shop by seven o'clock when the guests would start arriving. He stopped off at Le Pot on the way. He drank a glass of beer and then ordered a second. A succession of patrons drifted through the bar for a post-work nip, among them the corpulent hairdresser from the Restaurant de la Cloche who had been so venomous about Manfred Baumann. Thankfully he did not spot Gorski at his table in the corner. Gorski dreaded the twice-yearly ritual of Céline's show, but there was no question of not attending. He was expected to mingle with the guests and display the fine manners Céline had taught him.

Céline insisted that Gorski kept his wardrobe up to date. On more than one occasion, he had overheard remarks being passed at the station about his 'dandyish' outfits.

White shirts were banned. These were for clerical workers and waiters, groups even lower in Céline's elaborate social hierarchy than policemen. 'Just because you're only a cop doesn't mean that you can't dress properly,' she liked to tell him. 'I can't have the husband of the owner of *Céline's* going around looking like a vagrant.' She often used the phrase 'only a cop' and it never failed to rile him as, he assumed, was intended. When called upon to introduce him at one of her gatherings, Céline was in the habit of pulling an apologetic face when informing people of her husband's profession. Gorski would pretend that he had not seen it, but inside he seethed. A couple of drinks were required to gird himself for the evening. Gorski imagined Céline's face if she could see him now, sitting in this pleasingly grotty dive with the lowlife of the town. The thought gave him a moment's grim amusement.

He arrived at half past seven. Céline was at the back of the shop talking to a woman he did not recognise. She shot him a poisonous look. Gorski smiled at her and waved as if nothing were amiss. Clémence was standing nearby with a tray of champagne. Gorski pulled a face: *Am I in trouble?* She widened her eyes and nodded: *You sure are!*

There were about thirty people in the shop, bunched in little knots. Gorski made his way over to Clémence. She was wearing a black skirt and pale yellow blouse, as were the two other girls Céline had requisitioned to act as waitresses — or hostesses, as she insisted on calling them. She looked nice. To Céline's chagrin, she generally refused to wear anything other than jeans and T-shirts.

Gorski took a glass of champagne from her tray.

'How bad is it?' he asked.

'You are in deep shit,' said Clémence. 'Deep, deep shit.'

Gorski clicked his tongue, then knocked back the champagne and took another glass.

'This is good stuff,' he said. 'You tried it?'

'Just one.'

'You'll need more than that if you're going to get through tonight,' he said.

Clémence laughed, then darted her eyes in the direction of her mother. Céline was making her way over. She smiled her most charming smile, took his glass from him and placed it back on Clémence's tray. She took him by the elbow and steered him across the room. 'Try not to embarrass me any more than you already have,' she stage-whispered.

They reached a knot of two couples. The men looked as uncomfortable as Gorski. Céline introduced him: 'My husband, the great detective.'

Gorski shook hands. He did not register the names of the guests.

'Nice to meet you,' he said to each in turn.

Céline abandoned him to attend to some new arrivals. One of the men seemed quite pleased to have Gorski to talk to. He was in the insurance business. He asked Gorski about the rate of burglaries in the town and went on to explain how this impacted on the premiums charged to clients. Gorski watched Céline go about her duties. She was wearing a flowing green silk suit with wide trousers. The chemise was open almost to her midriff, but owing to her flat chest there was nothing obscene about it. She looked elegant. She greeted each new arrival with a great fuss. She had a habit of laying her hand on the forearm of whoever she was talking to and arching her midriff towards them, before making some witty or saucy remark. People found her charming and flirtatious.

Gorski had met Céline in this very shop. He was twenty-five and had been a detective for only a few weeks. He had not yet got used to wearing a suit to work. His *gendarme*'s uniform had bestowed authority. In plainclothes you had to identify yourself. People looked at him with disbelief — he was too fresh-faced to be a detective. He practised taking out his ID in front of the mirror in his tiny bathroom. He held it unfolded at his side, then raised it slowly to shoulder height, before saying, 'Georges Gorski, Saint-Louis police.' He did this over and over, but still felt like he was imitating cops in films.

Ribéry asked him to accompany him to a robbery at a ladies-wear shop on a side street next to the little park in front of the Protestant temple. It was only a few hundred metres from the police station, but Ribéry insisted on driving. He never walked anywhere. The citizenry, he maintained, expected to see a detective pull up in a car. The shop window showed a selection of corsetry and brassieres in beige and cream. Gorski had the impression that the display had not been changed in years. On the pavement Ribéry indicated with an outstretched arm that Gorski should enter first. 'You take the lead,' he said. A bell tinkled above the door. The wood of the jamb was splintered where the door had been forced. A woman in her mid-fifties was standing by the glass counter. She was wearing a tweed skirt, cream blouse and sensible brown shoes. Her hair was secured in a bun. The mascara around her eyes was smudged. Gorski fumbled for his ID in the inside pocket of his jacket and held it out.

'Detective Gorski,' he said, 'and this is Inspector Ribéry.'

He looked over his shoulder. Ribéry was carrying out a close inspection of a display of undergarments. Gorski asked a few routine questions. The cash register had simply been lifted from the counter and, as it was Friday, it had contained the entire week's takings. Nothing else had been stolen. Mme Bettine explained that her assistant had discovered the break-in. Céline appeared from the back shop. She was about twenty, dressed in a dark blue pencil skirt and a white blouse. She was tall and slender with no waist at all and small breasts. She had a tousled mane of chestnut hair. Gorski could see the outline of her brassiere through the sheer material of her blouse. She looked at Gorski with clear green eyes. She appeared perfectly composed.

'I understand you discovered the break-in,' he said.

'I arrived at about quarter to nine. The door had been pushed in.' Her tone was matter-of-fact.

Gorski nodded. 'Have either of you noticed any suspicious activity in the last few days?'

The two women looked blankly at him.

'Any suspicious characters loitering outside, a customer behaving oddly perhaps? The fact that the robbery occurred when the till was full suggests that the culprits may have known something about the routine of the shop.'

'You think they might have been watching us?' said Mme Bettine. She started to snivel into a tissue she was holding. The girl made no attempt to comfort her. Neither of them had seen anything.

Gorski nodded slowly. He explained that he would send round a fingerprint team that afternoon. In the meantime they should avoid touching any smooth surfaces.

'Is that it?' said Céline.

'We'll make enquiries in the neighbourhood. Perhaps someone heard the door being forced.' He turned to Ribéry, who was fingering a satin nightdress. He might have been a customer looking for a gift for his wife.

'Gypsies,' he said without looking up. 'It'll be gypsies.'

Gorski ignored his comment.

'I'll let you know how the investigation progresses,' he said. 'In the meantime, can I suggest you take your takings to the bank on a daily basis from now on. Metal shutters also make an effective deterrent.'

'Excellent work,' said Ribéry on the pavement outside. 'Most convincing. Not a chance of getting them, of course.'

Gorski spent the rest of the morning questioning residents in the vicinity of the shop. He could easily have requisitioned a couple of *gendarmes* to do this legwork for him, but he had not yet become accustomed to wielding his newfound authority over his colleagues, most of whom were older and more experienced than he was and tended to look askance when he asked them to do anything. His quest was as fruitless as Ribéry had anticipated. People looked blankly at him and shook their heads, before pushing their doors closed in his face. The amount stolen hardly merited this expenditure of time, but he could hardly report back to the shop without carrying out a rudimentary investigation. As he exited a building opposite the shop, he spotted Céline on the pavement smoking. She saw him and waved languidly. Gorski waved back, pleased that his efforts had not gone unnoticed. At one o'clock, he gave up and went to the Restaurant de la Cloche, where he knew Ribéry would be lunching. He joined him at his table.

'Any luck?' the inspector asked through a mouthful of food.

Gorski shook his head.

'I admire your enthusiasm,' said Ribéry, 'but that door would have given way with one decent kick. Nobody would have heard a thing.'

He poured Gorski a glass of wine from his *pichet*. Nothing more was said about the break-in. Gorski could think of no other reasonable lines of enquiry. He could ask at local bars whether anyone had been spending more money than usual, but the sum in question was not large enough to raise any eyebrows. In any case, he had already learned that bar owners did not take kindly to being questioned about the activities of their patrons and tended to be tight-lipped. It was not good for business to be seen to be too cosy with the police. Ribéry ordered a second *pichet* and insisted on pouring Gorski another glass.

'You've done more than enough work for today,' he said, filling his own glass to the brim.

Gorski returned to the station and wrote up a report of his morning's activities. The fingerprint team had not found anything usable. There had been plenty of prints on the glass counter, but they all belonged to the owner and her assistant. Before he returned to the shop, Gorski went to his apartment to change. It was a hot day and the light blue shirt he was wearing had large dark circles under the arms. He stripped to the waist and washed his armpits over the sink. Then he put on a clean white shirt and the same dark blue tie he had been wearing earlier.

It was five o'clock when he returned to the shop. A joiner was on his knees in the doorway, packing away his tools. Gorski had to step over him to get into the shop. Céline was leaning against the counter.

'Hello again,' she said.

'Where's Mme Bettine?' he said.

'I sent her home,' said Céline. 'I couldn't stand her snivelling anymore.'

Gorski nodded. The girl's comment struck him as needlessly spiteful.

'I'm afraid there do not appear to be any witnesses.'

Céline shrugged. 'The old bag's insured.'

Gorski wondered if the girl was striking this attitude in an attempt to impress him, to try to appear older and more worldly than she was. The joiner stood up and indicated that he was done. Céline thanked him and closed the door behind him. She turned the sign on the door to closed.

'You changed your shirt,' she said. 'The other one was better. You can't wear a white shirt with a dark blue tie. You should only wear a white shirt with a black suit.'

Gorski was embarrassed that she had noticed he had changed.

'Oh,' he said, 'I didn't know that.'

'That suit's not up to much either. Maybe I should take you shopping sometime.'

Gorski could feel himself beginning to blush.

'I was wondering if you might have thought of anything else.'

The girl smiled at him. She had a wide, attractive mouth. She leaned against the glass counter where the till had been. It was still dusted with fingerprint powder.

'Are you always this diligent?' she asked.

Gorski shook his head slowly. 'Not always,' he said.

They were only a matter of feet apart. He couldn't think of anything else to say. Céline put a finger to her lips. It was still stained with the fingerprinter's ink. Gorski took a step towards her. She clasped his neck and pulled his mouth towards hers.

Gorski's only previous sexual experiences

212

had occurred during the summer he spent labouring on a farm before his final year at school. One afternoon, he was creosoting the doors of an outbuilding. It was very hot and the fumes from the chemicals had made him feel nauseous. The daughter of one of the farmhands appeared at his side. She was an olive-skinned girl of fourteen or fifteen, with dark hair and brown eyes. Her name was Marthe. She might have been watching him for some time, but Gorski had not noticed her. Without saying anything, she pushed open the door Gorski was painting and went inside. Gorski followed. It was cool and dark in the barn. Yellow slats of sunlight stabbed through the gaps in the wooden walls. Marthe pulled up her chemise and placed Gorski's hands on her large breasts. Gorski squeezed them then lowered his mouth over a brown nipple. Marthe undid his trousers, pushed him to the floor and squatted over him. She ground her groin mechanically against him, gasping melodramatically. Gorski found the experience quite painful. (Later, he learned to spit on his hand to lubricate his member.) He came almost immediately, the smell of creosote in his nostrils. Marthe finished and climbed off him. She fixed her clothing, then asked Gorski if he had a cigarette, which he did not. She shrugged and left the barn.

Similar encounters occurred regularly for the rest of the summer. Gorski was left with the impression that sex was easy to come by and not the great mystery that people made it out to be. Marthe was matter-of-fact after the act. There was never any need to get dressed afterwards since they never actually removed their clothes. Gorski started to buy cigarettes and sometimes they would lie next to each other for a few minutes and smoke.

When Gorski returned to school it was with a certain swagger. He felt a great superiority as he listened to his classmates' comic accounts of their attempts to seduce girls. Around his female classmates, he adopted an off-hand, aloof manner, which did not produce the results he hoped. Towards the end of the year, after drinking a bottle of wine at a house party, he talked a girl into going upstairs with him. She was a tall, Germanic-looking girl called Jeanet Hassemer whom he had admired for months. They found a bedroom. Without preamble Gorski took the girl's hand and pushed it down the front of his trousers. The girl pushed him away and ran from the room. When he went downstairs a few minutes later, another boy punched him in the face.

In the years that had passed since his experiences with Marthe, Gorski had not so much as kissed a girl. He found that women became guarded when he told them that he was a policeman and consequently he became awkward in their company.

Céline undid the buttons of her blouse and unclasped her brassiere. She had prominent dark nipples. She rucked her skirt up around her waist and pushed Gorski's hand between her legs. Gorski slipped his index and middle fingers inside her and she pressed her groin against the heel of his hand. Gorski bit her neck and massaged her modest breasts. Céline ground her sex against his hand with increasing vigour. Her breathing quickened and then suddenly subsided. Gorski let his fingers slip out of her. Her face was flushed. Gorski was glad nothing more was required of him. He had spent himself almost as soon as he had touched her breasts. He hoped his emission would not seep through his trousers. Céline pulled down her skirt and fastened the buttons of her blouse. Gorski took out a packet of cigarettes and offered one to her.

'We're not supposed to smoke in here,' said Céline. 'Mme Bettine says it makes the clothes smell.' She seemed suddenly much younger. Her hair was disarrayed. They went outside and smoked.

Gorski knew from the outset that he was out of his depth. Céline's father, Jean-Marie Keller, was a wealthy businessman and a bigwig on the town council. On their first date Gorski took Céline to what he imagined was the best restaurant in Saint-Louis. He felt uncomfortable in the place, with its starched white tablecloths and elaborate array of cutlery. Céline was twenty minutes late. Gorski tried to affect a nonchalant attitude as he waited, drinking a glass of beer. Only two other tables were occupied and Gorski felt that the waiters were mocking him. He had bought a new dark grey suit for the occasion and, remembering Céline's dictum about white shirts, had chosen a mustard-coloured one.

'What a funny place,' said Céline on her arrival. She did not apologise for being late. Her family, she told him, only ever dined out in Strasbourg. A waiter took her coat and she ordered a gin and tonic. When her drink arrived, Gorski ordered one as well. The waiter bowed his head slightly. Céline barely touched her food. Gorski took this as a sign of sophistication, but he could not bring himself to leave anything on his own plate.

Céline talked a lot about her father. Perhaps, she said, he would be able to help Gorski in his career. She asked how long he planned to stay in the police.

'I've only just made detective,' said Gorski. He could not resist adding that he was the youngest detective ever appointed in Saint-Louis.

Céline asked what business Gorski's family was in and he told her that his father was now retired. She talked amusingly about working in Mme Bettine's shop, impersonating the customers and ridiculing the old-fashioned stock. She was only doing it to gain experience, she said, as she intended to go into business herself one day. After the meal, they stood awkwardly outside on the pavement.

'Mummy's picking me up at ten,' she said.

Gorski was taken aback. Being picked up by her mother did not square with the precocious girl he had encountered in Mme Bettine's shop. He wondered how old Céline actually was. They had fifteen minutes to kill. They walked slowly towards the park outside the shop where she had arranged to be collected. They sat down on the low wall.

'Don't you want to kiss me?' Céline said.

'What if your mother sees us?'

Céline laughed. 'She won't mind.'

They kissed, but mechanically, and Gorski broke it off. Céline smiled at him.

'Next time, we should go out in Strasbourg,' she said.

Gorski felt elated that there was going to be a next time. Céline's mother pulled up in a bottle green Mercedes. She waved cheerfully at the couple. Gorski stood up and returned her greeting, feeling rather foolish. Céline gave him a peck on the cheek and told him to call her.

Gorski telephoned the shop a few days later. He asked Céline if she would like to get together again. They could go to Strasbourg, if she liked. Céline laughed and said she had only been joking. She said she was free on Sunday afternoon. Gorski agreed to pick her up at two o'clock. In the meantime, he took to walking past Mme Bettine's shop at every opportunity, hoping to catch a glimpse of Céline smoking on the pavement outside.

That Sunday, Gorski pulled up outside the Keller house in his battered Fiat. There was a long gravel drive and two Mercedes were parked outside. To the side of the house was a series of outbuildings. Gorski got out and rang the doorbell. Céline's mother opened the door. She was wearing jeans and a sweatshirt. Her hands were dirty from gardening.

'You must be Georges,' she said. 'We've heard a lot about you. Céline tells us you're soon to be head of Saint-Louis police.'

Gorski laughed. 'I'm just starting out,' he said.

'And modest as well,' said Mme Keller. Gorski was surprised that Céline had been boasting about him to her parents. She called up the stairs to Céline and they stood waiting in silence for a few minutes. Céline came down the stairs in a summer dress with large buttons up the front, fastened at the waist with a thin brown leather belt. Gorski immediately thought how easy it would be to access. Mme Keller asked what they were up to.

'I thought we might go to the Camargue. For a walk,' said Gorski. The Petite Camargue was a small nature reserve some kilometres north of the town.

'How lovely,' said Mme Keller cheerfully. 'Watch out for snakes.' She gave a mock shiver.

They got into the car and drove off. Gorski had brought a rug and put a bottle of wine and two glasses wrapped in newspaper in a canvas knapsack. They walked for half an hour before finding a spot overlooking the lake. Gorski laid out the rug. The sun filtered through the foliage above them and made dappled patterns on their skin. Céline was quiet. Gorski poured two glasses of wine. He downed his first glass too quickly and poured himself another. Céline put hers on the ground next to the rug. It spilled and the wine soaked into the earth. She lay back and closed her eyes. Gorski was lying on his side next to her, leaning on his elbow. He put his hand on her bare leg and moved it under her dress. Céline did not protest. Then he undid the buttons at the top of her dress. She was not wearing a brassiere. Lying on her back, her breasts completely disappeared. Her clavicles protruded through her skin, as thin as wishbones. Gorski kissed her and stroked her breasts. Céline parted her legs a little. Gorski unfastened his trousers and climbed onto her. He got inside her and managed to sustain two or three minutes of thrusting before he ejaculated. Céline clutched the back of his neck. Afterwards he took off his shirt and lay on his back next to her. The sun was warm on his skin. He could hear the rustling of the leaves in the breeze and the lapping of the water of the lake. Céline lay with her dress open and rumpled around her waist. Gorski could not help smiling to himself as he thought of his animalistic fumblings with Marthe, with her rolls of puppy fat, great flopping breasts and peasant smell. Céline could not have been more cool and elegant. Even her body, like that of a skinny boy, seemed a study in good taste and restraint.

Sundays became their day. They would drive to the Camargue or some other isolated spot. Gorski's performance became more assured. Céline never spoke during the act, but there was a kind of grim determination in her will to orgasm. Afterwards they would go to an inn and have a simple lunch and a bottle of wine. Often there was little conversation during these lunches. Gorski did not know what to talk to Céline about and she made little effort. Sometimes she corrected the manner in which Gorski held his cutlery or wiped up his sauce with his bread. At times Gorski was embarrassed. Other couples chatted unselfconsciously and made fun of each other. He could never imagine teasing Céline.

After a few months, Mme Keller insisted that Gorski join them for Sunday lunch. Céline did not appear particularly thrilled by the idea and Gorski was frustrated that their weekly lovemaking would be disrupted, but he realised that the invitation represented a step up in the seriousness of their relationship. Gorski, under instruction from Céline, bought a new jacket and slacks for the occasion. He expected Céline to remain rather aloof from him, but, to his surprise, she was uncharacteristically warm. She sat next to him on the sofa in the large drawing room and clutched his hand in her lap. Gorski had rarely spoken to M. Keller, who was by then planning to run for mayor of Saint-Louis, but he too behaved warmly towards him. Over lunch it transpired that he knew Ribéry and made no secret of the fact that he had asked him about Gorski.

'He speaks very highly of you, my boy. "A very bright young man" were his exact words, I believe.'

Gorski did not know what to say. Céline squeezed his knee under the table.

'Of course,' M. Keller went on, adopting a more confidential tone, 'we all know that the inspector is not . . .' he made a show of weighing his words carefully, '. . . not the most diligent in the execution of his duties.' He mimed a drinking motion with his hand and winked at Gorski. Gorski did not say anything, not wishing to be disloyal to his superior.

'Which leads me to suppose,' he went on, 'that we'll be seeing a new chief of police installed in the not too distant future.'

The following Sunday, Gorski asked Céline to marry him. She shrugged her shoulders and accepted. She was, it turned out, nineteen.

Céline tapped a teaspoon on a champagne glass to gain the attention of those assembled in the shop. She graciously thanked everyone for coming and announced that the time had come for the presentation of her autumn collection. There was a ripple of applause. At the end of her little speech, she reminded her audience not to forget that the real purpose of the evening was not to enjoy themselves, but to spend money. 'Why else would I ply you with champagne?' she concluded. Everyone laughed. The lights were lowered and the music was turned up. A succession of girls appeared from the storeroom and made a turn around the shop. These were teenagers Céline had recruited from the local schools and had been rehearsing for weeks. Two or three of the girls were very beautiful. Gorski tried not to let his eyes linger on their bodies. After their circuit of the shop, the girls would dash back into the storeroom before reappearing in a different outfit. The audience applauded. Many of them, Gorski realised, were parents of the models. He had

to admit that it was very efficiently orga-
nised. He caught Clémence's eye. She
jabbed two fingers towards her mouth in a
gagging motion. Gorski ignored her. He
looked at Céline. She was not watching the
girls, but observing the delighted expressions on the faces of her guests, smiling
broadly. Gorski felt suddenly affectionate
towards her and determined not to do
anything more to spoil her evening. The
show lasted no more than fifteen minutes.
At the end, the models came out to take the
applause of the audience. They gathered
round Céline and hugged her. Céline af-
fected a modest expression and wiped a tear
from the corner of her eye. Gorski raised
his glass towards her in a gesture of congrat-
ulation. Then he slipped out.

A few people had gathered on the pavement outside and were lighting cigarettes.
Like Mme Bettine before her, Céline did
not allow smoking in the shop. Gorski lit a
cigarette of his own and walked slowly
around the perimeter of the little park. The
sky was clear and there was a chill in the
air. He held his cigarette in his mouth and
pulled on his raincoat. When he reached the
opposite side of the park he could still hear
the faint hubbub coming from the shop.
When he was sure nobody was looking, he

stubbed out his cigarette and stepped into the shrubs in front of the apartment building opposite. He stood for a few minutes observing the spot where, a week before, Alex Ackermann had waited for Adèle. The lights of the shop were still visible through the leaves, but he could no longer hear anything, as if he was viewing the scene from behind a pane of glass. There was a strange pleasure in standing unseen in the bushes. He remained there for a few minutes thinking about Adèle. He imagined her climbing onto the back of Ackermann's scooter and zipping off into the night. Then, on the pavement opposite, he saw Manfred Baumann. He was walking slowly in the direction of his apartment with a woman on his arm. Gorski stepped further back into the shrubs and watched them pass. The woman was walking a little unsteadily. Gorski did not recognise her. The couple did not appear to be talking. When they were out of view, the door to the apartment building behind Gorski opened. Gorski was startled and turned round abruptly. A middle-aged man with a terrier stared at him questioningly. Gorski fumbled in his coat for his ID, before whispering, 'Police.'

FOURTEEN

At lunch the following day, the new waitress arrived to take Manfred's order. It had taken her only a few days to settle into her role. She was a niece of Marie's, and Manfred had overheard Pasteur call her Dominique. She already seemed less harassed as she moved between the tables, even at this, the busiest time of day. Still, she was no Adèle, and Manfred suddenly missed the sight of the former waitress, traipsing about the place with her carelessly fastened blouse. Dominique wrote Manfred's order out in long-hand, before snapping her notebook shut and saying, 'Certainly, Monsieur Baumann.'

Manfred was sure that on hearing his name, the man at the adjacent table, who had previously been absorbed in his newspaper, suddenly glanced in his direction. When Manfred returned his look, he immediately averted his eyes. Manfred did not recognise the man. Had his name suddenly acquired the kind of notoriety that made someone, quite involuntarily, look up from his newspaper? Perhaps the man would later tell his wife that he had seen that fellow Baumann, whose name had been mentioned in connection with the disappearance of the waitress, sitting eating his lunch in the Restaurant de la Cloche as if nothing at all was amiss. And how, in any case, did Dominique know his name? Had Marie made a special point of pointing him out? Had she been one of those who had described him to Gorski as a creature of habit?

Dominique returned with his meat salad, a dish Manfred disliked, but which he nevertheless ordered once a week for fear of offending Pasteur, who regarded it as something of a *spécialité de la maison*. She showed no particular emotion as she placed the bowl on the table. Manfred told himself he was being foolish. Most likely the girl had merely overheard her aunt calling him Monsieur Baumann. Marie addressed all the regulars in this formal manner. It was part of the old world atmosphere she liked to cultivate for the place. Still, it grated a little with Manfred. He felt warmly towards Marie and enjoyed the moments when she paused to exchange a few remarks with him.

He never felt, as he did with other people, that she was about to ridicule him or accuse him of some misdemeanour, so when she addressed him in this way it was as if she was quite purposefully asserting the professional boundaries of their relationship.

As Manfred ate his lunch, he watched Marie go about her work. Was it possible that since the business with Adèle, she had been keeping her distance from him? There was nothing Manfred could put his finger on, yet he could not recall any occasion in the last few days when she had paused at his table to enquire about his wellbeing or pass a comment about the weather or some other uncontroversial subject. Today, for example, she had not so much as acknowledged him. She was attending to the tables on the far side of the room, as she always did during the lunch service, but even so Manfred would have expected her to mouth a greeting in his direction. The more he watched her, the more she appeared to be avoiding his gaze. Perhaps her nose was out of joint on account of his nonappearance the previous evening. Manfred felt a surge of annoyance. Was he not allowed to absent himself from the place for a single evening? He had even gone to the trouble of informing her husband in advance, not that he would expect Pasteur to have passed on the information. He ate the rest of his meal with a growing feeling of resentment. Perhaps in the future he would take his custom elsewhere. They could do without his money and gossip about him to their hearts' content.

At the counter, Manfred deliberately averted his eyes when Marie passed with an armful of empty plates. She reappeared from the kitchen as he was collecting his change from the salver. She paused at his side and leaned in close to him.

'So, Monsieur Baumann, what's this I hear about a young lady in your life?'

Manfred was quite taken aback.

'Young lady?' he said.

'Come on now,' she said, placing a hand on Manfred's arm, 'I want to hear all about her.'

Pasteur glanced at them over his spectacles.

'She's just a friend,' Manfred managed to mutter. He could not think of anyone who might have seen them together.

'Well, you bring her in here sometime. Otherwise I'll think you're keeping her hidden away.'

'Yes,' said Manfred, 'I will.'

He strode briskly back to the bank. Was it

not possible to step outside one's door without becoming the subject of conversation? Did people have nothing better to talk about than what he did with his evenings? He was further annoyed that Marie's final remark had clearly been intended to convey that she knew he had eaten in another restaurant.

Manfred sat brooding at his desk. How ridiculous he was! The idea that he could sustain some kind of relationship with Alice Tarrou was preposterous. He had not even enjoyed their evening together. All he had done was listen to her talk about herself and her abhorrent ex-husband. And then, in a wretched attempt to gain her pity, he had mentioned Juliette. Manfred was disgusted with himself. It was quite despicable. And, on top of that, he had, for the first time in his life, disclosed his connection to the murdered girl. He had not mentioned her by name, but with Gorski sniffing around every aspect of his life, who was to say he would not question Alice? He felt quite nauseous.

Midway through the afternoon, Carolyn knocked timidly on the door. Manfred spread some papers on the desk in front of him before telling her to enter. She stepped into the doorway of the office and said there was a policeman to see him. Manfred felt no surprise until, instead of Gorski, a young *gendarme* appeared behind her.

'Monsieur Baumann,' he said without preamble, 'Inspector Gorski would like to see you at the police station.'

Manfred was too surprised to respond, not because he was being asked to go to the police station, but because Gorski had not had the courtesy to come himself. Despite the awkwardness of their previous encounters there had been an atmosphere of civility, of two professional men talking, if not candidly, at least respectfully to one another. Now Gorski had sent a minion barely out of school to pick him up, as if he was a common criminal. And to compound the matter, he had done so at his place of work, in front of his staff.

'That's out of the question,' Manfred said, 'I can't just leave at the drop of a hat.'

He said this mainly for the benefit of Carolyn, who was standing inside the door, her exit blocked by the policeman. He had no real intention of refusing.

'I must insist,' said the policeman. He took a few steps towards Manfred's desk, as if he thought he might be about to make a bolt for it. Carolyn took the opportunity to slip out. Manfred remained seated for a moment.

'Am I under arrest?' He immediately regretted saying this. It suggested a guilty conscience.

'No, monsieur, as I understand, you are assisting Inspector Gorski with his enquiries into the disappearance of Adèle Bedeau.'

Manfred wished that Carolyn had stayed long enough to hear this. He was merely assisting the police with their enquiries.

'Can you give me five minutes?' he said.

The cop nodded but remained standing, the door to the office still open. Manfred made a show of finishing reading a document, then arranged the papers on his desk into a neat pile and stood up. He fetched his jacket from the stand and put it on. The policeman put out his hand as if to usher him towards the door and followed him closely out. The staff made no pretence of carrying on with their work. They were gathered round the desk of Mlle Givskov. Manfred instructed Carolyn to reschedule his appointments for the remainder of the afternoon. She looked puzzled as Manfred did not have any appointments. He ignored her expression and told Mlle Givskov to lock up if he did not return before the bank closed for the day.

'Of course, M. Baumann,' she said as if the situation were entirely normal.

A police car was parked outside, even though the station was barely three hundred metres away. The young cop opened the rear door and Manfred got in. Nothing was said on the short drive. Manfred rarely had occasion to ride in a car. The same street that he walked four times a day looked different, as if he were seeing it in a film. The tinted windows of the vehicle had the effect of heightening the colours of the sky and the yellowing leaves on the trees. They pulled up outside the station and the cop led Manfred up the little steps, his hand on his elbow. He resisted the temptation to look around to see if anyone was witness to this humiliating spectacle. Manfred had never set foot in the police station before. Although the facade was shabby, it was a rather grand building by the standards of Saint-Louis. A washed-out tricolour hung limply above the entrance. To the right was a notice board displaying faded recruitment posters for the police and the Foreign Legion.

The policeman told Manfred to take a seat in the reception area and said something to the officer behind the glass partition. The officer, a man in his fifties with a grey face and a drooping moustache, looked over and nodded disinterestedly. Fifteen minutes passed. The officer with the moustache did not so much as glance in his direction when he appeared at the window to deal with the trickle of callers. An old woman, evidently well-known to the cops, came in to report her dog missing. A delivery driver asked directions. Manfred had taken the seat nearest the door and every time someone entered he had to move his legs to let them pass. He gazed at the dog-eared posters on the wall opposite, urging citizens to keep their houses and vehicles locked and to be vigilant against crime. After another ten minutes, Gorski arrived. He did not greet or even appear to notice Manfred. He tapped his keys on the window and someone buzzed open the door to the right.

Another few minutes passed. Manfred wondered if he should ring the bell and remind the desk sergeant that he was here. That was what an innocent man would do. Someone with nothing to hide, someone who was assisting the police with their enquiries would not sit meekly waiting to be called. He decided to give it another five minutes. Above the window was a circle of clean paint where there had once been a clock. The telephone on the counter rang.

The grey-faced officer answered, his eyes staring blankly at Manfred while he spoke. He took down an address and promised to send someone round. Then he disappeared. Manfred heard an outburst of laughter. He imagined the cops behind the partition discussing how long they could make him wait. He felt his face colour and resolved to get up and ring the bell. As he was getting to his feet, Gorski appeared at the window. He had probably been clandestinely observing him.

'Monsieur Baumann,' he said, 'please come through.' He pressed a buzzer to open the door and ushered Manfred along a stale-smelling corridor into an interview room. He indicated that Manfred should take the seat with his back to the door and sat down opposite him. There was a tape recorder on a second table against the wall. Gorski did not switch it on. He put his elbows on the table and exhaled theatrically as if contemplating how to begin. He clasped his fingers together and rested his chin on them.

'Monsieur Baumann,' he began, 'I've asked you to come to the station because I wanted to give you the opportunity to correct the version of events you have given me.'

Manfred remained silent.

'It seems to me that . . .' he made a show of weighing his words carefully, '. . . that you must have been mistaken in some of the things you have told me.'

Manfred did not know what to say. *Be sure your sins will find you out,* one of his grandfather's favourite aphorisms, ran through his mind. Perhaps now was the moment to admit that he had seen Adèle. What, after all, would come of it? Certainly he could be accused of wasting police time, perhaps even obstructing the investigation, but such things were bureaucratic matters rarely resulting in charges. In truth, it would be a relief to admit to something Gorski clearly already knew, even if there were repercussions. And the repercussions of sticking to his story were undoubtedly worse. Clearly there must have been some development. Why else would Gorski have summoned him?

Before Manfred had the chance to speak, Gorski nodded curtly. The opportunity was gone. He got up and paced to the side of the tiny room.

'You recall, of course,' he continued, 'that before her disappearance, Adèle Bedeau was seen in the company of a young man.'

Manfred nodded.

'This young man — an Alex Ackermann

— has now come forward. He came to see me because he was rightly concerned that he was a suspect in the disappearance of the girl. He seemed sincere in his desire to provide information and, without burdening you with details, initial enquiries appear to bear out his story. There are, however, a couple of points which require clarification.'

He paused. Manfred's mouth was dry. Gorski's pedantic manner irritated him. Why didn't he just come out with whatever it was he had up his sleeve? It was too late now to admit that he had seen the young man. It would appear that he was only doing so because he had been cornered. And in any case, who was to say that Gorski would believe what he had to say? Had he not already proved himself to be a liar? Now anything he said would be treated with scepticism.

Gorski resumed his seat.

'According to Ackermann, on the Wednesday night when he met Adèle, she was in the company of another man. He described the man as being in his late thirties, about one-eighty, with short dark hair, wearing a dark suit and tie and a light raincoat.' Gorski widened his eyes and held out the palms of his hands. 'So you can see why I am confused.'

'That description could fit any number of people.'

Gorski tipped his head as if to concede the point. 'What were you wearing that night?'

Manfred did not answer. He was surprised at the number of thoughts that could flash through his mind in a short space of time. He could affect surprise: *Yes, of course, I remember now! I did walk a little way with Adèle that night. How stupid of me to have forgotten!* But Gorski would never fall for such a ploy. Perhaps, it was time for outrage. He was an upstanding member of the community, a professional person with not a blemish on his record, he had had enough of Gorski's insinuations. But Manfred lacked the decisiveness for either course. Instead he just sat there, awaiting the inevitable.

'I simply want you to admit that you saw the girl on the night in question, so that we can move on,' said Gorski.

'He must be lying,' Manfred said.

Gorski shook his head slowly. 'It would be something of a coincidence, I think you'd agree, if he invented this figure who just happened to match your description. In any case, having come forward of his own volition, why would he lie?'

'Perhaps he wanted to throw suspicion on someone else.'

'I don't think so,' said Gorski, as if he and Manfred were all of a sudden engaged in mutually trying to solve a puzzle. 'But it's an interesting question nevertheless: why would he lie? You'd agree, I imagine, that if a person lies they must have some reason for doing so.'

He let this last comment hang in the air for a few moments.

Manfred stared at the table. It had a chipped formica top and a metal rim. Previous visitors had scratched their names on the surface. It seemed a curious place, Manfred thought, to advertise one's presence. Gorski sighed, leaned forward over the table.

'After this mysterious figure walked off — in the direction of your apartment, I might add — Ackermann asked Adèle who he was. She replied that he was a customer from the restaurant and that he "gave her the creeps".'

Manfred felt like he had been kicked in the stomach. *He gave her the creeps.* The phrase made him nauseous. Why would Adèle say such a thing? Their relations had always been polite, cordial even. He had never treated her with anything other than

239

courtesy. If anything, he had gone out of his way to be pleasant in order that she would understand that he did not look down upon her as a mere waitress. On top of that, on the night in question, they had passed a few pleasant moments together and she had called him by his first name. And yet she had told this young upstart that he gave her the creeps. It did not make sense. Perhaps she had said this because in fact she felt some attraction to Manfred and had not wished to arouse the jealousy of her boyfriend. Perhaps he was the hot-headed type and would have made a scene. This tallied with the fact that when they had said goodnight, she had addressed him as *monsieur,* clearly in an attempt to cast their relationship in a more formal light.

Gorski had paused and was looking at Manfred, but his words had washed over him. He had obviously asked a question. 'I'm sorry?' said Manfred. He could hardly explain how offensive Adèle's words were since he had previously claimed that he had no feelings one way or the other about her. If this were the case, why would he be so concerned with what she thought of him? Or perhaps Gorski had reached the same conclusion about the hurtful words Adèle had used — that there was more to

240

their relationship than either of them wished to admit, something which would be quite understandable given the difference in their ages and standing in the community.

Gorski shook his head. 'Manfred, I've given you every opportunity to put your version of events right. All I want to do is piece together Mlle Bedeau's movements before she disappeared. By your own admission, on the night in question, you left the Restaurant de la Cloche shortly after the girl. You walked in the same direction, yet you claim to have seen neither Adèle nor this young man. And now Ackermann, who has never seen you before, describes a man precisely answering your description. You must recognise that I can hardly do anything other than conclude that you're hiding something from me.'

Was it, even now, too late to revise his story?

'I understand,' said Manfred.

'So you maintain that you saw neither Adèle Bedeau nor Alex Ackermann that night?'

Manfred nodded sadly.

Gorski stood up and walked towards the door. Manfred took this to mean the ordeal was over, but he merely shouted along the corridor for two cups of coffee. He sat down again, and the two men waited in silence for the coffee to arrive. Manfred stared at the names on the tabletop. Perhaps like him, the previous occupants of this room felt that they were disappearing into the netherworld of the penal system. The impulse to write a tabletop epitaph to oneself seemed suddenly less strange.

The cop with the drooping moustache brought the coffee in two plastic cups and wordlessly placed some sachets of sugar on the table. Gorski tore three open and emptied them into his cup. Manfred found it incongruous that the detective would load his coffee with so much sugar. He took a sip before resuming, leaning across the table, his face close to Manfred's.

'The following night, the night of Adèle's disappearance,' Gorski was speaking rapidly now, 'Ackermann saw the same man pass the park at the Protestant temple, then wait in the shrubbery at the edge of the park until Adèle arrived. When they rode off on his scooter, the man ducked into a doorway, clearly in order to conceal himself.'

Manfred felt his throat tighten. He should say something. What would someone falsely accused say?

'He must be mistaken.'

'Mistaken?' said Gorski. He shook his

head slowly.

Manfred did his best to maintain eye contact with Gorski. Then he looked at the table. There was a wasp on the lip of his coffee cup, moving sluggishly as they always did at this time of year. Gorski pushed down on the table, his fingertips evenly spread. He had small delicate hands. The wasp dropped to the table and struggled to right itself. Gorski scraped his chair back, stood up and leant on the wall to Manfred's right. He adopted a more conversational tone, as if they were two friends passing the time of day over a drink in a bar. That night, he informed Manfred, Adèle and Ackermann had visited what could only be described as a shebeen, where they had drunk a large quantity of alcohol and smoked joints.

'Afterwards they went to a house party in a basement on Rue de la Gare,' he went on. 'To cut a long story short, they had an argument and Ackermann left. That, he claims, was the last he saw of Mlle Bedeau. From what I can gather, she later left the party alone and in a state of some intoxication.'

Manfred lowered his eyes. He took a sip from the plastic cup in front of him. It tasted foul. The wasp was slowly making its way around the metal rim of the table. He was relieved that the interview had at least moved on from his own actions that night. Gorski appeared to be waiting for him to respond, but he said nothing. What could he expect him to say about Adèle's actions on the night in question?

'Surely you can see why I'm telling you this,' said Gorski.

'I'm sorry, I can't,' Manfred replied.

'Rue de la Gare is not three hundred metres from your apartment.'

'And?'

'You say you went home directly that night.'

'Yes.'

'What did you do?'

Manfred thought for a few moments. 'I read for a while, drank a whisky or two and went to bed.'

'Watch any television?'

'I don't own a television.'

'Make any telephone calls?'

'No.'

'Anyone call you?'

'No.'

'Did you speak to anyone in the building?'

'No.'

'So, really you could have been anywhere.'

'I was at home.'

'But you couldn't prove that.'

Manfred shrugged.

Gorski drained the remains of his coffee, placed the cup carefully back on the table.

'Have you ever harboured any thoughts about Adèle Bedeau?' he asked.

'What sort of thoughts?'

Gorski fixed him with his gaze. 'You know what sort of thoughts, carnal thoughts.'

Manfred could hardly tell Gorski that he spent his evenings surreptitiously spying on her and often went home and masturbated thinking about her heavy breasts and wide behind.

'Certainly not,' he said, 'I have nothing but respect for Mlle Bedeau.'

'So you think it would be disrespectful to have sexual thoughts about a woman?'

Manfred felt besieged. 'I don't think about Adèle Bedeau that way.'

'Are you a homosexual?'

'No,' said Manfred.

'Some people seem to think you are.'

This came as no surprise to Manfred. He had heard whispers to this effect in the bank. Lemerre often liked to taunt him with such insinuations. He could all too clearly imagine the hairdresser gleefully telling Gorski that he was that way inclined.

'I'm not queer,' he said.

'A pity that,' said Gorski, 'since it's un- likely that a homosexual would be involved in a crime like this.'

'A crime like what?' said Manfred. He raised his voice slightly. Gorski ignored his question.

'What about women?' he went on. 'Do you have a lover?'

Manfred thought of Alice. He felt suddenly that he would never see her again.

'No,' he said.

'But a man of your age has needs.'

'I take care of those,' said Manfred. He had started to grind his back teeth.

'In what manner?' Gorski's tone was affable, curious, as if he was enquiring about an innocuous hobby.

Manfred clamped his jaw firmly shut. He wanted to cry out for Gorski to stop. He could not bear this relentless delving into his business. His fingernails whitened as he gripped the table.

'Has Adèle Bedeau ever been in your apartment?'

The suggestion came so out of the blue that Manfred exhaled sharply. He attempted to pass off his response as laughter.

'I'm glad you find this amusing, Manfred,' Gorski went on. 'The last time this girl was seen alive was in the vicinity of your apartment. You have consistently lied about seeing Mlle Bedeau on the two nights in question, leading me to conclude that there is something in your relationship with her that you wish to conceal.'

'I have no relationship with Mlle Bedeau.'

'Then why lie about it?'

Manfred said nothing.

'Did Adèle Bedeau visit your apartment in the early hours of Friday morning?'

'No,' said Manfred. 'She has never been in my apartment. She doesn't even know where I live.'

'Very well,' said Gorski. He shook his head slowly, as if Manfred had disappointed him. Then he pushed himself off the wall he had been leaning against and left the room. Manfred exhaled. His heart was pounding. Slowly his breathing subsided. He wiped the sweat from his forehead with his handkerchief. Things were getting out of hand. He felt nauseous.

The officer from the reception desk appeared and asked Manfred to follow him. They walked back along the corridor leading to the reception area. The policeman pressed a buzzer and held the door open for Manfred.

'Am I to wait?' Manfred asked.

The policeman shook his head. 'You're free to go.'

Manfred stood bemused in the reception

area for a few moments. Plainly Gorski was toying with him. He hesitated before exiting. Nobody intervened. He came to a halt on the pavement at the foot of the steps. His hands were shaking. The late afternoon air was still hot. He felt conspicuous in front of the police station, but the few passers-by paid no attention to him. Why should they? There was nothing out of the ordinary about him. He was just a man wiping his brow on a warm day. He stepped to the side of the pavement to allow a woman in North African dress and her three children to pass.

FIFTEEN

Manfred looked at his watch. It was quarter past four. The bank would still be open. He should go back to work to put a stop to any gossip. He could say that he had been called in to identify a witness or something of that sort. He could even make light of the experience. That was what an innocent man would do — go back to work as if nothing untoward had occurred. Or perhaps an innocent man would be so shaken by the experience of being hauled into a police station that he would duck into the nearest bar and down a good measure of alcohol to calm his nerves. Manfred set off along the street in the opposite direction from the bank.

It struck him that Gorski must surely be having him watched. Having come close to accusing him, as he just had, of having something to do with Adèle's disappearance, he would hardly let him walk free from the station without placing him under surveillance. Manfred stopped abruptly and looked around. Nobody ducked into a doorway or appeared to suddenly avert their gaze. There were no men in dark glasses leaning against lampposts reading newspapers. Of course, these were stereotypes. It could be anyone — the woman across the road scolding her son, the teenager loitering at the kiosk, the man looking out from inside the door of the travel agent's waiting for customers. More likely, it would not be any single individual, but a whole team. Perhaps Gorski had already asked those who knew him to keep an eye on him and report back if he behaved strangely. He must act naturally. All along, his mistake had been not to act naturally. He kept walking. He must behave exactly as he would if he were not being watched. It should not be too difficult. Did he not, after all, already live his life as if he was constantly being watched, as if he expected at any moment to be challenged to explain his actions or to answer charges unknown? Did he not fully expect everyone around him to be called at any time to give evidence against him?

He passed a side street and then, as if on the spur of the moment, double-backed and turned into it. It was a quite ordinary road with houses that opened directly on to the pavement. An old woman in a headscarf with an overweight lapdog on a leash approached on the opposite side, but otherwise the street appeared to be deserted. Manfred looked over his shoulder. Nobody was following him. In the next street was a seedy-looking bar that he occasionally passed. He had never been inside, but it had always held a certain attraction for him. He turned the corner and entered the place, as he had secretly known he would since he left the police station. It was dark and cool inside. There was a smell of indeterminate meat and dark tobacco. The walls, ceiling and even the light in the place were the colour of mustard. Behind the counter hung the drinks tariff and a calendar with pictures of half-naked women. Nobody so much as glanced in Manfred's direction. He quickly surveyed the room before taking a table next to the wall. The proprietor appeared, wiping his hands on his apron.

'Monsieur?' His manner was neither friendly nor unfriendly.

Manfred ordered a glass of red wine and then, as the proprietor turned away, changed his order to a carafe.

'A carafe, it is,' the man said.

The carafe and tumbler arrived without

ceremony. Manfred filled the glass to the brim and downed it. The wine was cheap and had a metallic tang, but it was like having a cool compress placed on his brow. Manfred refilled his glass and took another long swallow. He closed his eyes for a few moments, letting the alcohol take its soothing effect. Then he rolled his head back on his shoulders. His hands were still shaking slightly.

Three men in workman's overalls were standing at the counter, arguing about immigration. The proprietor dropped the odd comment into the conversation as he went about his business. At another table a single man in a slightly shabby suit was reading a newspaper and drinking a white wine. He suddenly raised his eyes and caught Manfred looking at him. He nodded a short greeting and returned his attention to the paper. He did not appear to recognise Manfred, nodding merely as one afternoon drinker to another. Manfred felt a sudden sense of liberation. Here he was nobody. If he got up and left, no one would even notice, far less comment. He meant nothing at all to anyone in the bar.

Manfred imagined throwing it all in with the Restaurant de la Cloche. He could come here to Le Pot instead. Of course, within a very short time the proprietor would learn his name and start to greet him with the words 'The usual?' or perhaps even set out his carafe as soon as he stepped through the door. The men who stood at the counter would quickly come to regard Manfred as too good for them, on account of his choosing to sit at a table — the same table every day — rather than drink at the bar. Before long they would have come up with a nickname that they would use behind his back. No, this anonymity was inevitably short-lived. The only way to preserve it would be to constantly drift from bar to bar, but Saint-Louis was not large enough to sustain such a practice for long. Soon he would lapse into some sort of routine, of visiting certain bars on certain nights. What Manfred needed was to get out of Saint-Louis for good, to head to a city like Strasbourg or Paris where one could drink every night in a different bar for the rest of one's life. The idea was intoxicating. And yet there was no question of actually upping sticks and doing such a thing, at least not while this business with Adèle was hanging over him. It would look as if he was absconding.

Manfred poured himself more wine. The man with the paper got up and left, bidding a cursory goodbye to the proprietor. Manfred was surprised that he did not feel more self-conscious. Normally in such a situation he craved some reading material in which to bury his head and avoid eye contact. A newspaper made one invisible. He thought about his grandfather's nickname, how as a teenager he had skulked around the shadows of the house, sometimes taking off his shoes to avoid disturbing his grandparents. He had always felt like an imposter in their home and sought to avoid reminding them of his presence. And hadn't he even now, in this bar, taken an inconspicuous table by the wall? When he arrived at work it took a supreme effort for him to walk in boldly, in a manner befitting his status as 'the boss' and greet his staff in an audible voice. Every morning he breathed a minor sigh of relief as he slipped onto the leather chair behind his desk.

Yet, Manfred reflected, he felt a rare sense of comfort in this slightly rancid smelling bar where no one knew him. He felt like a man, entitled to stop where he wanted and drink a carafe of wine, alone, at four o'clock on a weekday afternoon. The proprietor cleared the glass and water jug from the nearby table, then unhurriedly wiped it down. He did not so much as glance in Manfred's direction.

Manfred finished his wine, but he did not feel like leaving. He felt like he was abroad. He raised his hand to the proprietor and ordered a second carafe. To hell with the Restaurant de la Cloche. Pasteur would have to do without his money tonight. And the rest of them? Let them gossip all they liked. If they had nothing better to talk about, that was their problem.

The second carafe arrived and Manfred got stuck in. Things had to change. He was in a rut, but now was time to get out of it. For years he had told himself that there was nothing he could do about his situation, that circumstances, his temperament, dictated how he behaved. But he had been deceiving himself. There was nothing to prevent him doing anything he wanted. He could easily apply to the bank for a transfer to another city, to a place where he could live unencumbered by the weight of his past, a place where nobody called him 'Swiss'. But why stop there? He recalled how, as a teenager, he had burned with the desire to write, how he had sat up through the night scribbling in notebooks. Why not take up writing now? Perhaps he had talent. He only had to rediscover the fire-in-the-belly of his youth. It was not even impractical. For years he had earned a good salary and spent no more than he needed. His savings were substantial, more than enough to fund himself as a writer for years. Manfred became oblivious to his surroundings. In his reverie he saw himself sitting in front of a typewriter at the open window of an *atelier* in Paris, strolling along a cobbled street in Montmartre in bohemian clothes, notebook in hand, casually greeting the whores and tradesmen of the district. Was there really anything to stop him? He was brought back to earth by a familiar voice. Lemerre was standing by his table.

'Slumming it a little, aren't you, Swiss?' he said with characteristic hostility.

Manfred felt disorientated, as if he had been abruptly woken from a deep sleep. Before he had time to tell himself that he had no need to excuse his presence in the bar to Lemerre, he began to feel his way towards an explanation.

'I . . . I sometimes pop in here for a quick one after work.' He regretted the lie as soon as he had said it.

Lemerre weighed this up with theatrical bewilderment. He looked at the two carafes on Manfred's table. Manfred remembered that his barber's shop was not five minutes' walk away.

'Strange that I've never seen you in here.'

He turned to the proprietor. 'You seen our Swiss in here before, Yves?'

The proprietor gave an almost imperceptible shake of his head, as if reluctant to provide Lemerre with the confirmation he desired.

Lemerre massaged his jowly chin and shook his head slowly, as if stumped by the puzzle and went over to the bar, where the proprietor had already placed his drink. Manfred cringed. Lemerre engaged in some coarse banter with the men at the bar. Then he lowered his voice and the men turned in unison to look at Manfred, before he muttered something else and they all burst into laughter. Manfred felt the colour rise in his cheeks. He wanted to jump up and run out into the street, but he hadn't paid for his drinks and doing so would entail either going over to the counter or summoning the proprietor, both of which were out of the question.

Lemerre downed his drink swiftly and left without another word to Manfred.

Manfred suddenly felt the gloomy effect of the wine. His head swam. The bar had fallen silent. The regulars had suddenly run out of topics of conversation, or perhaps felt self-conscious on account of the previously unnoticed stranger in their midst. The place was tainted now. He was no longer a nobody, but somebody who had been observed and whose behaviour was being noted. His carafe was two-thirds full. He would look ridiculous if, having ordered it only minutes before, he got up and left. He refilled his glass and forced himself to drink. He tried to return to his daydream about escaping Saint-Louis, but the idea that he had even for a moment entertained the thought of running off and becoming a writer was ludicrous. And all the more so with Gorski sniffing around. Manfred drained his glass as if making a private toast to the death of his dream.

There were more pressing issues with which to occupy his thoughts. Gorski had already questioned Lemerre and his cohorts and might well do so again. Already Manfred had broken his golden rule and failed to follow his routine. And now that Lemerre had caught him red-handed, it was bound to come to Gorski's attention. The detective would be sure to ask why he had come to this out-of-the-way dive where one could not be seen from the street. Who was he hiding from? Why, since the disappearance of Adèle, had he been behaving in this out-of-character manner? Manfred would have no plausible explanation. Regardless of having been caught by Lemerre, it had been a mistake to come here, but he must not compound one mistake with another. He must revert to his routine and go to the Restaurant de la Cloche as usual. Manfred struggled to drink the rest of his carafe. The workmen at the counter left and for a few minutes Manfred and the proprietor were the only people in the bar. Unlike Pasteur, who could always find some task with which to occupy himself, this man — Manfred had heard Lemerre call him Yves — stood staring blankly into the space above the tables. He was stocky and unattractive, with narrow beady eyes. The fawn sports shirt he was wearing was stained with grease or mustard. He did not appear to be watching him, but Manfred felt that every movement he made was being noted. The effect of the wine was no longer pleasant. If called upon to speak, he felt that he would slur or stumble over his words. Neither man spoke. Manfred glanced at his watch as if to suggest that he had some appointment to keep. His bladder pressed against the waistband of his trousers. The WC was on the opposite side of the bar. Under the scrutiny of the barman, Manfred felt it was beyond him to get up from the banquette and walk across the room. He wondered what Alice would make of the sight of him, sitting getting sozzled in this dive, incapable of walking to the WC to relieve himself. Yves unfolded his arms and exhaled loudly. Manfred wondered whether he was about to speak.

Thankfully, the door opened and two men in their twenties entered. They were talking loudly in derogatory terms about their boss. The proprietor greeted them with a single word, 'Messieurs,' and an upward motion of his head. The young men ordered large beers and stood at the bar. Manfred took the opportunity to leave his seat and make his way to the WC. When he returned, the two young men were crudely discussing the attributes of various females colleagues. They paid no attention to Yves and had not so much as glanced around the bar. Manfred simultaneously despised them and envied their lack of self-consciousness. Still, they formed a kind of barrier between him and the proprietor. He was no longer the centre of attention. When another older man came in and sat at a table beneath the high windows, he barely seemed to notice Manfred, before taking out his newspaper and carefully opening it on the table in front of him.

Manfred finished his carafe and paid. Outside the sun was low over the buildings and the air had taken on a chill. His stomach was rumbling, but there was no time to go home and eat. Of course, he could eat at the Restaurant de la Cloche, but he would not do so. He never took his evening meal there and if he were to do so, it would certainly be commented upon. In any case, he would not have time to eat before the infernal card game began.

Manfred entered the restaurant at more or less the usual time. Lemerre and Cloutier were already there. Neither of them acknowledged Manfred as he passed. Lemerre absentmindedly shuffled the cards and spoke to Cloutier in an unusually low voice. Under normal circumstances, the Restaurant de la Cloche was the one place where Manfred felt at ease. His routine was so well-established that he did not feel, as he did elsewhere, that he had to act naturally. People generally paid him little heed. He approached the bar. Pasteur would have thought it presumptuous to set out his drink before he ordered. As he did every night, he greeted Manfred with a nod and the words, 'The usual?' and Manfred replied, 'The usual, yes.'

Tonight, however, those familiar nods and greetings, the very walk to the counter were challenging, as if he was walking into a bar in a foreign country where he did not speak the language or understand the customs. He felt as if he was reading a sentence from a phrasebook. Pasteur, for his part, merely nodded curtly, poured his drink and placed it on the counter before returning his attention to polishing the glasses beneath the gantry. Manfred attributed this aloofness to the fact that he was drunk. Lemerre would already have informed Pasteur of their encounter in Le Pot. Of course, it was none of Pasteur's business if Manfred once in a while took a glass in another bar, but the chilly atmosphere suggested that his nose was out of joint.

Dominique squeezed past Manfred at the hatch and carried two *steak frites* to a couple in the corner. Manfred watched her reset two tables in the mirror above the bar. She could not have been more different from Adèle. She was skinny and flat-chested. Manfred could still perceive the outline of her slim buttocks beneath her skirt. After she had placed the plates in front of the customers she remained at the table fidgeting until the couple satisfied her that they did not require anything else. As she passed through the hatch on her way back to the kitchen, she almost flattened herself against the counter in order, it seemed, to place the maximum distance between herself and Manfred.

'How's the new girl getting on?' he asked Pasteur.

Pasteur glanced up as if he had forgotten that Manfred was there.

'Fine,' he said.

'Your niece, I understand?' said Manfred. He didn't know why he was trying to continue the conversation. Was it a perverse response to the curt answer Pasteur had just given or was it the effect of the alcohol he had already drunk? He felt himself slur a little on the word 'niece'.

'That's right,' Pasteur replied without looking in Manfred's direction.

Petit arrived and took his seat. He poured himself a glass from the carafe on the table. Manfred awaited the summons that signified the commencement of the dreadful ritual. But, instead, the three men engaged in a huddled conversation over the table. Then Pasteur carefully folded his dishtowel and, without a word, walked across the restaurant and took the remaining seat at the table. Manfred was astonished. He watched the vignette unfold in the mirror above the bar. Pasteur took his place as if it was the most natural thing in the world. Lemerre placed the pack in the centre of

263

the table and the four men cut the cards as if it was a custom they had been performing for years. None of them looked in Manfred's direction. His cheeks burned. The whole thing must have been arranged with Pasteur in advance. Even the niece, who now took his place behind the bar, the proprietor's place, which Pasteur never gave up for anyone, must have been in on it. Not to mention Marie, who must be holed up, mortified, in the kitchen. They could not have humiliated him more if they had blatantly accused him of murdering Adèle. Of course, he should march right over to the table and demand to know what was going on. Was he supposed to just stand there for the entire evening drinking his wine as if nothing untoward had taken place?

Manfred's heart pounded in his chest. Of course, they would like nothing more than for him to make a scene, to demand to know what was going on, to start protesting his innocence. Manfred could imagine what the other customers in the restaurant would make of such a spectacle. How amusing it would be. And the four men would just sit there, cards in hand, expressions of mock innocence on their faces. Lemerre's victory would be complete. Manfred determined not to give them the satisfaction. He was under no obligation to assert his innocence to Lemerre, Pasteur or anybody else. So what if he was excluded from the infernal game! They were welcome to it. And they were welcome to their petty conspiracies. Manfred finished his glass and calmly ordered another from the girl. She poured it out and placed it in front of him. Manfred thanked her and took a sip.

It was a long, long evening. At regular intervals Dominique took a fresh carafe to the table by the door. Slowly the restaurant emptied of diners until the only customers were Manfred and the card players. The clatter of dishes and cutlery from the kitchen died away. The only remaining sound was of the players' bids. There was none of the usual banter between hands. Even Lemerre refrained from his usual provocations. By the time Manfred neared the end of his bottle, he was aware that he was swaying slightly. His back had become painful from the effort of standing rigidly at the bar. He finished his bottle and asked for the bill. The waitress placed it on the counter and Manfred paid, leaving, for once, a generous tip in the pewter salver. He did not blame her for her part in his humiliation. Probably she had little idea of the significance of the plot in which she had been an accomplice. She accepted the tip with a barely audible thank you and gave Manfred what he interpreted to be an apologetic smile.

Manfred took his raincoat from the hanger and clumsily put it on. Then he turned and walked unsteadily towards the exit. The men kept their eyes conspicuously on their cards as he passed.

SIXTEEN

Manfred woke with a headache. His mouth was dry and he reached for the tumbler of water he kept on the bedside table. It was not long before the events of the previous evening returned to him. He felt a kind of numbness. He lingered in bed a few minutes longer than normal, listening to the sounds from behind the apartment building, the clunk of car doors closing and engines being started, the faint murmur of birdsong. It was quite normal, but Manfred experienced it as if his head was submerged in water. Everything was muffled.

He sat up and drank the remains of the glass of water. His clothes lay in a crumpled heap on the floor rather on the chair where he normally left them neatly folded. A horizontal slat of sunlight crept in at the foot of the window where the blind did not quite reach the sill. A paperback lay on its spine on the floor, its pages fanned out. He must have knocked it off the bedside table. Manfred felt a sudden sensation that he was not *in* his room, but instead standing outside looking on, as if he was a detective leafing through photographs of a crime scene. Then quite suddenly, he saw himself in the room, bare-chested, propped up against two pillows and he had a strong sense of being watched. Manfred shook his head and dismissed the idea. The feeling must merely be the effect of having drunk, the previous evening, three times as much as he normally did. Nevertheless, when he got out of bed, contrary to habit, he put on a robe to walk the few steps along the passage to the shower room. He felt like an actor playing the role of himself. The headache did not worry him. It was dull and throbbing, quite unlike the migraines which felt as if shards of glass had become lodged in his skull. He found some aspirin in the bathroom cabinet and swallowed three tablets, before splashing cold water on his face.

He turned on the shower and stepped into the cabinet before the water reached a comfortable temperature. He imagined a surveillance team making derogatory remarks about the size of his penis. The drumming of the water on the floor of the cabinet was comforting and he was glad when the glass began to steam up. He turned his face to the water and held it there, close to the showerhead. He must put these silly thoughts from his mind. Of course, the technology existed to place people under surveillance in their homes, and no doubt such technology was at the police's disposal, but the idea that Gorski would have gone to the trouble of breaking into his apartment and fitting concealed cameras was ridiculous. Sketchy as Manfred's knowledge of the law was, such an operation would surely entail the consent of a magistrate, not to mention the manpower required to install the equipment and monitor the footage. Surely, even if the law permitted it, Gorski would not go to such lengths. On the other hand, perhaps it was precisely this operation which had necessitated his removal to the police station the previous day. Gorski would have had to be certain that Manfred would not suddenly arrive home during the installation of the equipment.

Manfred concentrated on the business of his shower. He shampooed his hair and used a rough loofah on his back before taking the showerhead from its bracket and washing away the lather from the crevices of his body. He stepped out of the cabinet and dried himself. He resisted the temptation to put his robe back on, instead wrapping a clean towel around his waist. He wiped the steam from the mirror above the wash-hand basin. His skin was grey and his eyes were bloodshot. He had inherited his father's rapid growth of stubble and he enjoyed the ritual of transforming his face each morning. This morning, however, his skin felt loose and his hands were shaking slightly so that he had to take great care not to cut himself. He patted his face dry and walked back along the passage to the kitchen, still with the towel around his waist. He set a pot of coffee on the hob and looked out of the kitchen window over the children's play park. Perhaps Gorski's men had taken an apartment in the building opposite and were photographing him through an oversized telephoto lens. The thought caused Manfred a wry smile. The only rooms that overlooked the play park were the kitchen and the bedroom, and he rarely bothered to raise the blind in the bedroom.

He dressed, combed his hair and put on his watch. Back in the kitchen he laid out two croissants in a basket, butter and jam, a plate and a knife. He poured the coffee into a large bowl and sat down at the table. As he ate his breakfast, he looked around the room. There was no sign of his apartment being disturbed, but there was no shortage of places in which a camera could be hidden. Manfred was tempted to get up and start squinting at the light fittings and air vents. But it would be impossible to institute a search thorough enough to convince himself there were no devices in the apartment, and, in any case, would the very fact that he was searching for them not be interpreted as a sign of guilt?

It was 8.07. Manfred forced himself to finish his breakfast at his usual pace and left the apartment, as he always did, at 8.15. He paused at the bank of mailboxes in the foyer. Some leaflets were sticking out of the slat of Alice's box. It was curious that they had only once encountered each other in the morning. Manfred was quite sure he would have noticed her. And now it appeared that Alice's mailbox had not been emptied. Probably there was a quite innocent explanation. Perhaps she had gone away or had simply grown tired of discarding the accumulated junk mail.

Outside, Manfred scanned the street for Alice's sports car. He had not noticed what make it was, but he was sure he would recognise it. Instead of turning right and walking towards the bank, Manfred retraced the route he had followed the morning he had met Alice. Most likely she always parked her car behind the building. Perhaps residents even had designated parking spaces, but Alice's car was not there. Manfred reprimanded himself for snooping around in this way. Still, as he headed towards the bank, he could not shake the thought that it was strange that he had never once seen Alice before he found her blouse in the dryer. The more Manfred thought about how they had met, the more suspicious it seemed. The fact that he had happened to bump into her only days after the incident in the laundry room seemed too much of a coincidence. Then there was the absurd charade of her finding his gauche conversation amusing. Manfred cursed himself for having been taken in. He had even secretly congratulated himself on being in possession of a certain charm. What a vain, naive fool he was! And worse, he had actually begun to harbour feelings for her. Since they had met, his mood had lightened at the thought of her. And that all this had occurred while the business with Gorski was going on had not caused Manfred even a moment's pause. When one pieced the thing together it became quite clear that Alice must have been planted by the police in order to inveigle her way into his confidence.

Gorski must have a very low opinion of him if he thought he would fall for such an obvious set-up.

Despite this, as he walked to the bank, Manfred could not resist the temptation to scan the streets for Alice's car. Part of him still wanted to catch a glimpse of her. A brisk breeze rattled the papery leaves of the trees which lined the street. Manfred buttoned his raincoat. To the east, the sky was darkening. The aspirin had had no effect on his headache. Manfred kept his eyes trained on the pavement and quickened his pace. At the bank, he was greeted by silence. The staff made no pretence of continuing their conversation. Perhaps they had assumed he would not appear that morning and that the next they would hear of him would be from the front page of *L'Alsace.* Manfred did not bother to bid them good morning. He called Carolyn into his office and had her bring him some coffee. It was an aberration from his routine. Normally he waited for her to bring him a cup midway through the morning, but in the current circumstances, it seemed a trifle.

Carolyn looked at him with concern and asked if he was all right. Manfred snapped that he was fine and immediately regretted his harsh tone. When the girl returned with his coffee, he apologised and explained that he had a headache. Carolyn nodded and slunk out of the room as if she was afraid to turn her back to him.

Manfred spent the morning staring blankly at the documents on his desk. It must have been quite obvious that he was not doing any work. Manfred reminded himself of his resolve to act naturally, but his thoughts about Alice had thrown him off kilter. The more he thought about it, the more bloody-minded he felt. He went over and over their encounters in his head and the more he reflected, the more he concluded that it could be nothing other than a conspiracy. The timing and details — the fact, for example, that she had been wearing the pale blue blouse on the morning he had met her — and most of all the idea that a woman like Alice Tarrou would be interested in him, all contended against his desire to believe that she was unconnected to the investigation. Manfred had come across such plots in many a novel. It seemed an unlikely tactic for a provincial police force to employ, but the evidence spoke for itself. His headache increased. Everything he had said to Alice would have been reported back to Gorski, including his ill-judged comments about Juliette. Despite his previous resolve to follow his routine, he decided that he should not have come to work. What would have come of it? What if he had disappeared just as Adèle had done? The bank would still have opened. After a few days, head office would send someone to replace him. There would be some gossip, then it would all be forgotten. *He* would be forgotten.

At lunch, Pasteur did not look up from behind the counter when Manfred entered the Restaurant de la Cloche. Dominique arrived at his table and Manfred ordered the *andouillette* as he always did. Most of the tables were occupied, but there was little of the normal hubbub of a lunchtime service. Was the curiously subdued atmosphere on account of his presence? He was sure the eyes of the room were upon him, but whenever he looked up from his food no one was looking in his direction. Nevertheless, Manfred sensed that the occupants of the restaurant would breathe a collective sigh of relief when he left. Pasteur did not glance in his direction for the duration of the meal and, when he paid his bill, no reference was made to the events of the previous evening. It was the proprietor's part in his exclusion from the game that most wounded Manfred. He had always thought of Pasteur as an ally.

It was true that he did not greet him with any special warmth or favour him over other customers. But he had on occasion shot Manfred a conspiratorial look when Lemerre was behaving unpleasantly. It was a meagre foundation upon which to construct a friendship, but Manfred had, nevertheless, thought of Pasteur as his friend.

All the same, as Manfred walked back to the bank, his mood lightened a little. It was a bright day and no one so much as glanced at him. It was not, Manfred told himself, because people were avoiding his gaze, but simply because there was nothing exceptional about him. His headache had subsided and his earlier thoughts about Alice seemed silly. It was absurd to think that Gorski would have gone to so much trouble to entrap him. He had met Alice only the day after Gorski had first visited him in his apartment. Manfred smiled at how ridiculous the idea that Alice was working for the police had been. Of course, there had been a degree of chance to their encounters, a degree of chance which could, when one enumerated it, make the whole thing seem highly improbable, but was that not always the case when two strangers met?

In his office Manfred took the telephone book from the bottom drawer of his desk.

There was no harm in setting his mind to rest once and for all. All he had to do was call all the stationery firms ms in town and ask for Alice Tarrou. If Alice's story was not true, there would be no entry for her company in the directory. It was as simple as that. Manfred flicked through the pages. There were no stationery companies listed in Saint-Louis. He found two printing companies. That was almost the same thing. Manfred picked up the receiver, then hesitated before calling the first number. He did not know if Tarrou was Alice's married or maiden name. Perhaps she still used her ex-husband's name at work. He would just ask for Alice. He would recognise her voice if she came on the line. Then he could just hang up.

He dialled the first number. It rang for some time before a gruff male voice answered.

'May I speak to Alice?' said Manfred.

'Alice who?' the man said.

Manfred hesitated. 'I'm not sure of her second name,' he said. 'I wrote it down, but I seem to have lost the slip of paper.'

'You've got the wrong number, pal,' said the man. 'There's no Alice here.'

Then he hung up.

Manfred replaced the receiver. His heart

was beating a little faster. He tried the second number. This time a young woman answered and told him that no one called Alice worked there. Manfred apologised for troubling her. He ran his hand over his chin. It had the texture of sandpaper. Was it possible, after all, that Alice had concocted the story of the stationery company? He realised that she had not said that the firm was located in Saint-Louis. He looked again in the directory. Two stationer's and three printing firms were listed in Mulhouse. Manfred dialled the first number. A girl answered.

'I wondered if I could speak to Alice,' said Manfred.

'Alice isn't here,' said the girl. 'Can I help you?'

Manfred paused. He could hardly ask the girl what Alice's surname was. 'No,' he said, 'it's a personal matter. Will she be back later?'

'I'm not sure,' said the girl. 'If you give me your number, I'll get her to call you.'

'That's all right,' said Manfred, 'I'll try again later.' Then he put the phone down.

He spent what was left of the afternoon going over the conversation in his mind. There was nothing distinctive about his voice, but the girl was sure to mention that a man had called. Would Alice guess it was him? Perhaps she would think nothing of it, but Manfred did not wish her to know he had been snooping on her, that he had called her office in order to verify what she had told him. That was not how normal people behaved. On top of that, the whole exercise had been futile. Unless he did call back, which he had no intention of doing, he had no way of knowing that it was the same Alice. It was a common enough name.

Manfred asked Mlle Givskov to close up the bank and left early. He was tempted to nip round to Le Pot for a quick glass, but the thought of running into Lemerre deterred him. He could not think of another suitable establishment. Instead he stopped off in a grocer's shop and bought two bottles of red wine. Apart from his usual nightcap, which he took only to help him sleep, he did not make a habit of drinking in his apartment. There was something wretched about drinking at home. The bottles clanked noisily in the brown paper bag in which the grocer had placed them. Manfred removed one of them and slipped it into the outer pocket of his raincoat.

As he approached the apartment building, he was surprised to see Gorski emerge from the entrance. He looked around, as if to ascertain whether anyone had seen him, and started to walk in Manfred's direction. Manfred did not know what to do. It was too late to cross the road and there was no suitable place to conceal himself. In any case, he would not want Gorski to think that he was trying to avoid him. He had no choice but to keep going. The detective gave no indication of having seen him. Then, when they were no more than five metres apart, Gorski nodded curtly and walked straight past him. Manfred continued to his apartment. If Gorski had not wished to speak to him, what was he doing in the apartment building? Manfred placed the two bottles on his kitchen table. He opened one and poured himself a glass. He stepped out onto the balcony overlooking the play park. Alice's silver sports car was parked in its usual place.

SEVENTEEN

Gorski was sitting in the communal area of the station behind the reception window, leafing through his interview notes. He didn't like to closet himself in his office. It gave the impression that he was aloof and he did not like the idea that the other cops might be talking about him. Some of his colleagues still resented Gorski's status as Ribéry's protégé. All that had been twenty years before, but his reputation for currying favour with authority had stuck, at least with the older members of the force.

Schmitt was manning the desk. He had a newspaper spread in front of him on the counter. Gorski had on a number of occasions requested that he refrain from reading his newspaper in view of the public, but Schmitt simply ignored him and eventually he had let it drop. By the time Gorski joined the station, Schmitt had already been confined to desk duties due to some ill-defined

281

medical complaint. He made no secret of his disdain for the young detective. Gorski for his part would have dearly loved to get rid of him. He fantasised at length about forcing him into retirement. He had the power to do so, but he lacked the appetite for confrontation. In any case, such an action would only provoke further resentment among the fraternity of older officers.

Without looking up from his paper, Schmitt said, 'There was a call from Strasbourg. They pulled a floater out of the river.' He mentioned it as if was a matter of no consequence which had simply slipped his mind.

'Sorry?' said Gorski. He had been in the station twenty minutes before Schmitt decided to share this piece of news.

'They said they fished a body out of the Rhine.'

'What kind of body?' said Gorski. He made no attempt to hide his irritation. It was not uncommon for bodies to be found in the Rhine, but even Schmitt could hardly have failed to register the potential importance of the information.

'A female, they didn't say much.'

'No age, no description, no cause of death?'

Schmitt shrugged. 'I got the impression

282

they'd only just pulled her out.'

'But you didn't ask?'

Schmitt exhaled noisily through his moustache, as if the thought hadn't crossed his mind.

'They left a number.'

He made a show of searching for it amid the debris on the counter. He found it on a scrap of paper and held it up. Gorski snatched it and went to his office to make the call. He sat down and went through what he would say. He disliked calling the stations in the city. Even the receptionists never failed to make him feel like a provincial bumpkin. Not that anything was ever said. It was a matter of tone. But there was no getting around making the call. A woman answered.

'Inspector Gorski of Saint-Louis calling for Inspector Lambert.'

And there it was: 'Sorry, from where?'

'Saint-Louis, Haut-Rhin,' Gorski repeated.

The receptionist connected him to the extension. Gorski had met Lambert on a number of occasions, but he never seemed to remember him.

Lambert picked up. 'Georges, how are you?'

Gorski could not help feeling gratified that

he remembered his first name and had greeted him in a friendly manner.

'I hear you've got something I might be interested in,' he said.

'Maybe,' said Lambert.

'Do you have any further information about the remains?' Gorski regretted the formal manner in which he phrased this. It ruined the affable tone with which the conversation had begun.

'Young female, that's all. They only pulled her out a couple of hours ago. She's on a slab in the mortuary. Come up and take a look if you like.'

Ten minutes later Gorski was heading north on the A35. He was excited. He was no expert in such matters, but he understood that it took a few days for gasses to form in the stomach of a corpse and bring it to the surface. The fact that the body had been found one hundred kilometres downstream meant nothing. Bodies often drifted great distances before they snagged on a branch or caught a current and washed up in the shallows. Gorski was equally pleased by the way Lambert had spoken to him and immediately invited him to accompany him to the mortuary to view the body. All being well, by the end of the day, he could have a time and cause of death, perhaps even some other forensic evidence.

The landscape between Saint-Louis and Strasbourg was flat and monotonous. The road was quiet and Gorski used the drive to gather his thoughts about Adèle. Until Alex Ackermann had turned up, she had remained an enigma to him.

That first night, the couple had crossed the border to Basel where they had gone to a bar, well known to Gorski's Swiss colleagues as a haunt of the alternative scene. Ackermann admitted he had taken Adèle there in an attempt to impress her. They had a few drinks and he bought a small quantity of hashish from a man whose name he claimed not to remember. Gorski had not pressed him on the point. He was not interested in a small-time dope dealer and he wanted the boy to feel that he could speak freely. Once the youth had confessed this transgression, he visibly relaxed. He explained that it was because of this that he had not come forward sooner. The Adèle that Ackermann described was quite different from the sullen waitress of the Restaurant de la Cloche. While she had revealed little about herself, she was talkative and worldly. Ackermann confessed that he had felt a little out of his depth. It was hard to reconcile the two pictures of Adèle, but

Gorski reminded himself how little he knew about what his own daughter got up to when she was out with her friends. Perhaps she too went to disreputable bars and smoked marijuana. Ackermann had struck him as a pleasant enough young man whose primary concern was that his parents did not hear about his activities. Had he met him in the company of Clémence, he would not have been overly concerned.

Gorski negotiated the one-way system around the station in Rue de la Nuée Bleue with some difficulty, eventually leaving his car a few streets away. Lambert came down to the foyer without delay and shook Gorski warmly by the hand. He was a tall handsome man with sandy hair and pale blue eyes. He was wearing an expensive well-cut suit. For once, Gorski was pleased to be smartly turned out.

'How's the case?' he asked.

'We're following up a few leads,' said Gorski. He did not want to admit that he was getting nowhere.

'That bad, eh?' His tone was sympathetic rather than mocking.

'I could certainly do with a body,' said Gorski.

Lambert suggested that they take his car to the mortuary. He asked Gorski a few more questions about the case, but when it became apparent that he had little or nothing to go on, he dropped the subject. Gorski was embarrassed. He wondered if it was his own incompetence that had resulted in the lack of progress. He would have liked to ask Lambert's advice. He would have dealt with far more cases of this nature than Gorski. But he did not do so and the final minutes of the journey were passed in silence. Lambert parked his BMW in a restricted area outside the mortuary and strode past the reception area. He appeared to know the corridors of the building well. He marched along so quickly Gorski almost had to run to keep up. They were greeted by a technician in a white coat and Lambert explained why they were there. When the technician glanced questioningly in Gorski's direction, Lambert introduced him as if he had forgotten momentarily that he was there. The technician led them to a bank of stainless steel doors. He told them that the post-mortem would not take place until later that evening, but they were welcome to attend. Gorski hoped that would not be necessary. In his early days as a detective, he had, out of a sense of bravado, volunteered to attend the autopsy of a suicide. Much to the amusement of the pathologist and his assistant, he had thrown up only minutes into the procedure. News of the incident mysteriously filtered back to the station and for weeks afterwards he had had to endure his colleagues pretending to vomit into wastepaper baskets whenever he entered the room. The technician slid the drawer open. Gorski took a deep breath. It was immediately apparent that the body was not that of Adèle Bedeau. The girl was blonde and skinny. Her ribs showed through her skin. The flesh had taken on a greenish-grey hue. Lambert looked at Gorski, who shook his head. He felt nauseous.

'Been dead a good couple of weeks, I'd say,' said the technician.

'Sorry, pal,' said Lambert.

They drove back to the station in silence. Gorski felt that Lambert was embarrassed on his behalf, that he had shown his naivety by jumping in his car so hastily. He could easily have waited in Saint-Louis for a description of the body to be sent to him. Instead, he had got ahead of himself, like a child who couldn't wait to open his Christmas presents. On the drive to Strasbourg he had practically solved the crime in his head and got himself a transfer to the big city force in the process. Indeed, had he not partly raced here merely for the opportunity to rub shoulders with some big city cops, and so that later he would be able to mention in an off-hand way to Céline that he had been up to Strasbourg?

Gorski and Lambert parted in the street. Lambert wished him luck with the case and told him to get in touch if he needed anything. Gorski thanked him. They shook hands and Lambert disappeared back into the station.

Gorski took the longer route along the Rhine back to Saint-Louis. He drove slowly. He had no wish to return to the station and admit that his trip to Strasbourg had been a wild goose chase. He could already see the mocking expression on Schmitt's face. The brown water of the great river to his left moved at funereal pace. The crops in the fields to his right were cut to a stubble. There was a sweet smell of manure in the air. He felt deflated. The investigation was cold and he could see little chance of it taking a turn for the better. If it did, it would be a matter of good fortune rather than through any inspiration on his part. All avenues of investigation had been exhausted. There was only Manfred Baumann, but aside from the fact that he was lying, there was no real evidence to connect him to Adèle Bedeau's disappearance.

He pulled into a lay-by a little to the north of Saint-Louis and sat for some minutes, smoking. Then he got out and walked through the woods towards the clearing. As he trudged along the path he told himself that the clearing was as good a place as any to gather his thoughts, but there was more to it than that. As he took his usual seat on the fallen tree trunk, he wondered if a cop like Lambert would have made more progress with the case. His Strasbourg colleague would certainly have taken a more forceful line with Manfred Baumann, perhaps arresting him in the hope of forcing him into a confession. Or perhaps he would have staged some reconstruction of the events leading up to the girl's disappearance. Gorski's credo was that police work was a matter of routine, of following procedure, but he feared his scorn for speculation was nothing more than a defence against the suspicion that he was incapable of taking a more intuitive approach to his work. Twenty years ago, he had failed and now he was failing again. Yet he refused to countenance changing his methods. But had he not, in fact, returned to the clearing because of the nagging feeling that there was some connection between the disappearance of Adèle Bedeau and the murder of Juliette Hurel?

He had, as a matter of course, considered and rejected the notion. Yet the idea persisted. He carefully stubbed out his cigarette on the tree trunk and lit another.

Gorski loathed hunches. They were an excuse for ill-disciplined thinking, part of a vocabulary cops liked to use to cloak their work in mystique. Speculation led nowhere. One 'what if' led to another and, before long, supposition was piled on pointless supposition. It was like the opening of a game of chess. After every move the permutations increased exponentially. Gorski had no inclination to lose himself in a pointless chain of conjecture, a chain which would in all likelihood turn out to be built on false premises. In any case, such thinking gave Gorski a headache. Yet his plodding adherence to empiricism had got him nowhere. And, had he not from the outset proceeded on the premise that Adèle Bedeau was dead, and more than that — that she had been murdered? It was a very basic assumption, but even now Gorski had no evidence to support it. Indeed, the very lack of evidence pointed to the opposite conclusion: that Adèle Bedeau was alive and had simply disappeared. Was this not why Gorski had become so excited when Schmitt had informed him of the body in the river? The assumption he had made had been vindicated. And in the process Gorski could applaud himself on the correctness of his instincts. He had already been congratulating himself on the drive to Strasbourg.

The air in the forest was cool and still. A woodpigeon cooed incessantly. Gorski cast his eyes up towards the foliage, but he could not see any birds. He drew on his cigarette. The ground was tinder dry. For a second Gorski saw the forest ablaze, the invisible birds around him suddenly taking to the skies to escape the flames. Then he heard a rustling in the bushes behind him. He started. He dreaded the idea of someone coming along to whom he might have to explain his presence. He looked over his shoulder. There was nobody there. Perhaps a bird or animal had disturbed the undergrowth. He looked at his watch. It was only quarter past four. He could not go home. Clémence would be back from school and think it odd that he was in the house. These days he spent as little time as possible at home. He got up from the tree trunk and for no particular reason walked in the direction of the sound he had heard. There were some ripe blackberries in the bushes. He paused to pick some, snagging the sleeves of his jacket on the thorns. They were sweet and juicy. The flavour reminded him of the weeks he had spent working on a farm as a teenager. He pushed through the brush-wood. After a while he came across an overgrown path.

Twenty minutes later he arrived at a brick wall, around three metres tall and veined with creepers. The pale yellow bricks were crumbling and much of the mortar had come loose, so that it appeared to be held up only by the ivy that grappled its way to the coving. The wall stretched some distance in either direction and Gorski could not step back far enough to see over it due to the dense bushes from which he had emerged. There was a wooden door. It had once been painted blue, but most of the paint had long since peeled off, leaving the wood exposed and rotting. The undergrowth reached halfway up the door and the hinges were covered with ancient cobwebs. It had clearly not been used for years. Neverthe-less, Gorski stepped into the shrubbery and tried the rusty doorknob. It rattled uselessly in his hand. He contemplated scaling the wall. There were plenty of crevices that could serve as footholds, but the idea of ar-riving on someone's property in such an undignified manner did not appeal to him. Besides, he could not be sure the wall would not collapse under his weight.

Instead Gorski headed north, away from Saint-Louis. Gorski was confident that the wall formed the rear boundary of the large villas on the outskirts of the town. After three or four hundred metres it ended, giving way to some vegetable plots, which might have belonged to the nearby houses, or were perhaps rented by townsfolk. Gorski cut through a pathway leading towards the road and doubled back towards where he had first emerged from the woods. The houses on the northern edge of the town were large imposing buildings set back from the road, their privacy protected by stone walls and mature trees. Aside from the occasional burglary, he had not had occasion to visit these properties since the murder of Juliette Hurel.

Gorski recognised the name on the mailbox at the foot of the drive of one of the houses. He put on his jacket to hide the large sweat marks under his arms. His footsteps crunched conspicuously on the gravel as he approached the house. Certainly he had been here before, but he struggled to recall the details of his previous visit. Gorski felt ill at ease approaching the house. He half-expected the owner to come out and berate him for trespassing. Even now as a police inspector, he felt uneasy in the presence of the bourgeoisie who inhabited these grand houses. Since their marriage, Céline had been relentless in her intolerance of Gorski's lower class mannerisms, endlessly correcting his speech and reprimanding him for wiping his mouth with the back of his hand or holding his cutlery incorrectly. As a result, Gorski was, as Céline put it, just about able to pass in polite society, but in her absence, Gorski often reverted to his old ways, betraying his origins through a certain obsequiousness in the presence of his social superiors.

He rang the bell. It was a full minute before the door was opened by a uniformed maid. She looked enquiringly at him. Gorski resisted the temptation to apologise for the intrusion and handed her his card. He asked to speak to Monsieur or Madame Paliard. As soon as he stepped into the cool of the entrance hall and inhaled the musty aroma of the old house, his previous visit returned to him. The interview had been conducted in a reception room through the door to his left. It was a grand, high-ceilinged room with elaborate cornicing, an old-fashioned brass candelabra and somewhat gaudy furniture. There was a bay window, hung with pale green velvet drapes and a large fireplace with an enormous gilt-framed mirror above it. Gorski recalled catching a glimpse of his younger self in that mirror. The air had been still and cool. It was clear that the room was rarely used. Gorski had asked Monsieur Paliard and his wife a few rudimentary questions about the murder of Juliette Hurel. Paliard, he recalled, was a lawyer. Gorski had remarked that he had not encountered him in the criminal courts and Paliard had told him that he practised family law.

The maid left Gorski in the hall and returned a few moments later to show him into the reception room. It was exactly as he recalled. The air in the room was dead, as if it had not been disturbed since his last visit. The maid informed him that M. Paliard would join him in a few minutes and offered him a refreshment while he waited. Gorski asked for a glass of water.

'It's very hot,' he said, immediately scolding himself for feeling the need to justify such a modest request. The maid disappeared and returned with a jug of iced water and two glasses on a silver tray. When she left, Gorski poured himself a glass and downed it. He was still sweating from his walk through the woods. He took out his handkerchief and mopped his brow. Céline maintained that sweating was a lower class habit. And it was true, in twenty-two years of marriage, Gorski had never seen his wife perspire.

The old man arrived. He gripped a walking stick in each hand and leant heavily on them. A plastic tube was attached to his nose with medical tape. His skin was a greyish yellow and hung loosely on his face. Nevertheless Gorski recognised him immediately. Despite his frailty, he retained an air of authority. He struggled to a sofa and dropped down into it with difficulty. He motioned with a crooked finger that Gorski should sit, which he did. Paliard's fragile state of health sharpened Gorski's feeling that his visit was an intrusion.

Paliard made no attempt to initiate proceedings. There was no *What can I do for you?* or *How can I help you, Inspector?* Only those cowed by the presence of a police officer began in such a manner. Old money, Gorski had long since learned, treated the police with disdain. They were received as, in the past, the gamekeeper or the stableboy might have been.

'You've risen in the ranks since our last meeting, Inspector.'

'Yes,' said Gorski.

'That probably says more about the mediocrity of our police force than any ability on your part.' A thin smile flickered across Paliard's lips. The effort of this prompted a wheezing cough from the back of the old man's throat. He indicated that Gorski should pour a glass of water from the jug on the table. Gorski did so and handed it to Paliard, who waited for the wheezing to subside before taking a sip. Gorski was reminded of the hours he spent sitting silently with his father in the latter days of his life. He waited for Paliard to catch his breath.

'I'm investigating the disappearance of Adèle Bedeau,' Gorski said by way of justifying his reappearance, despite the fact that the current investigation had no bearing on his visit or at least not one that he could easily have explained. In any case, Paliard ignored him.

'I remember your last visit. I was as unimpressed with you as I was with the conclusion of the case you were investigating. What was the name of the girl?'

'Hurel, Juliette Hurel.'

'Yes,' said Paliard. 'It was a vagrant that got done for it, was it not? Malou, if I recollect?'

'That's right,' said Gorski. He was embarrassed that the old man recalled the details of the case.

'Not a shred of evidence, if I remember correctly. A real stitch-up.'

'There was an eyewitness that placed him in the vicinity,' said Gorski without conviction.

Paliard tutted slowly and shook his head.

'I'm quite sure even a man of your limited intelligence would not place too much credence on the evidence of an attention-seeking old woman.'

'Malou was tried and found guilty,' said Gorski.

'And thus you absolve yourself of responsibility. Splendid!' said the old man.

Gorski said nothing. He was beginning to regret calling upon Paliard, especially given the ill-defined grounds for his visit. At the end of the day, the conviction of Malou was not his responsibility. He had been obliged to follow up a lead and likewise he was obliged to divulge the testimony of the widow. It had not been his decision to prosecute Malou, nor had it been he who had found him guilty. There was, however, little to be gained from putting this to Paliard.

'As I said,' he began again, 'I'm investigating the disappearance of Adèle Bedeau.'

Paliard shook his head again. 'I find it

hard to believe that even a man such as yourself could think that I might be able to furnish you with any information in that connection. Rather, I imagine you are here because you believe there is a connection between the two cases. And, as such, it stands to reason that you think that Malou was falsely convicted.'

Gorski could see no way of progressing the interview without conceding the point.

'Yes,' he said. He was not sure he had ever admitted this to anyone other than Céline. In a way it was a relief to do so.

Paliard showed no sign of satisfaction at his small victory. 'So, given that you are, as I gather from the newspapers, getting nowhere in your current investigation, you think that the case you failed to solve twenty years ago might shine a light on the present one.'

Hearing Paliard articulate his thoughts made it sound every bit as ridiculous as Gorski feared it would.

'You're clutching at straws then?'

'Yes, I am,' said Gorski.

'A man who doesn't clutch at straws drowns,' said Paliard. He looked at Gorski. He had narrow pale blue eyes. Gorski wondered if he detected a hint of encouragement in Paliard's words.

'Inspector Gorski, in a matter of minutes my nurse is going to appear at the door there and tell you that your time with me is up. I suggest that if you've got something on your mind, you come to the point.'

Gorski felt he had nothing to lose. It did not seem likely that Paliard could have a lower opinion of him than he already did.

'Ever since the trial, I've gone back to the clearing where the murder took place. It's ridiculous, of course, but I thought there might be something that had been overlooked. I suppose I was hoping for a moment of inspiration.' He paused, expecting Paliard to inject some sarcastic remark, but he said nothing.

'After a while, I just went up there out of habit. Often I didn't think about the case at all, or I just thought about whatever case I was working on at the time. It's quiet up there. You couldn't pick a better spot for a murder.'

Gorski felt that he was beginning to ramble. To his surprise, however, Paliard was listening attentively. 'Since this girl disappeared I've been thinking about the Hurel case again. One thing's for sure, if Malou was not the culprit then the real killer is still at large. I always believed at the time that the perpetrator must have been local, which was one of the reasons I never believed that Malou was the guilty party. So it stands to reason that he may still be in the area, assuming he's still alive, of course. So when Adèle Bedeau disappeared I couldn't help wondering if the same killer was at work.' He shrugged. 'As you said, I'm clutching at straws.'

Paliard said nothing.

'I was in the woods a short while ago. For no particular reason, I left the clearing in a different direction than usual and found myself at the gate in the wall to the back of this property.'

The door opened. A young woman in a blue medical smock entered.

'I'm afraid you'll have to leave now. Monsieur Paliard is not able to receive visitors for long. It exhausts him.'

Paliard jerked his thumb towards the nurse. 'She likes to talk about me as if I'm not here.'

Gorski smiled thinly.

'I'm afraid I've wasted your time. I came on a whim. I'm sorry for disturbing you.'

Paliard waved away his apology. 'Not at all. I've found our talk quite stimulating. Feel free to call again. Only . . .' He was interrupted by another fit of wheezing.

The nurse walked across the room and

stood proprietarily behind her charge.

'Inspector,' she said firmly.

Gorski nodded and stood up. He bid the spluttering Paliard good day and saw himself out. Despite Paliard's derision, he was glad he had paid the visit. Although nothing concrete had come of it, he was at least engaging with the investigation. And there was something in the atmosphere of that tomb-like room which he felt he was missing. He thought of Ribéry's dictum to look for what was not there. His footsteps crunched down the gravel exactly as they had twenty years before. There was a heavy aroma of laburnum. Then he remembered there had been a boy, a teenager. He turned and half-ran back up the driveway. The front door was not locked. The maid appeared in the passage at the rear of the hall.

'Inspector, you can't . . .'

Gorski ignored her. The drawing room door was open. Paliard was still on the sofa, an oxygen mask now attached to his face. He was struggling even to catch the shallowest breath, one craggy hand gripping the arm of the sofa, the other over his chest. The nurse was fussing around him. She saw Gorski in the doorway and ordered him out.

EIGHTEEN

Manfred had always hated Saturdays. During the week, even if one hated one's job, one went to work because one had to, because there was no choice in the matter. People congregated in their work places with a sense of communal resignation. It was relatively easy to give the appearance of being a normal member of society. Weekends were different. One was expected to enjoy oneself, to take part in healthy outdoor pursuits, family or social events. Manfred had never enjoyed such activities. If he read books or went to the cinema, it was not so much because he enjoyed doing so, but because it filled the hours. He dreaded Monday mornings when the staff at the bank would regale each other with tales of how packed with activity their weekends had been. Each seemed determined to be the one who had eked the most pleasure out of their hours of liberty. Without fail, when she brought in his coffee, Carolyn would ask her boss if he had had a pleasant weekend. Manfred always assured her that he had. If pressed, he sometimes said that he had been to the cinema in Strasbourg. This seemed to satisfy the girl's curiosity and she would then recount her weekend's activities for as long as Manfred would tolerate. He barely listened and often sat imagining what she would say if he told her in a matter of fact way that he had visited a disreputable club where he had committed a sexual act with a girl of about her age whose name he did not even trouble to ask.

On this particular Saturday, however, there was no question of Manfred visiting Simone's. The prospect of that part of his routine coming to Gorski's attention was not appealing. On top of that, since his evening with Alice, the seedy allure of Simone's had dissipated and Manfred felt a sort of shame in ever having visited the place. His weekend required some thorough reorganisation.

He began by telephoning his grandmother to tell her he would not be coming for lunch on Sunday. She made no attempt to conceal her disappointment. Manfred explained that he was meeting a friend.

'A friend?' Mme Paliard repeated. 'What kind of friend?'

Manfred had expected her to be pleased to hear this news. Instead her tone was one of incredulity.

'A woman who lives in my building,' he explained.

'I see,' she said, as if the phrase was some kind of euphemism. 'Couldn't you meet this friend some other time? Your grandfather will be upset. He hasn't been well. You know how your visits cheer him up.'

'I'm sure he'll get over it,' Manfred said, immediately regretting his harsh tone. He knew, of course, that it was his grandmother who was disappointed not to see him. 'Perhaps I could come during the week. Thursday, perhaps?' If he visited on that evening, he could avoid a repeat of his exclusion from the card game.

'It doesn't matter,' she said. 'We'll see you next Sunday.'

Manfred put the phone down feeling angry towards his grandmother, but he was glad she had not accepted his off to visit during the week. His routine was disordered enough as it was. He decided to do his laundry this afternoon. Even Gorski could hardly interpret anything untoward in an alteration to the time at which Manfred carried out this task. Alice had agreed to call for him at two o'clock the following afternoon to 'do something together'. Manfred had little idea what doing something together might entail, but certainly it was at least possible that it would carry on into the evening, when he would normally do his washing. Manfred did not expect this to be the case. Nevertheless it was prudent to be prepared for such an eventuality. He felt uneasy as he took the back stairs down to the scullery with his sack of washing. He did his washing on Sunday evenings precisely because the laundry room was always empty at that time. Perhaps on a Saturday morning it would be teeming with residents with whom he would be obliged to exchange pleasantries. The room was empty. The other residents of the building were most likely busy eking pleasure out of their Saturdays.

Manfred hurriedly pushed his shirts and undershorts into one machine and his socks and other garments into a second. He sat down as he always did on the plastic chair by the door and opened his book, but he could not concentrate. He was concerned that Alice might come in. He had no wish to witness the spectacle of her sifting through her underwear, but he could hardly withdraw if she arrived. They would be forced to engage in conversation for the hour or so it took the machines to do their work, exhausting topics of conversation that might be required the following afternoon. Alice would in all likelihood take such a situation in her stride, but the scenario alarmed Manfred. He decided to go upstairs to his apartment and return when the cycle was over. It was not uncommon for people in the building to leave their washing unattended. Machines were often running when he came down and clothes sometimes seemed to have been left in them for hours. Manfred disapproved of this practice, and had on occasion left anonymous notes to this effect, but the circumstances were exceptional. He would return as soon as the cycle was over and remove his washing from the machine. He spent an hour pacing restlessly around his flat. He decided that he would, after all, spend the evening in Strasbourg. Since he often told Carolyn he went to the cinema, that was what he should do. He took it as read that Gorski was fully appraised of his movements and he would place some negative interpretation on any deviation from his routine. In any case, he had no desire to spend the evening cooped up in his apartment.

Manfred returned to the laundry room just as the machine was ending its cycle. A man was loading his washing into one of the free machines. He was in his sixties and Manfred had often seen him walking his little terrier around the play park behind the building. He suspected that his dog might be responsible for the faeces that had recently been found in the stairwell but, as he had no real evidence to back up his suspicions, he did not mention it. The space was too cramped for them both to move around, so he was obliged to loiter in the doorway while the man finished loading his machine. Neither of them said anything. The man turned on his machine and, to Manfred's relief, left the room. Contrary to his normal practice, Manfred bundled his wet clothes into his laundry sack and took them back to his apartment. There was an old clothes horse on the balcony. Manfred unfolded it and pegged up his shirts. In an hour or so the sun would reach the balcony and they would be dry in no time. Manfred leant for a moment on the metal balustrade. Alice's car was parked below. Manfred was tempted to wait there on the balcony just for the opportunity of seeing her come out and get into her vehicle. It would be quite normal to wave and call out a greeting to her. Of course, he would do no such thing. He would press his back to the wall of the balcony for fear of being spotted spying on her. Children were playing noisily in the park. A group of Arab women sat gossiping on a bench. One of them turned and looked up towards the balcony. Manfred retreated into the kitchen.

When Manfred went to the station to catch the 17.35, Alice's car had gone. He wondered what she might be doing. Perhaps she was seeing her repellent ex-husband. Manfred purchased his ticket and arrived at the platform a little earlier than usual in order to ascertain whether he was being followed. It was a pleasant evening. To the east, the sky above Basel was already taking on a pinkish hue. A smartly dressed man in his mid-thirties was standing on the platform holding a folded newspaper in his right hand. Manfred was not sure if he had already been on the platform when he arrived. He walked across the man's eye line and continued to the end of the platform. There were few other people around, but the man appeared to be consciously avoiding looking in Manfred's direction. As he approached the man for a second time, he turned and raised his eyes to the departure board. The Strasbourg train was due in two minutes.

Manfred positioned himself behind the man, in the doorway of the little brick waiting room. He had no doubt that the man was aware that Manfred was now watching him. He enjoyed the idea that he had turned the tables. He was quite sure his actions would be noted and reported back to Gorski: that he had not been at all cowed by the fact that he was being watched; indeed, that he had behaved like a man who had nothing on his conscience. When the train pulled in to the platform, the man had no choice but to get on first, clear evidence that he already knew where Manfred was heading. Manfred was tempted for a moment to stand on the platform and watch the train pull away with the detective aboard. He imagined the cop leaping to his feet and banging on the door to be let out and then having to shame-facedly inform Gorski that he had lost his quarry. Amusing though the idea was, it would ruin the carefully constructed illusion that Manfred was behaving exactly as he normally would. Besides, would it not seem peculiar if, having bought a ticket only a few minutes before, he failed to board the train?

The man had taken a seat at the end of the carriage. He gave every appearance of being engrossed in his newspaper. Manfred sat at the opposite end of the carriage and took his book from the pocket of his raincoat. The man did not once raise his eyes from his newspaper. But why should he? He already knew Manfred was on the train.

As the train sped through the countryside, Manfred realised there was a flaw in his plan for the evening. He would be observed going to the cinema. That in itself was not a problem. It would be easy enough to recount, if required, the actors and narrative of the film he went to see. But, as his trip was intended to give the impression that he was in the habit of going to the cinema in Strasbourg, he might be asked what other films he had seen on other occasions, at what time, in which cinema and so on. Such information could easily be checked. On top of that, there was a cinema in Saint-Louis not five hundred metres from Manfred's apartment. Why would he travel eighty minutes by train to go to the cinema when he could do the same thing on his own doorstep? Manfred resolved to buy a newspaper in the station to ensure he did not see a film that was showing in Saint-Louis.

Manfred imagined the questioning that would ensue:

You bought a newspaper when you reached the station?

Yes. I wanted to check which films were showing.

So you didn't know which film you were going to see before you took the train to Strasbourg?

No.

Why not go to the cinema in Saint-Louis?

I didn't want to see any of the films that were showing there.

What films were showing?

And, thus, he would be found out. Instead, he should make directly for a cinema — the little one on Rue du 22 Novembre that showed obscure foreign films — and buy a ticket for the first film that was on. If there was time to kill, he would have a glass of wine or something to eat in a nearby café. What could be more normal than that?

By the time the train pulled into Strasbourg, Manfred was feeling quite pleased with himself. The man with the newspaper was first to leave the carriage. Manfred followed him off the train. The man walked rapidly along the platform onto the concourse, not once looking over his shoulder. He appeared to be in a hurry. He dropped his folded newspaper into a litter bin without breaking his stride. It seemed a strange thing to do. Why, if he had finished with the newspaper, had he not left it on the seat of the train? Perhaps, knowing that he had been spotted, it was a pre-arranged signal to another operative waiting at the station. Quite spontaneously, Manfred decided to follow the first man. He almost broke into a run so as not to lose him as he strode across the concrete expanse of Place de la Gare. For a moment, Manfred felt quite exhilarated. He was in control of events. The man crossed into Rue de Maire Kuss and continued to walk briskly. At no point did he look over his shoulder.

Manfred kept about twenty metres back. The man was not difficult to follow. He was taller than average and was wearing a light linen suit. He was, in fact, rather conspicuous. After a few minutes he entered a brasserie. An attractive woman sitting at a table in the window stood up. There was a glass of wine on the table in front of her. They greeted each other with a kiss on the lips before the man sat down at the table and summoned the waiter. Manfred stood dumbly observing this vignette from the pavement outside. The waiter arrived and the man ordered a drink. Then he glanced out of the window and saw Manfred on the pavement outside. A puzzled expression flitted across his face as if he was trying to place him, but his gaze did not stay on him for more than a second and he quickly returned his attention to his companion. Manfred suddenly felt ridiculous. He could hardly remain there spying on them. And to what end? He turned away abruptly and bumped into a woman walking in the opposite direction. She muttered a derogatory comment under her breath.

Manfred felt a sudden and vicious desire for alcohol. Not for his usual glass of wine, but for something that would provide swifter inebriation. He turned into an alley where he was sure he could find a suitable watering hole. He almost burst through the door of the first suitable establishment, a dimly lit place where alcohol was consumed in the candid pursuit of intoxication. Such was his relief at reaching the counter, he could not for a moment decide what to order. The barman looked at him impassively.

'Monsieur?' he said.

'A whisky, please,' Manfred said. The barman indicated with a gesture of his arm the array of bottles behind the bar.

'It doesn't matter,' he said, trying to keep his voice even. 'Anything.'

The barman nodded, selected a bottle and poured the drink at a leisurely pace. Manfred fidgeted at the counter. His hands were shaking. He wanted to yell at the barman to hurry up. The barman placed the drink in front of him and, without any thought for decorum, Manfred downed it in one swig. He breathed out slowly, eyes closed. The whisky warmed the back of his throat and worked its way down to his stomach. When he opened his eyes, the barman was watching him impassively.

'Another?' he asked.

Manfred nodded gratefully. He downed the second whisky as he had the first, then a third. He found himself a stool and sat down. The fourth he nursed for a while. What an idiot he was. This whole trip to Strasbourg was a charade, enacted for an audience of one. Yet there was no one to witness his performance, no one to report back to Gorski. It mattered not if he went to the cinema, to Simone's, or sat here in this dive or any other getting blind drunk. Nobody was watching him. Nobody cared where he was or what he was doing. Not even the barman, who was plainly unperturbed by Manfred's determination to get sozzled. His actions were not going to be called before a court of law and picked over. What Manfred chose to do was of no consequence to anyone other than himself. And yet, even as he realised this, had he not sought out a bar without windows in a secluded street where he could not be seen?

Manfred swivelled around on his stool and took in his surroundings for the first time. The place was dingy and brown. Until that moment, he had thought he was the only customer, but, in fact, the place was well populated by grim-faced men in various stages of inebriation. As Manfred surveyed the room, none of his fellows so much as glanced in his direction. He had become invisible. He drank down his whisky and ordered another. He felt giddy.

At a certain point Manfred made an attempt to engage the barman in conversation. He was a young chap with an open, pleasant face. He did not seem averse to conversation, but Manfred had difficulty following his responses and the exchange soon fizzled out. Later, a man took the stool next to Manfred's at the counter and ordered a *pastis*. He was wearing a three-piece suit with a lilac handkerchief in the breast pocket. He clumsily placed a briefcase on the floor at his feet and struggled to pour the water from the little jug into his glass. He was well on his way to oblivion. Manfred made a comment to this effect. The man turned his head towards the source of the sound, took some time to focus and then returned his attention to his drink without a word. Manfred repeated his remark, this time accompanying it with a sharp prod to the man's upper arm.

The man looked round, steadying himself on the bar.

'Do I know you?' he said.

Manfred grinned at him. 'The name's Baumann, Manfred Baumann.'

The man looked blankly at him. Manfred thought of inviting him to accompany him to Simone's. He seemed like the kind of fellow with whom one might enjoy a night on the town.

NINETEEN

Gorski spooned three sugars into his coffee. Céline looked on disapprovingly. She did not drink coffee and she never tired of telling Gorski his sugar intake would lead to diabetes. It was eight o'clock. He was sitting in his shirtsleeves, his jacket slung over the back of his chair. The coffee stimulated Gorski's desire for the first cigarette of the day, but he did not dare light up over the breakfast table. Not that either of them ate breakfast. Gorski's stomach always felt unsettled in the morning. Usually he bought a croissant or a *pain au chocolat* at the bakery on Rue de Mulhouse and ate it at the station midway through the morning. Céline poured out her tea and sat down. They had barely seen each other since the evening of her event at the shop.

'The show was good,' he said.

'Thanks for coming,' said Céline. She had a strangely inexpressive way of speaking, so that it was often difficult for Gorski to discern whether she was being sarcastic. He chose to take her words at face value.

'I thought it was very good,' he said.

Céline raised her eyebrows sceptically. Clearly he was still in the doghouse.

'Did you sell much?' he persisted.

'It's not all about selling,' she said. 'It's about promoting the brand.'

Céline often talked about 'promoting the brand', but Gorski had little idea what she meant by it.

'Of course,' he said. He drank his coffee. Céline stood up.

'I hope you're not planning to wear that tie,' she said.

Gorski resisted the temptation to respond antagonistically. 'I was, yes,' he said in an even tone.

Céline shook her head in exasperation and left the kitchen without another word. A few minutes later he heard the front door close and the sound of her car starting. Gorski topped up his coffee and lit a cigarette. As it was Saturday there was little chance of Clémence making an appearance before noon. He took a tube of antacids from the pocket of his jacket and dropped two into a glass of water. He watched them froth up then disperse in the glass. When he looked up, Clémence was standing in the doorway. She was wearing a pair of his old pyjamas, the sleeves rolled up to the elbow. Gorski could not hide his pleasure at seeing her. Clearly she had only come down when she had heard her mother leave.

'Heartburn?' she said.

'Just a little,' said Gorski.

'You should eat better. You look terrible.'

'Do I?'

Clémence sat down at the table. Gorski poured her some coffee. He did not know what to say to her. It was unusual for them to be alone together. Usually they bonded through childishly making fun of Céline behind her back. Perhaps she had come downstairs because there was something she wanted to talk to him about. She got up and found the remains of a baguette in the bread bin. She nibbled at the end of it, allowing crumbs to fall onto the floor.

'What you up to today?' Gorski asked. He tried to make it sound casual, as if he was not prying into her business.

Clémence looked at him. 'I'm meeting some friends in Mulhouse.'

Gorski nodded, but he had no idea who her friends were or what they might do together. He thought of what Alex Ackermann had told him of his evenings with

Adèle Bedeau. Of course, Adèle was older than Clémence, but at his daughter's age he had already had his fumblings on the farm with Marthe. The thought of Clémence engaged in similar activities horrified him.

'You need a lift?' he asked.

Clémence smiled indulgently.

'We're getting the train. Thanks.'

Then she took a mouthful of coffee and went back upstairs.

At ten o'clock Gorski was back at the foot of the drive leading to the Paliard house. He had taken the precaution of phoning ahead, but still, without thinking, he had left his car on the road, rather than driving up to the house. The nurse came to the front door. She made no pretence of welcoming him.

'You've got ten minutes,' she said.

Paliard was waiting in the drawing room. His skin looked even greyer than it had the previous day. The nurse followed Gorski in and stood by the door.

'Good to see you again, Inspector. You'll excuse me if I don't get up.'

'Of course,' said Gorski. He could not work out if Paliard's breezy greeting was meant in jest. The old man motioned for him to take a seat. On the table a silver tray with a decanter of sherry and two glasses had been set out.

'You'll have a drink with me, Inspector?' said Paliard.

Despite the early hour Gorski nodded his consent. He had no wish to do anything to dampen the old man's good humour. Paliard struggled forward on the sofa and poured out two large measures. Gorski took his glass and toasted Paliard's good health. He had made up his mind not to beat around the bush.

'Thank you for seeing me again, M. Paliard,' he began. 'I only have one question for you.'

Paliard interrupted him. 'Before you begin, Inspector, if you'll indulge me, I have a question for you. The tramp, Malou — what happened to him?'

Gorski glanced towards the nurse. 'I'm not sure we've got time for that.'

'Don't worry about her,' said Paliard. 'She's my employee. She might not act like it, but she is. We were discussing our friend Malou.'

'He died in prison,' said Gorski.

Paliard nodded. 'And you did nothing to clear his name?'

Gorski shrugged. 'The case was closed. There was nothing to be gained from opening old wounds.'

'No?' said Paliard. 'But you said yourself that if Malou was not the culprit then the real killer was still at large. Was it not the case that you just didn't want to ruffle any feathers? Perhaps you didn't want any black marks against your name that might hinder your speedy rise through the ranks?'

Gorski stared at him. Paliard raised his eyebrows. 'Well?' he said.

'I did what I could. The fact is there were no other suspects. There were no more leads to follow.'

'Nevertheless, you continued to return to the woods?'

'Yes.'

'But nothing came of that?'

'No.'

'So what are you doing here?'

Gorski took a sip of his sherry. It was horribly sweet. For a moment he had forgotten the purpose of his visit.

'As I said, I have one question. After I left yesterday, I remembered that you had a son. When I came here before, I asked him a couple of questions.'

Paliard said nothing.

'I was wondering where he is now.'

'Why do you want to speak to him?'

Gorski did not have a ready answer to this question.

'When I walked here from the clearing yesterday, I arrived at the door in the wall at the back of your property. Would I be correct in saying that the door has not always been in the state of disrepair it is in now?'

Paliard nodded.

'It struck me that the gate afforded ready access to the woods.' Gorski was aware that this did not constitute a great insight.

Paliard smiled thinly. 'You're right about one thing, Inspector, the boy was never out of those woods. Used to disappear in there all day, at least until the murder. But he wasn't my son.'

Gorski waited for him to continue. He raised his eyebrows questioningly.

'He was my grandson.'

'Your grandson?'

'Manfred.'

'Manfred?' repeated Gorski. 'Manfred Paliard?'

'He's not a Paliard. His name is Baumann, son of the Swiss good-for-nothing that ruined my daughter.'

Gorski ran the palm of his hand across his forehead and exhaled slowly.

'He was a queer boy. Still is, if you want my opinion.'

Gorski nodded.

'If you want to talk to him, my wife will give you his address.'

Gorski told him that wouldn't be necessary. He finished his sherry and stood up.

'Thank you for your time,' he said. 'You've been most helpful.'

The old man appeared disappointed that Gorski was leaving. The nurse opened the drawing room door to usher him out. He could hear the old man struggling for breath as he closed the front door. He stood for a few moments on the step of the big house. A plump woodpigeon was pecking at the gravel of the drive. Gorski's footsteps did not disturb it.

TWENTY

Manfred was woken by a loud knocking and a voice shouting something he was too drowsy to make sense of. He half opened his eyes. Sunlight filtered through dirty voile curtains. He was not at home. His head hurt and his mouth was dry. He closed his eyes. His trousers were loosened round the waist but he was still wearing his shirt and shoes. He squinted through his eyelids. The light from the window hurt his eyes and he raised a hand from under the blanket to shield them. The knocking at the door came again, more insistently. It was followed by a male voice that made no concession to Manfred's fragile condition.

'Monsieur! Eleven o'clock, time to clear out.'

Manfred turned towards the source of the sound. The movement triggered a shooting pain at the back of his skull. He was in a hotel room. Next to the door was a chest of drawers. At the foot of the bed was a cracked wash hand basin. There was a small plastic bucket on the floor beneath it to catch drips from the supply pipe. Manfred's jacket lay in a crumpled heap on the floor. The chipboard at the bottom of the door was broken where someone had put their foot through it. There was no bathroom. Manfred hauled himself into a sitting position on the side of the bed. He became aware of a keen pressure in his bladder. He got up and relieved himself in the basin. He ran some water and, with some difficulty keeping his balance, splashed cold water on his face. His left cheek stung. He looked around for a towel. He picked up his jacket and took his handkerchief from his pocket and patted his face dry. He looked in the mirror above the basin. His left cheekbone was bruised and the right-hand side of his face and temple was grazed. The scratches were superficial, but the skin around them was red. Dried blood was congealed around his nostrils.

The door opened and a cleaner came in. She did not appear surprised to see Manfred, and she withdrew in the same languid manner as she had entered, muttering a cursory apology. Manfred hurriedly washed the blood from his nose and wiped it with his handkerchief, which already had blood-stains on it. He glanced around the room to see if any of his possessions were there. His wallet was safe in the inside pocket of his jacket. He left the room and found himself in a passage that had the sickly smell of vomit. The cleaner gazed at him impassively. Manfred squeezed past her trolley. The smell made him retch. He found the stairs and half ran down four flights. He found himself in a dimly lit reception area. A middle-aged man in a cardigan with half-moon glasses looked up from a newspaper spread on the counter. He greeted Manfred cordially enough. Manfred wondered if he was the same man who had rousted him from his room a few minutes before.

Manfred said good morning and reached into his jacket for his wallet.

The man waved his hand and spoke as if he didn't expect him to understand French. 'You paid last night,' he said.

'Oh,' said Manfred, 'thank you.'

Outside, he found himself in a narrow lane. He was still in Strasbourg, somewhere in the vicinity of the station. He spotted a kiosk at the end of the lane and bought a bottle of water. He sipped a little and swilled it around his mouth before spitting into the gutter. Then he took a proper swallow. He was unaware of the people milling past him on the pavement. He felt dizzy and sticky with sweat. He went into a café and ordered a black coffee. The last thing he remembered was being in the bar, drinking whisky. He had no memory of leaving the bar or of going to the hotel. Nor could he remember how he got the scratches on his face. Probably he had fallen over. He was sure he had not been in a fight He would remember such a thing. The unpleasant odour had followed him from the hotel. He realised that there was dried vomit on his shoes and the cuffs of his trousers. He downed his coffee, placed some coins on the table and left. The coffee oriented Manfred a little in the present. He remembered his arrangement with Alice for that afternoon and looked at his watch. It was twenty past eleven.

On the train back to Saint-Louis, the light began to flare, as if hot sunlight was being smeared on the inside of his eyelids. Manfred lodged the heels of his hands in his eye sockets. The familiar drilling sensation in his right temple commenced. Manfred was the only person in the carriage. He drew his knees up towards his chest and sat there, rigid, waiting for the journey to pass. The trick was to empty his mind, to ignore the coming onslaught. He tried to think gay thoughts and imagined himself walking hand in hand with Alice through a pleasant, verdant wood. Birds were singing. The sun was warm. Manfred's jacket was slung casually over one shoulder. He made amusing small talk. But it was no good, the pain continued to mount.

A hand was placed on his shoulder. Manfred jumped.

'Your ticket, monsieur.'

Manfred took his hands from his eyes and drew his knees down. The ticket inspector's face was a pink blur. Behind his head, light flared like a halo. Manfred raised his hand to shield his eyes. The official repeated his request.

Manfred reached into the breast pocket of his jacket where he always kept his ticket. He handed it to the inspector who gave it a cursory glance. He asked Manfred if he was all right. He nodded that he was. The conductor did not move away. Manfred could not tell what expression he wore. It might have been concern or perhaps disgust.

'I'm fine, thank you, I have a headache,' he said. He was suddenly anxious that he had missed his stop, but the conductor, having looked at his ticket, would have informed him if this had been the case. The official made his way off along the aisle without another word. Manfred squinted out the window and saw that they had only just left Strasbourg. As the train picked up speed, the motion made Manfred want to vomit. He did not trust himself to make it to the WC at the end of the carriage. He threw up a little in his mouth and forced himself to swallow. He wiped his lips with his handkerchief. He longed to be at home in his darkened bedroom with the covers pulled over his face.

Later, Manfred did not remember getting off the train, walking the short distance to his apartment or getting undressed and into bed, but all these things must have occurred, because at a certain point, he was disturbed by a knocking on the door of his apartment. He had arranged to meet Alice in the foyer of the building. He looked at the alarm clock by his bed. It was ten past two. The knocking came again, a little louder, then Alice's voice:

'Baumann, are you in there?'

Manfred crawled out of bed. He was completely naked. He found his robe and padded along the passage to the door.

Alice looked taken aback.

'What happened to you?' she said.

Manfred focussed on her face. Her hair

was tied back in a ponytail.

'I'm sorry, I . . .' He did not want to admit to feeling unwell. Migraines were not a manly complaint. 'I must have slept in,' he said.

Alice gripped his chin and jerked his head around, examining his injuries.

'Fall out of bed, did you?' she said. She pushed past him into the passage, wincing as she inhaled his breath. She was wearing a waterproof jacket and tight blue jeans tucked into thick socks. Manfred followed her into the kitchen. She suggested that he take a shower and get himself ready. It did not occur to Manfred to do anything other than comply. In the bathroom, he swallowed four painkillers and forced himself to drink three glasses of water. The shower helped. He brushed his teeth, but did not bother to shave. He dressed and returned to the kitchen. Alice had made coffee and was sitting at the kitchen table. She laughed when she saw Manfred in his suit.

'I thought we might take a walk at the Camargue,' she said. 'Don't you have anything more suitable to wear?'

Manfred shook his head. Alice poured him some coffee and he sat down and drank it. It was quite clear that he would do whatever Alice had decided. It was liberating. He was not required to make decisions or even venture an opinion. He need only submit to Alice's will.

Although there was an autumnal chill in the air, Alice insisted on taking down the roof of the car. She did not speak for the duration of the journey, but concentrated on driving at alarming speed along the country lanes, which were barely wide enough for two cars to pass. The pain in Manfred's head became a backcloth to the sensation of hurtling along through the hedgerows. At every bend, it seemed that the little car would career off the road. Manfred experienced a feeling of calm. Whether the car remained on the road was a matter of no consequence to him. He felt a kind of disappointment when Alice pulled safely into the pot-holed car park at the nature reserve.

They got out. Alice opened the rear of the car and retrieved a pair of muddy walking boots. She sat down on the bumper to change into them. Manfred watched her. Even in her manly outdoor clothes she was tremendously attractive. She was not at all like the other women he knew. Her thighs were taut and defined under the denim of her jeans and her skin had a pleasing elasticity. The women who worked at the bank were flabby and loose-skinned, their flesh barely contained by a scaffold of brassieres and corsets. When Manfred addressed them, it always appeared that they had been woken from a trance. Alice, by contrast, was alert to everything going on around her. There was a precision and purpose in her movements, even in the way she threaded the laces around the eyelets of her boots.

When she had finished, she looked up. Manfred was too groggy to disguise the fact that he had been staring at her.

'Your feet are going to get wet,' she said.

He exhaled wearily. 'It doesn't matter.'

Alice led the way out of the car park towards a narrow gravelly path. Manfred was surprised how many people were around. They were all dressed like Alice and most of them had small children or dogs straining on leads. Whenever they met another group of walkers they were obliged to fall into single file to let them pass. People generally uttered some kind of greeting or cheery comment about the weather as they passed. Manfred left it to Alice to return these greetings on his behalf. As he inevitably fell in behind Alice it would have seemed superfluous for him to contribute. Once or twice dogs pushed their noses forcefully towards Manfred's crotch before their owners laughingly hauled them back. This seemed to be quite acceptable behaviour among the habitués of the path.

Manfred assumed that a walk such as this must be one of the activities with which his colleagues filled their weekends. The people they met appeared to be enjoying themselves and to feel some sort of camaraderie towards each other. Manfred was aware that his unsuitable attire drew puzzled glances from some of the passers-by, but this did not bother him. Perhaps he looked like a detective on his way to examine a crime scene deep in the woods.

Alice strode ahead, now and again passing comment on the scenery or some plant or other. Manfred realised that he was not required to contribute much to the conversation. The further they walked, the fewer people they encountered. After twenty minutes or so they reached a large, flat lagoon surrounded by trees in varying shades of yellow and brown. A light breeze brought the occasional leaf spiralling slowly to the ground.

Alice paused. 'There's a path around the lake, if you'd like to go on,' she said.

'Of course,' said Manfred. The walk had at least had the effect of soothing the pain in his skull. It was now no more than a dull throbbing.

The path, which was now just hardened earth, narrowed. Alice put her hand round the crook of Manfred's elbow, just as she had when they had walked back from the restaurant together. She gave every appearance of feeling some affection for him. He could smell her hair. She broke away and crouched at the side of the path.

'Ceps,' she said lightly fingering some yellow-brown fungi growing at the foot of a tree. 'We should have brought a basket.'

'Aren't they dangerous?' said Manfred.

Alice gave a little snort through her nose. 'I've been coming here since I was a girl,' she said. 'I used to cycle out and find a quiet spot and just lie back and watch the clouds go by. Sometimes in the summer, I'd go skinny-dipping with friends.'

Manfred found himself blushing at the thought of the teenage Alice leaping naked into the water.

'But this is my favourite time of year,' she went on. 'I love the colours of the trees and the smell of the earth.'

'Yes,' said Manfred, 'it's nice.'

She stood up and took Manfred's arm again. Their footsteps crunched on the dry leaves. There was nobody about. Somewhere a woodpigeon cooed. Manfred did not feel the need to say anything. He was thinking about the days he had spent with Juliette in the woods behind his grandparents' house. Alice paused at the edge of the lake. A formation of geese approached and landed clumsily on the water in a cacophony of honking.

'They come here for the winter,' Alice said.

Manfred nodded.

When they reached the furthest point of the lake, Alice scrambled onto some rocks on the shore and sat down. Manfred sat next to her. It was very quiet.

Alice took a packet of cigarettes from the pocket of her jacket and lit one with her chunky lighter. Manfred inhaled the metallic odour. He wondered if she was going to lean over and kiss him. He would not resist if she did. She drew deeply on her cigarette and, tipping her head back, exhaled slowly through her lips. Manfred watched the stream of milky smoke disperse into the air.

'I had a visit from a policeman,' said Alice, turning to look at him. Her cheeks were flushed from the fresh air. Manfred was taken aback.

'A stocky guy, about fifty, short hair. I've forgotten his name.'

'Gorski,' said Manfred.

'Gorski, yes,' she said. 'He was asking

about you.'

'What about me?'

'He wanted to know what sort of relationship we had, how long I'd known you, that sort of thing.'

'What did you tell him?'

'I told him it was none of his business.' Manfred nodded. 'What did he say?'

'Not much. He gave me his card and left.'

'He came to your apartment?'

'Yes.'

'How did he find out where you lived?'

Alice shrugged. 'I don't know. I didn't ask. He gave me the creeps.'

Manfred stood up. Had she cooked up this story to explain why he had seen Gorski leave the apartment building two days before? Sunlight glinted on the ripples of the water. His head hurt. He could not make sense of things. Perhaps Gorski had put her up to this little outing. Perhaps she was recording their conversation and the woods were crawling with cops waiting to spring out when he said something incriminating. Manfred scanned the trees around them. Alice was staring at him.

'Manfred?' she said.

Then it hit him: *He gave me the creeps.* It was the same expression Gorski said Adèle had used about him. His head swam. He closed his eyes tight, then opened them and looked at Alice. He was having trouble focussing.

'I don't believe you,' he said.

Alice's eyes widened. 'I'm sorry?' she said.

She stood up and took a couple of steps away from him.

'You're lying,' he said. The sunlight on the lake was dazzling. Manfred closed his eyes for a moment. He felt dizzy. He turned and faced the trees. He imagined the men in the woods, waiting for a sign from Gorski to move in. His eyes darted around the undergrowth. Nothing stirred. His breathing subsided a little.

Alice took a step towards him. 'Is there something wrong with you?' There was a hint of fear in her eyes.

Manfred shook his head as if to rouse himself from sleep. He was aware that he might, at this moment, appear quite insane. He must try to seem reasonable.

'I just want you to tell me the truth about you and Gorski,' he said, keeping his voice as even as possible. Alice tucked her chin to her chest and looked at him, open-mouthed.

'There is no me and Gorski,' she replied.

'He put you up to this whole thing,' Manfred blundered on. He took a step towards her.

Alice stood her ground. Her face had hardened.

'I just wanted to know why the police are asking questions about you. If you've done something wrong, you can tell me.'

'Of course I can.' Manfred laughed through his nose and shook his head. 'I actually thought you liked me.'

'I thought I liked you too,' said Alice. She looked at him as if she had never seen him before. Then she turned and started back towards the path. Manfred watched her. They appeared to be quite alone. He could hear the distant honking of the geese. The water lapped gently on the rocks. It was a pleasant spot.

Manfred called her name. She did not turn round. He felt a strong desire to run after her and tell her everything: how he had lied to Gorski; what had occurred between Adèle and him; even how he had killed Juliette. He suddenly felt that it would all seem quite reasonable — that he would seem reasonable. He called her name again. She strode on, making a dismissive gesture with her hand over her shoulder. She vanished into the woods. Manfred stood staring dumbly at the spot where she had disappeared for a few minutes, then followed her.

TWENTY-ONE

Manfred had grown accustomed to the feeling of being watched. It was stronger than ever as he sat on the front pew of the chapel. His grandmother was on his right, twisting an embroidered handkerchief between her fingers. Manfred had felt no emotion on hearing that his grandfather was dead. He had no fondness for the old man and could not see his death as anything other than a release for his grandmother. The turnout was unexpectedly large. Manfred had never known his grandfather to have any friends and whenever his grandparents had to attend a social engagement, he grumbled about it. Twenty or thirty bent old worthies, some wearing military honours on their lapels, filled two or three rows of the chapel. There was also substantial representation from the law firm. Manfred imagined that each of them had their eyes trained on the back of his head, hoping to discern some sign of emotion. He bowed his head a little as if in contemplation.

The priest described in a matter-of-fact tone how Bertrand Paliard had now been accepted into the kingdom of God. Manfred tried not to smile at the thought of how his grandfather, a confirmed atheist, would rankle at such a sentiment. Manfred had not been in a church for many years. He found it oddly agreeable. The air was cool and heavy with incense, and the priest's monotonous drone had a soothing, narcotic effect. The flagstones were rounded like pebbles by centuries of footfall. Likewise the oak pews were worn and faded. The circular stained-glass window high on the wall behind the priest produced a pleasantly subdued light. Manfred paid little attention to the service. At some point he noticed that his grandmother had taken his hand and was gripping it with surprising tenacity. The time came for the coffin to be carried to the grave. Under the direction of the undertaker, Manfred and the five other pallbearers, only one of whom Manfred recognised, arranged themselves around the box. Manfred was half a head taller than the rest of them, and as the box was raised onto their shoulders he had to bend at the knee to shoulder his part of the burden. The others gave every impression of being old hands at this business.

As they began the ponderous waltz up the aisle, Manfred spotted Gorski standing at the back of the church. He was indeed being watched. Manfred felt a flush of anger at the intrusion. Gorski was not to know that he did not feel any sadness at his grandfather's demise. Manfred adopted a mournful expression for the cop's benefit. He turned his mouth down at the edges and kept his eyes fixed on the stone floor. He glanced up only as he passed Gorski at the door. Gorski acknowledged him with a curt, unapologetic nod. The congregation filed out behind the coffin. It was early in the afternoon and after the dim atmosphere of the chapel, the sunlight was quite dazzling. There was an incline towards the Paliard plot, and Manfred had to stoop even lower to keep hold of his corner of the coffin. One of the old men had to pause, wheezing, to wipe his brow. The undertaker, no doubt accustomed to such occurrences, relieved him of his place and they made swifter progress towards the plot. Manfred's mother's grave was to the right. It was surprisingly well maintained. There were fresh flowers in a pot at the foot of the headstone. Manfred never visited it and he wondered if his grandparents had looked after it or if such things fell under the remit of the municipality.

The box was lowered onto some planks that had been placed across the grave and then, with the use of canvas straps, lowered into the hole. Manfred admired the efficiency with which this potentially awkward task was carried out. He took his place at the graveside next to his grandmother, who now tearlessly clutched his hand. The old man had always despised displays of emotion and over the years Manfred's grandmother had absorbed the lesson. As the priest read the benediction, Manfred could not resist the temptation to look over his shoulder. Gorski was leaning against the wall by the wrought iron gates to the churchyard, smoking a cigarette. He felt a hand at his elbow and realised he was being directed to add his handful of soil to the grave. The hollow sound of earth on wood was quite agreeable. The mourners filed past, offering their condolences to Manfred and his grandmother, before making their way to the vehicles assembled on the road. There was to be a reception at the family home. As Manfred accompanied his grandmother towards the gate, Gorski approached.

'My condolences, Madame Paliard,' he said.

'What are you doing here?' Manfred said, his customary meekness cast off.

Gorski reiterated his condolences to Manfred. 'I thought we might take a little drive together,' he said.

'That's out of the question,' he said.

They reached the limousine that was to take them back to the house and Madame Paliard was helped in. Gorski subtly blocked Manfred's entrance to the vehicle and, in a single motion, bent inside the car showing his ID.

'Madame, my apologies, but I have some pressing business with your grandson. Could you spare him for an hour?'

The old woman appeared confused, but nodded her assent and Gorski led Manfred towards his car. Gorski waited patiently as Manfred was accosted by one of the decorated old men. 'I was with your grandfather in Algeria,' he told Manfred, shaking him vigorously by the hand. 'I could tell you a few tales.'

Manfred had no idea his grandfather had ever been in Algeria. 'I have a piece of business to take care of first' he said. 'I'll be back in an hour. Look after my grandmother for me.' The old man gave a little salute, comic in effect if not intention, and Manfred followed Gorski to his car.

Gorski's Peugeot smelt strongly of smoke. Manfred did not say anything, embarrassed that his determination of a few moments before had crumbled so easily. He knew he should behave as if he was outraged at Gorski's intrusion, but it seemed pointless after so meek a surrender. In reality, he was relieved not to have to attend the reception.

Gorski made a U-turn and headed north. He lit a cigarette and wound down the driver's side window. 'You weren't close to your grandfather?' he said.

'Not especially,' Manfred replied.

'Not especially?' said Gorski, 'My impression is that Monsieur Paliard had very little regard for his grandson.'

Manfred felt his forehead prickle. 'Your impression?' he repeated dumbly, fully aware that this was exactly the response Gorski wished to elicit.

'Yes,' said Gorski, 'I spoke with M. Paliard a couple of times shortly before his death. We talked a little about you.'

Manfred said nothing. He was trying to absorb the implications of what Gorski had just told him. He could not imagine his grandfather having anything positive to say about him. Gorski turned the car into a minor road that ran north, parallel to the Rhine. They drove along in silence for a few minutes.

'Where are we going?' Manfred asked eventually, although it was becoming increasingly clear.

'You'll see,' said Gorski. 'Somewhere quiet.'

'If you have more questions for me, I'd like to be interviewed in the presence of a lawyer.'

Gorski nodded slowly. 'Let's not worry about that for the time being.'

They drove for a few more minutes before pulling up in a lay-by. There was a white painted gate leading to a footpath into the woods. Gorski turned off the engine and got out. He took off his jacket and hung it on the hook above the window in the back seat. Manfred got out. Gorski asked if he would like to leave his jacket in the car. Manfred was perspiring, but he declined and instead loosened his tie and opened the top button of his shirt.

Gorski led the way through the gate. The air was cooler in the forest. The path was too narrow for them to walk two abreast and Gorski indicated that Manfred should lead the way.

'I've been coming up here for years,' Gorski began, his tone conversational. 'Almost exactly twenty years, in fact. You know, there aren't too many murders around here, but two decades ago a young girl was strangled in these woods. I was just a young cop then. The case fell in my lap through circumstance. I was out of my depth.'

Manfred was relieved that the detective could not see his face. He recalled the sight of the younger Gorski standing with his back to the mantelpiece in the chilly reception room where the funeral-goers would now be gathering. He had not changed so much. His hair was grey and he was perhaps a little thicker around the midriff, but his face retained some of its youthfulness. They came to a fork on the path.

'To the left here,' Gorski said from behind his shoulder. 'In the end, we secured a conviction — your grandfather remembered all this — a tramp named Malou, but I was never convinced. It stays with you, a thing like that. That's why I kept coming back. Your grandfather told me you were very fond of these woods back then. Never out of them in fact.'

He paused and tapped Manfred on the arm, indicated with his finger that they should leave the path. They scrambled down a slope, their trousers snagging in the thorny undergrowth. The forest floor was tinder dry. A woodpigeon cooed incessantly. Then they were there, in the clearing.

Manfred swallowed audibly. The back of his eyes stung. When he closed them, he saw Juliette's body lying broken in the middle of his grandparents' rug. He felt his knees weaken and for a moment thought he was going to faint. Gorski pointed to a fallen tree on the far side of the clearing and suggested they sit down. The tree trunk had not been there previously, but otherwise the place was as Manfred remembered it. The two men made their way across the clearing and sat down. Manfred took off his jacket and laid it carefully next to him. Gorski lit a cigarette. Manfred could smell the dryness of the forest floor. It had not rained for weeks.

'So,' Gorski said, 'here we are.'

Manfred did not say anything. He understood that his silence was tantamount to an admission of guilt. But Gorski could not expect him just to come out with it — to blurt out that he killed Juliette, that he had choked her to death and calmly packed up his belongings before running off into the woods. Nevertheless, like twenty years before, he had no intention of denying anything. If Gorski had done his job the first time around, Manfred would have served his time by now and been done with the matter.

Gorski got up from the trunk and walked to the middle of the clearing. He was still smoking. Manfred imagined the ash from his cigarette igniting the tinder and engulfing the forest in flames.

'It was just here that the girl was found. The body was in a peculiar position, as if she had been dumped here. Of course, we considered the possibility that she had been killed elsewhere and then brought here, but it didn't add up. Why carry a body this far into the forest and then make no attempt to conceal it? Why not weigh it down and throw it in the Rhine? Of course, I considered the idea that the killer actually wanted to be caught, to take credit for his crime, but I didn't place much credence in that kind of theory. Still don't.'

He said all this as if he was reliving his thought processes for his own benefit. He paused and looked at Manfred.

'My mistake was that I was looking for the wrong kind of person. I'd never investigated a murder before and all I had to go on was what I'd read in books.' He stopped and looked at Manfred. 'What the books don't tell you is that sometimes murder is just a matter of chance. And you can't investigate chance. Two people meet and something bad happens. Maybe even by accident.' He carefully stubbed out his cigarette with the toe of his shoe and resumed his place next to Manfred. The two men sat in silence for a few moments staring ahead at the spot where Juliette had died. Manfred bore Gorski no ill will. It had never occurred to him before that if he had taken the opportunity to confess all those years before, he would by now have been free of the thing. Perhaps due to his age and the circumstances, he would have been shown leniency and would have spent only a few years in jail. He might have been out by his mid-twenties. Instead, every moment of his life since had been determined by what happened here in the clearing.

'So,' Gorski prompted, 'do you want to tell me what happened?'

Manfred told him the story from the beginning. Gorski listened impassively, his gaze fixed on the trees on the opposite side of the clearing. Now and again he lit a cigarette. Manfred felt quite calm as he described what had happened. He even enjoyed recalling some of the details of his meetings with Juliette, of his feelings as he had returned from the woods each evening.

He faltered only when it came to the killing itself. He turned his head away from Gorski as he described pulling the rug from beneath Juliette's body and carefully gathering up their belongings. From the corner of his eye he could see Gorski nodding his head slightly, as if what he said made perfect sense. When Manfred had finished, he said nothing. The woodpigeon continued to coo in the trees.

Eventually Gorski stood up. 'Let's go,' he said. He stretched out his hand as if to shepherd Manfred in the direction of the car.

Manfred followed him back through the clearing to the path. He felt quite calm. They drove back to Saint-Louis in silence. At certain points the Rhine loomed into view, its brown water as slow-moving and sluggish as mud. Manfred expected Gorski to take him directly to the police station, but he drove past it and pulled up further along Rue de Mulhouse outside his apartment. There was nobody about. Manfred looked at him.

'Aren't you getting out?' said Gorski.

Manfred was confused. 'Am I not to be arrested?'

Gorski shook his head slowly. 'We'll talk again tomorrow. I'd like you to tell me the truth about Adèle Bedeau.'

He leaned over and pushed open the passenger door. The hair on the back of his neck was neatly trimmed. Manfred got out.

'Don't go anywhere,' said Gorski.

Manfred stood on the pavement and watched as he made a slow turn and headed back towards the police station. He stood there on the pavement for some time. The man from the laundry room passed with his terrier, pausing for a few moments on the verge as the dog snuffled in some leaves. He did not appear to recognise Manfred.

TWENTY-TWO

Gorski parked in Rue des Trois Rois. The florist greeted him as cheerfully as ever. The weighty scent of flowers reminded him of the church. Perhaps it was the funeral that had made him come here. His own father's funeral had attracted only a handful of people. Ribéry had attended and sat discreetly at the back of the chapel. A few of his father's cronies from the Restaurant de la Cloche had scattered themselves among the pews behind Gorski and his mother. None of M. Gorski's customers had come.

Gorski bought a little bouquet of lilies. Mme Beck tried to refuse his money, but he insisted.

'I took a little soup up earlier,' she said.

'I'm very grateful,' said Gorski.

He took the stairs up to the apartment. He knocked lightly on the door, before pushing it open. It was never locked. His mother was asleep in her armchair. She looked very peaceful and Gorski thought about leaving without disturbing her. He found a vase in the old darkwood sideboard and went into the kitchen to arrange the flowers. When he returned his mother was awake.

'Hello, Georges, I wasn't expecting you.' She smiled weakly at him.

'I didn't mean to wake you,' he said.

'I was just resting my eyes.'

'I brought you some flowers.'

'So I see. You should be buying flowers for your wife, not for me,' she said. 'But thank you. They're beautiful.'

She struggled out of her chair and hobbled into the kitchen. She did not like to be helped. Gorski sat down at the table. He always sat in the same place. Mme Gorski returned some minutes later with a tray. Gorski poured out the tea. They sat in silence for a few minutes. It was very quiet in the little apartment.

Mme Gorski asked about Clémence.

'She's good,' said Gorski. 'Doing well at school.'

'And your wife?'

Mme Gorski never referred to Céline by name.

'Good,' said Gorski. 'Busy with the shop.'

Céline rarely visited and when she did she

made little effort to conceal her disdain for the little apartment, with its old-fashioned furnishings and decor. Gorski always felt ashamed of her behaviour. M. Gorski's chair was still in its place between them. Gorski could see the old man sitting there, his pipes arranged on the little side-table, newspaper draped over the arm of the chair.

'You remember the murder of the young girl in the woods?'

He was not sure what made him say it. He never spoke to his mother about his work.

'Of course,' she said. 'What was her name?'

'Juliette Hurel.'

'Yes,' she said. 'I remember it well.' She kept her eyes fixed on the window.

'We finally got the guy that did it,' he said.

Mme Gorski nodded almost imperceptibly. 'Your father would have been pleased,' she said.

Gorski swallowed hard and nodded. There was a bitter taste in the back of his throat. He let his breath out slowly. Then he got up and carried the tea things back to the kitchen.

'I'd better go,' he said.

He kissed his mother on the cheek. She gripped his hand for a moment.

'Bring Clémence round some time. I'd like to see her.'

'Yes, I will,' said Gorski. 'Soon.'

He had no desire to return to the police station. Gorski imagined how a cop like Lambert would celebrate the resolution of a twenty-year-old case, surrounded by admiring colleagues. Probably they would take over an entire bar and carouse into the night, a few favoured journalists hanging on the detective's every word. Lambert would not be troubled by a bad conscience about a tramp who had been quite content to spend his final years with a roof over his head.

Instead, Gorski took refuge in Le Pot. The bar was busy with post-work drinkers, unconsciously observing the unwritten law which dictated that workers stood at the counter while clerical and professional men occupied the tables. Gorski took what was becoming his usual seat and gestured to the proprietor that he would take a beer. The former teacher was at his place beneath the high window, a glass of white wine on the table in front of him. At the table in the corner were three youths, around twenty years old. They were fresh-faced, bourgeois boys clearly revelling in the rebelliousness of drinking in such a dive. Yves brought his beer. Gorski did not know if the proprietor knew he was a cop. If he did, he gave no sign of doing so. Bar owners did not welcome the patronage of policemen. The presence of a cop made the other customers uneasy, no matter how law-abiding they were. Gorski downed his beer in a couple of swallows and signalled to the proprietor to bring another.

If Gorski felt any satisfaction at the resolution of the Juliette Hurel case, it was of a melancholy kind. Had he been more competent, the case would have been resolved the first time round. He had been face to face with the guilty party and suspected nothing. And now, even if it were possible to bring charges against Manfred Baumann, it would do nothing for Gorski's reputation. In any case, the authorities would not consent to granting a posthumous pardon to Malou, and Baumann's confession would never be deemed admissible. Any lawyer worth his salt would see to that. And what would be gained by prosecuting Baumann? He was not a murderer in any meaningful sense. In the eyes of the law he was responsible for the death of Juliette Hurel, but he had not set out to kill her. In some ways, he had suffered the consequences of his actions as much as anyone.

Thus the conclusion of the case must remain a private matter. Gorski could not even go home to Céline and tell her that he had finally solved the murder that had blighted the early years of their marriage. Since the conviction of Malou, he had kept his thoughts about the matter to himself. Céline had found his fixation with the case distasteful and the knowledge that he had conspired in the conviction of an innocent man shamed him. It was better all round to keep up the pretence that the case was closed.

The only remaining question was whether Baumann's confession had any bearing on the case of Adèle Bedeau. The bank manager was, undeniably, a peculiar character. He had lied about his involvement in the waitress's disappearance and, as Gorski now knew, he had committed a murder on at least one occasion. Nobody Gorski had spoken to had anything positive to say about him. On paper, Baumann was a compelling suspect. Certainly the newspapers would have little trouble persuading their readers of his guilt. Yet Gorski was unconvinced. He did not place much importance on the fact that he had lied. Gorski had learned long ago that for even the most blameless people lying to the police was a reflex. As a cop, one's default position must be to believe nothing one was told. What mattered was not the bare fact that someone had lied, but their motivation for doing so. In the case of Manfred Baumann it was not yet clear whether he was lying because he had something sinister to hide or because he simply did not wish to become involved in a police investigation. Given what Gorski now knew of his history, the latter was possible, even understandable. On the other hand, perhaps he had been too quick to be taken in by Baumann's story. He had, after all, had twenty years to concoct his version of events. Perhaps it had not happened the way Baumann described it at all. Perhaps he had followed Juliette Hurel into the woods and done her to death to satisfy some murderous urge. Perhaps the whole story of the days they had spent together was nothing more than the inventions of a psychotic. By Baumann's own admission, his teenage self had displayed remarkable composure in covering his tracks and then, in the days and weeks that followed, betrayed no sign of what he done. Still, had Baumann wished to exonerate himself, he could simply have left out the unflattering details of how he had acted in the aftermath of the killing. The fact was that his story had the ring of truth to it. In any case, there was little Gorski could do to verify it one way or another.

Gorski ordered a third beer. The obese hairdresser came in. He walked to the bar, his thick legs splayed apart, and ordered a white wine. He had clearly had a couple already. He turned and surveyed the bar and spotted Gorski, who avoided his gaze.

'Inspector, how pleasant to see you in our humble establishment.'

Gorski looked up and acknowledged Lemerre with a curt smile. The former schoolteacher had looked up from his paper. Gorski found the hairdresser quite repellent. He waddled over to his table and spoke in a conspiratorial tone.

'Tell me, Inspector, how's the case coming along?'

'I'm sorry,' said Gorski, 'I can't discuss it.'

Lemerre leaned in closer. He smelled strongly of sweat.

'Come on, Inspector, I heard you gave Baumann the third degree.'

Gorski fixed him with a steely gaze.

Lemerre gave him a theatrical wink and tapped the side of his nose.

'So Baumann's for the high jump, eh?'

It mattered little what Gorski did or did not say. Lemerre was no different from the majority of individuals. People loved nothing more than a murder on their doorstep, preferably a bloody and vicious murder. The idea that something dramatic had happened in their midst lent a passing thrill to their lives. It fuelled conversation in bars like this for weeks.

'I can't comment. If you don't mind . . .'

Lemerre nodded meaningfully, as if by failing to deny his assertion, Gorski had favoured him with a choice morsel of inside information. He moved back to the bar. Gorski imagined how he would later regale anyone in the vicinity about how he had it on good authority that Manfred Baumann was soon to be done for the murder of Adèle Bedeau.

Now that Lemerre had blown his cover it would have been prudent to leave the bar at this point. He was no longer an anonymous drinker. He was a cop, around whom other drinkers must watch what they said. The conversation at the counter had become more subdued. It was not politic for Gorski to be seen getting quietly sozzled on his own. But he had no desire to go and sit around the dinner table with Céline. He should have telephoned to say he would not be home. Céline liked him to call if he was going to be late. But the beer had made him bloody-minded. He ordered another, a large one this time, like the ones the men at the bar were drinking. Did Gorski detect a change in Yves' demeanour towards him? Did he avoid making eye contact as he placed it on the table in front of him? It was probably his imagination.

The large glass felt pleasingly weighty in Gorski's hand. He took a healthy slug. Céline could go hang. Let her sit and seethe over her paltry, ruined dinner. They had nothing in common. They had never had anything in common. She resented him, and he resented her.

Lemerre did not stay long. After he left, the conversation at the bar picked up a little. Perhaps it had been on account of the hairdresser's presence, rather than Gorski's, that it had subsided. Still, the men at the bar also finished their drinks and drifted away. The three youths at the corner table remained absorbed in earnest conversation. They had not paid any attention to Lemerre's exchange with Gorski and appeared no more self-conscious than before. Clearly they were from well-off families, the sort of young men who were brought up to believe that they could achieve whatever they wanted to in life. Gathering in this least salubrious of Saint-Louis's bars was probably an act of revolt against the fathers who expected them to follow them into the family business or profession. They had long hair and wore heavy corduroy trousers. They held their cigarettes between their thumb and index finger and narrowed their eyes as they inhaled. One of them blew smoke rings, which made a slow ascent towards the now darkened window above them. They were discussing a writer Gorski had never heard of, listening earnestly to each other's opinions. No doubt they dreamt of defying their fathers and running off to Paris to write poetry or play jazz. Gorski empathised with them. Had he not become a cop simply to defy the expectations of his father, to assert some control over his life? Yet, he reflected, was it not the case that he would have been better suited to a life pottering around a pawnshop, in a brown store coat with a pencil behind his ear?

The youths became progressively drunker. Yves seemed unperturbed and continued to serve them round after round. What concern was it of his if they wanted to spend their fathers' money getting smashed? Gorski too began to feel the effects of the alcohol. The beer made him bloated, and he switched to wine. Later on, two men in suits, their ties loosened around their necks, came in and sat at the table next to Gorski's. They were in town on business and clearly out for a night on the tiles. They engaged Gorski in conversation.

'Where do you go for a bit of fun around here?' one of them asked.

Gorski shrugged. He was having trouble focussing. Yves observed the little scene from behind the counter.

The other man asked Gorski what line of business he was in and he told them.

'A cop?' said the man. 'Sorry, I . . .'

Gorski looked at them. They leaned back on their chairs and then returned to their own conversation. One of the youths got up and staggered towards the WC. He leant on the back of a chair, which toppled over under his weight. The boy collapsed on the floor, to the cheers of his companions. Yves came out from behind the counter and unhurriedly hauled the youth to his feet. The boy grinned stupidly at him. Yves planted him back on his chair.

'Time to go, boys,' he said matter-of-factly. The youths paid and piled out of the bar. They could be heard singing in the street.

Later, when Gorski returned home, he staggered upstairs without seeing the note Céline had left on the kitchen table and fell

asleep without noticing that she was not in
the bed.

TWENTY-THREE

The following day, Manfred rose at the usual time. He showered, set the coffee on the hob and dressed before sitting down to breakfast. He felt calm. He harboured no bitterness towards Gorski. If anything, it had been a relief to unburden himself. Gorski had made little or no comment as he related his story. He had betrayed no sign of judging him. Still, he was an officer of the law and it was his role to set in motion the mechanisms that the state had evolved to deal with such events. And, naturally, Gorski would use his confession to pin the business with Adèle on him as well. Manfred could hardly blame him. Would he not draw the same conclusions if he were in Gorski's shoes? But none of that mattered much anymore.

He left the building, as he always did, at 8.15. Despite the events at the Petite Camargue, Manfred still found himself hoping to bump into Alice. Of course, he would not blame her if she were to walk straight past him. On reflection, it was better that he did not see her. He would never see her again. The thought made him sad. Instead of turning right and walking along the Rue de Mulhouse towards the bank, he turned left and doubled back behind the building. Some Arabs were already loitering outside the Social Security office. He walked past the play park towards the railway station. It was a crisp, sunny morning. There were a few people around, but nobody gave him a second glance. Why should they? There was nothing remarkable about him and he had always kept himself to himself.

They would not miss him in the bank today. It would be assumed that he was taking care of his grandfather's affairs. It was quite normal to take a period of leave following a bereavement. Mlle Givskov would relish being left in charge. The Restaurant de la Cloche was another matter. As it was market day, Marie would reserve his table in the corner for 12.30. His non-appearance would certainly be noted. Marie would pass comment on the matter to Pasteur, who would reply with his customary shrug. Next Thursday his table would not be reserved for him and someone else would take his place, most likely ignorant of the fact that they were sitting at Manfred Baumann's table. The following week, his absence would not even be mentioned.

The station was busy with commuters. Some read newspapers. Others kept their eyes on the platform or occasionally glanced at the departure board. Nobody spoke. As Manfred arrived on platform three, a train pulled in. It was for Mulhouse. Several people boarded in an unhurried fashion. The carriages were not crowded. Manfred watched the train slowly pull out, then walked to the far end of the platform where there were fewer people. He was not familiar with the train schedule at this time of day, but another train was sure to arrive presently. It did not matter to Manfred where it was going. He had chosen platform three out of habit, since this was the platform from which trains for Strasbourg departed. It would be a simple matter to step off the platform. It was, after all, an action he had carried out hundreds of time. Today would be no different.

The sun was already warm. Perhaps Manfred should have waited in the shadow of the awning or checked when the next train would arrive, but that had not been part of his plan. In any case he did not want to draw attention to himself by walking back along the platform. He took out his handkerchief and wiped a few beads of sweat from his forehead. He had always disliked standing or sitting in direct sunlight. Years ago he had formed the opinion, rightly or not, that it contributed to the onset of his headaches.

A train approached the platform opposite. Manfred felt a tingling in his stomach. Nobody got off at Saint-Louis. When the train pulled out, the platform was empty, as if a magician had pulled his cloth from a birdcage. Manfred watched the heavy steel wheels of the train slowly pick up speed as the train drew away from the station. It was stupid not to have checked the timetable. Perhaps there would not be another train along for half an hour or more. He would begin to look conspicuous. But the fact that there was still a handful of people waiting suggested that a train would be along soon. Manfred's gaze followed the tracks beyond the station to the outskirts of the town. In the distance, a factory chimney belched grey smoke into the sky. He had been waiting for some ten minutes. Mlle Givskov would be arriving at the bank.

Finally a train pulled into view. It appeared to be travelling exceptionally slowly.

Manfred took a few steps back along the platform. He felt light-headed, perhaps on account of the sun. He had no idea if Gorski had any men watching him or whether they would make any attempt to intervene. It did not matter greatly. Manfred stepped up to the edge of the platform. He closed his eyes for a few moments, then felt a disturbance of air in front of his face as the train pulled in and came to a halt. Manfred opened his eyes, feeling as if he had been asleep for a moment. Then, without looking round, he opened the door and stepped onto the train. He did not hear anyone call his name or feel a hand on his shoulder.

The train remained in the station, as it always did, for a minute or two. Manfred's heart was racing. His brow was prickled with sweat. The other passengers buried their heads in books and newspapers. A man in his fifties stared blankly out of the window, registering nothing that passed before his gaze. Probably he had been making the same journey every day for years. Manfred expected Gorski to board the carriage at any moment and escort him onto the platform. The train seemed to remain stationary for longer than usual. Perhaps the driver had received a radio message informing him that there was a fugitive on board. But the police did not come and, at last, the guard sounded his whistle and the train jolted and eased out of the station. As it cleared first the platform, and then Saint-Louis, Manfred felt exhilarated. He sat completely still as if any movement would alert his fellow passengers to his presence. They were oblivious to the momentous events to which they bore witness.

The train picked up speed and Manfred watched farm buildings and scrubby fields flash by. And, quite suddenly, he was a fugitive from justice. He had, it appeared, evaded the clutches of the police. It was quite thrilling. All he needed to do when he reached Strasbourg was to change trains. Trains departed Strasbourg for destinations all over France, indeed, for all over Europe. Even if Gorski were to discover Manfred's absence in the next hour or so, no one appeared to have recognised him as he boarded the train. He would be in the clear.

Of course, there was the matter of money. Manfred had in his wallet sufficient identification to make a large withdrawal from his savings account. But it would not be difficult for the police to trace the time and location of any withdrawals he made. Perhaps a freeze would be placed on his assets. The thing to do was to close his account to cash before he changed trains in Strasbourg. There was a branch of Société Générale on Rue Moll, not ten minute's walk from the station. He could go there, take care of his business and be back at the station in half an hour. It was an additional risk, but preferable to giving away his whereabouts at a later date. Then he would board the next train out of Strasbourg. It did not matter where the train was heading; in fact, the more arbitrary the destination the better. He must not choose where he was going. He must leave it to chance. In any case, whatever his destination, he would travel on from there. At some point he could buy new clothes and get a haircut. Perhaps he would grow a beard. It was all quite simple. If a dimwit like Adèle Bedeau could disappear without a trace, surely he could do the same? Thousands of people disappeared every year. He had once read a magazine article about it. Within a few weeks he would be forgotten or presumed dead. As far as the state was concerned he would cease to exist.

Contrary to his usual practice, Manfred had not bought a ticket before boarding the train. Although it was possible to buy a ticket from the conductor, Manfred always imagined that doing so would lead to trouble of some kind. Perhaps the conductor's machine would be out of order or it would be suspected that he was attempting to travel without a ticket. In any case, conductors often seemed disgruntled by having to issue tickets on the train and made no attempt to disguise the fact. Today, however, there was no alternative.

Manfred waited nervously for the appearance of the official. Perhaps he would have received a message to keep an eye out for a man answering Manfred's description. A train conductor was, after all, in a minor way an agent of the state. The train pulled into Mulhouse. Manfred resisted the urge to get off. He must hold his nerve. The important thing was to put as much distance as possible between himself and Gorski.

The conductor appeared shortly after the train left Mulhouse. He was a young man, in his twenties. He wore his uniform in a slovenly manner and did not look like the type of person who was likely to carry out his duties with particular diligence. The other passengers in the carriage had all obtained their tickets before boarding, and the conductor gave them no more than a cursory glance. He made rapid progress along the carriage. Manfred asked for a return to Strasbourg. There was no point advertising the fact that he had no intention of coming back. The conductor nodded and drew round the ticket machine that was slung on a thick leather strap over his shoulder. Manfred explained that he had been in a hurry and had not had time to buy a ticket at the station. The conductor did not appear in the least bit interested. He issued the ticket and counted out Manfred's change.

When Manfred examined his ticket, he saw that the conductor had made it out from Mulhouse rather than Saint-Louis. Normally, Manfred would have drawn the conductor's attention to the error, but in the current circumstances it seemed a trifle. If questioned, Manfred need only say that he had put the ticket in his wallet without looking at it. In any case, the mistake had been the conductor's rather than his.

Countryside and towns sped past the window. Manfred was sitting, as he always did, with his back to the engine. He preferred to watch the scenery recede into the distance than loom up ahead. It gave him a sense of leaving places behind. He thought of the Restaurant de la Cloche, where Marie and Dominique would now be setting out the tables for lunch. One or two locals would be lingering over their morning coffee, a copy of *L'Alsace* spread on the table in front of them. The bank would now be open as normal. Carolyn would be going through his diary, cancelling his appointments. Perhaps she would have thought of calling his apartment to find out when he intended to return to work. But Manfred was sure she would not do so. She was too timid for such an intrusion. He thought of his apartment. After his rent lapsed, his possessions would be cleared out, and it would be rented to another occupant. It was a matter of some sadness to imagine his books and clothes being packed into boxes and most likely given away, but in the scheme of things it was a small sacrifice to make. It was part of the process of becoming a nonperson, of ceasing, for all intents and purposes, to exist.

The train was now twenty minutes from Strasbourg. Manfred began to feel anxious. Gorski must surely by now have discovered his absence. He had stated quite clearly that they would speak in the morning. Manfred pictured him pulling up outside his apartment in his dark blue Peugeot, dropping a cigarette to the pavement as he approached the building. Probably he would have brought another man, the young *gendarme* who had escorted him to the police station

377

perhaps, in case Manfred made trouble. How long would he remain at the door before he became suspicious? Would he kick it in or merely make his way to the bank in the expectation of finding Manfred there? In any case, he must by now be aware that Manfred had made a break for it and would be roundly cursing himself. Manfred, for his part, felt somewhat ashamed of how he was behaving. Gorski had treated him with a degree of civility he in no way deserved, and he had repaid him by fleeing in this cowardly manner. It was quite dishonour-able.

The train had slowed and was pulling through the industrial suburbs of the south-ern flank of Strasbourg. Manfred turned his thoughts to the business of closing his ac-count. The matter was fraught with difficul-ties. Manfred knew the procedure as well as anyone. Were a customer in his own branch to request such a large withdrawal, Manfred would expect the teller to summon him to supervise the transaction. And under such circumstances, Manfred would certainly enquire as to whether the client was no longer satisfied with the bank's services. Of course, no client was obliged to discuss the motives for their financial dealings, but the closure to cash of such a large account would, at the very least, raise eyebrows. Then Manfred remembered that he had on one or two occasions met the manager of the branch on Rue Moll. He would be sure to remember him and would think it strange, outlandish even, that Manfred wished to close his account and had come to another branch in order to do so. No, the whole enterprise was out of the question. Manfred took his wallet from the inside pocket of his jacket to confirm what he already knew: he had enough cash to cover his expenses for no more than a day or two. His exhilaration of an hour before was waning. The idea that he could evade Gorski's clutches and disappear without a trace was implausible enough, but without money it was unthinkable. What was he supposed to do? Turn to a life of crime, find some menial job in the black economy? He was hardly cut out for such things. Still, he had, without intending it, embarked on a course and he had no alternative but to follow it to its conclusion.

The train pulled into the station. Manfred was careful to conceal himself among the mass of passengers as he disembarked. Nobody checked his erroneous ticket as he left the platform. The concourse was busy. Clusters of travellers stood gazing up at the departure board, briefcases and bags at their feet. Commuters criss-crossed his path. Indecipherable announcements echoed from the tannoy. There did not appear to be any out-of-the-ordinary activity on the platform, nevertheless Manfred expected at any moment to be wrestled to the ground by a team of men, tipped off to his presence by Gorski. He would not resist. He had no desire to resist. In a way it would be a relief.

In an attempt to appear inconspicuous, Manfred strode purposefully across the concourse. He would go to the bank, after all, but withdraw only a modest amount of money, enough to see him clear for a week or two. He could worry about the long term later. The only thing he need think about at this juncture was to make good his flight Manfred slowed his pace. Two *gendarmes* were standing by the entrance to the station. They did not appear to have seen Manfred. He changed course and headed towards a kiosk which nestled beneath the departure board. Manfred watched the *gendarmes* for a few minutes from behind a newspaper stand. They did not appear particularly vigilant. Indeed, they seemed more interested in appraising the women who walked by than scanning the crowd for fugitives. Still, Manfred did not want to risk walking right past them. He bought a news-paper and moved towards the centre of the concourse, keeping the cops in his peripheral vision. They were a good twenty metres away. One of their radios crackled into life and the younger one spoke briefly into it. But they did not move from their post. Gorski must by now have gone to the station in Saint-Louis. It would be the first place he would look and he would surely call ahead to Strasbourg with a description of his quarry.

Manfred had to board a train without delay. He raised his eyes to the departure board. It was now 10.43. The next train was for Munich. Manfred rejected this. It was too risky to attempt to cross the border. The next three trains were local. That was no use either. The fifth was an express to Paris. Manfred's heart leapt for a moment. How easy it would be to disappear in such a metropolis. He could keep his head down for a few days and then, when things had settled down, move on. He had nothing but the clothes he was standing in and the few banknotes in his wallet, but, Manfred told himself, that was the way it had to be: that in order to disappear he had to leave everything behind. But Paris would be a mistake. The capital was the first place Gorski would expect him to go. After the Paris train was the 10.53 for Basel via Saint-Louis.

Manfred looked anxiously towards the entrance. The two *gendarmes* were now making a leisurely circuit of the perimeter of the station. The terminal was quieter now and he felt exposed in the middle of the emptying concourse. He opened his copy of *L'Alsace* and held it in front of his face. Perhaps tomorrow it would carry a picture of his face above a caption reading, *Fugitive sought in connection with disappearance of Saint-Louis waitress.*

Manfred glanced out from behind the paper. The two cops were now standing directly beneath the departure board, next to the kiosk. The smaller of the two, who had spoken into his radio, was looking directly at him. He was young and fresh-faced and was growing a moustache, in an attempt, Manfred thought, to make himself appear older. Manfred held his gaze for a moment. His heart was beating rapidly. It was not clear whether he was observing Manfred or merely happened to be looking in his direction. Then the older of the two, who had been perusing the headlines of the day's papers, nudged him and they moved off towards the centre of the concourse. Manfred folded his newspaper and started to walk towards the platform where, at any moment, the Munich train would pull in. It was all he could do to prevent himself from breaking into a sprint.

A few moments after 10.49, a crowd of onlookers gathered midway along platform nine and on the platform opposite, appearing as if from nowhere like pigeons around scraps of food. Some stepped forward to look down onto the rails, before turning away with their hands over their mouths. Those at the back craned their necks to catch a glimpse of what had occurred. The two duty cops pushed their way to the front of the crowd and stood for a few moments transfixed like the others, before remembering their official role in proceedings. They turned, as one, with their arms spread and began to shepherd the crowd back towards the concourse. The older one spoke into his radio. Further passers-by continued to gather at the back of the crowd and those who were already there provided them with accounts of what had happened.

'He was sprinting towards the train, then he tripped and fell onto the tracks.'

'No, he threw himself, he definitely threw himself,' said another.

'I saw the whole thing,' said a third man.

'He walked quite calmly along the platform and then stepped off. It was as if he was sleep-walking.'

The driver of the train was helped from the cabin. He was shaking his head, ashen-faced. Later, at the inquest, he would testify that he had not seen the man until he had stepped in front of the train and that he had had no chance whatsoever of applying the brakes in time. The station manager, having been alerted to the incident, arrived on the scene and, with the assistance of a gang of railway employees, began to cordon off the two platforms. The incident would cause a great deal of disruption to the day's timetable. The crowd of onlookers reluctantly began to disperse. When he had been assured that it was safe to do so, the younger of the two *gendarmes* climbed down onto the tracks and began to search through the victim's pockets for identification.

TWENTY-FOUR

The Restaurant de la Cloche was unusually busy for a Thursday evening. Two couples in their early thirties were eating together at the corner table. The women were attractive and fashionably attired. They had placed their orders only a few minutes before half past eight. They did not appear to be from Saint-Louis, at least neither Pasteur nor Marie had seen them before, and they were evidently in no hurry over their meal. They had ordered a second bottle of wine even before their main courses had arrived and a third was duly ordered. They chatted loudly and unselfconsciously and laughed raucously at each other's jokes. Pasteur glared at them from his station behind the counter, but they were oblivious to his black looks. He muttered to Marie as she passed that they must think they were in a Parisian bistro, his standard put-down for customers who he regarded as too loud, flashy or otherwise not to his liking. Marie smiled indulgently. She was in a good mood and was not going to let her husband's grouchiness spoil it. In any case, she enjoyed playing hostess to a younger, more fashionable clientele. The better class of customer liked to eat late and linger over their food. It would have been horribly provincial to refuse to serve them on account of an arbitrary rule. The Restaurant de la Cloche might not be a Paris bistro, but neither was it a canteen. Twice Marie had approached the table to enquire if everything was to her guests' satisfaction, resisting the urge to apologise for the rustic nature of the cuisine, and on both occasions had been heartily reassured. The young man in spectacles had even sent his compliments to the chef on account of the ham hock *terrine*. Marie had blushed deeply, the *terrine* being her own creation.

The two other parties still eating had obligingly agreed to have their coffee brought at the same time as their desserts. The tables by the window were occupied in the main by local people. Lemerre, Petit, and Cloutier were naturally in their place at the table by the door, the pack of cards in the centre of the table in readiness for the game that would soon begin.

Manfred was not at his place by the bar, and a man Pasteur believed to be a travelling salesman had taken his place. He lunched at the restaurant on an irregular basis. Pasteur was not surprised at Manfred's absence given some of the rumours that had been circulating. It made sense for him to keep his head down for a few days, but Pasteur was sure he would soon be back. The hubbub of conversation emanating from the tables by the window and from the crowd of customers gathered at the counter drowned out even Lemerre's voluble pontifications on the day's developments. Pasteur was in no doubt that the sudden popularity of the Restaurant de la Cloche was due entirely to its central role in the recent goings-on. He would be loath to admit it, but he gleaned a certain pleasure in his establishment's sudden notoriety and place at the centre of local life. Of course, things would quickly return to normal, but the publicity would not do business any harm.

Only the focal point of the day's drama seemed oblivious to the commotion. Adèle took the main courses to the group in the corner of the dining area at her usual languid pace and with her customary sullenness. She betrayed no sign of being aware that all eyes in the room were following her every move and that her reappearance was the subject of the most lurid speculations. When she had turned up shortly before lunchtime service, Marie had taken her upstairs for a talk. Pasteur was not privy to what had been said and nor would he ask. If Marie chose to divulge what had passed between them, she would do so in her own good time. Later, the cop, Gorski, had turned up and Adèle had again been summoned to the apartment. All Pasteur knew was that it had been agreed that Adèle would return to her former place on the rota. In addition, Marie had decided to keep her niece on to assist at lunchtime service. Pasteur had looked askance at this suggestion, but Marie had brushed off his objections. It would hardly be fair to dismiss the girl when she had so obligingly stepped into the breach caused by Adèle's absence. In any case, they were often short-handed at lunch and Dominique had only just learned the ropes. Pasteur had shrugged. Sometimes things changed. It couldn't be helped.

At the appointed hour, and despite the large number of customers still to be served, Pasteur joined Lemerre, Petit, and Cloutier at their table. His participation in the weekly game had already assumed the weight of tradition.

TRANSLATOR'S AFTERWORD

That this is the first appearance of *The Disappearance of Adèle Bedeau* in English is remarkable. In France, the novel has been almost continuously in print since its publication in 1982 and, since Claude Chabrol's screen version of 1989, it has achieved the status of cult classic. Certainly it is a novel in a minor key. Its protagonist, Manfred Baumann, is an ill-at-ease outsider, an observer of life rather than a participant. The novel is set in the unremarkable town of Saint-Louis on the French–Swiss border, a place where, as the opening pages make clear, few visitors wish to linger. And yet, for thirty years, readers have chosen to spend a little time there and to pass a few hours in the company of the maladroit Baumann.

Raymond Brunet was born in Saint-Louis, Haut-Rhin, on 16 October 1953, the son of a successful family lawyer. His mother, Marie, was barely out of school when she married Bertrand Brunet in 1948. He was forty-two. Marie was an exceptionally pretty girl from a family of shopkeepers. Childhood photographs show a smiling, vivacious girl often in the company of her pet terrier. Bertrand Brunet — undoubtedly the prototype for Manfred Baumann's grandfather in the novel — was a strict Protestant who disapproved of frivolity and did not enjoy socialising. It must have been a grim life for his young wife, and it seems likely that, confined to the family home, Marie succumbed to what we would now call depression. Certainly, she frequently retired to bed for days on end. Like a flower deprived of water, she wilted. It is no surprise that Raymond remained an only child.

Despite these unpromising circumstances, Raymond seems to have been a cheerful little boy. The grand family house on the outskirts of the town provided an excellent playground. He enjoyed hiding away in the nooks and crannies of the wood-panelled passages and, in summer, building dens among the trees at the bottom of the large gardens. For company he would hang around the kitchen, getting in the way of the housekeeper as she went about her chores. There was also a succession of maids to follow around, but they never stayed long enough for him to become attached. Like many an only child, Raymond could often be heard talking to himself or in earnest dialogue with his toys. At school he was well behaved and always close to the top of the class.

As a teenager, though, he became surly and withdrawn. Young children accept whatever situation they find themselves in as normal. As they grow older, however, they begin to see that not all families are like their own. Perhaps Brunet began to resent the austere atmosphere at home. In addition, he was lanky, socially awkward and suffered badly from acne, a condition that left his face scarred into adulthood. He was expected to follow his father into the legal profession, something he had no interest in doing, and the feeling that his destiny was not in his own hands weighed heavily on the young man. He began to read voraciously. In the summer he would go off on his bicycle with a packed lunch and a satchel of books, often to the woods of the Petite Camargue to the north of the town.

When Brunet was sixteen, his father was killed in a car accident. Late one night, his car left the A35 from Strasbourg and hit a tree. Most likely the lawyer had fallen asleep at the wheel. There were no suspicious circumstances, but nobody knew what he had been doing in Strasbourg that evening. It was a minor mystery which merited a few lines in *L'Alsace* newspaper. For Brunet, however, his father's death meant only a reprieve from the obligation to become a lawyer. Freed from parental pressure, he left school at the earliest opportunity and took a job in the office of a local insurance company. It was mundane clerical work but, according to his employer, he showed no signs of dissatisfaction. He arrived punctually and carried out his work diligently. He did not take much part in office banter; indeed, his predominantly female colleagues regarded him as somewhat aloof and superior. It was at this time that Brunet began to frequent the Restaurant de la Cloche, which was to become the principal setting of *La Disparition d'Adèle Bedeau.*

Brunet's first literary effort was a play in the absurdist tradition, based entirely in the restaurant. Many of the characters of the later novel appear in the play. *Au Restaurant de la Cloche* is a highly stylised, somewhat pretentious piece in which snatches of dialogue are repeated by different characters, mundane actions recur rhythmically and the ever-present proprietor comments on the action directly to the audience. It's a mish-mash of Beckett, Brecht, and Robbe-Grillet and of interest only as an insight into Brunet's influences at the time. In the autumn of 1978, Brunet sent it to the Paris theatre producer Max Givet, who rejected it as dated and derivative. The playscript was found among the producer's papers after his death in 1997. Aside from the present novel, it is Brunet's only surviving work.

Brunet continued to live in the family home, as he would for the rest of his life. His father's death had not altered the routine of the household much. As often as not, Brunet took his evening meal alone in the dining room, while his mother remained in bed. Afterwards, he would go upstairs and chat to her for a few minutes before retiring to what had been his father's study to read or write. Sometimes he went out and wandered around Saint-Louis, stopping off in one or another of the town's bars for a glass of wine or a *pastis*.

Brunet's awkward character made it difficult for him to form normal relationships, and it is possible he remained a virgin throughout his life. As far as we know, he never had a regular girlfriend. He may have visited establishments like the one depicted in Chapter Four of the present novel, but, other than the accuracy of the description, there is no evidence that he did so. Later, when he spent some time in Paris, some speculated or assumed that he was gay, but apart from his apparent lack of interest in women, this too is without foundation. His reported disinterest in the opposite sex should probably be more correctly ascribed to chronic shyness.

Brunet first submitted *La Disparition d'Adèle Bedeau* in March 1981. It was rejected by a number of publishers before being accepted by Éditions Gaspard-Moreau and appearing without great fanfare in the autumn of 1982. A number of favourable, though not rapturous, reviews were enough to justify a second and then a third edition. The book sold steadily for the next couple of years, but with no prospect of a follow-up on the horizon, it was allowed to fall out of print.

Around this time, Claude Chabrol, doyen of the cinematic New Wave of the early 1960s, came across a copy in a second-hand bookshop in Paris. The director was very taken with the novel's portrayal of provincial life and contacted the publisher. After a brief consultation with Brunet, the rights were sold to the famous director for a nominal sum. For both Gaspard-Moreau and Brunet it was a no-lose situation: the novel was out of print, and if a film were ever made, it would provide the book with a second wind. A script was swiftly written, but French cinema was at that time in thrall to the flashier talents of Luc Besson and Jean-Jacques Beineix, and the downbeat realism of *La Disparition d'Adèle Bedeau* was hopelessly out of step with the times. It was only when Chabrol passed the script to Isabelle Adjani, star of *Subway* and *One Deadly Summer,* that the project got off the ground. The then queen of French cinema agreed to play the role of Alice Tarrou, whose part in the story was greatly expanded. Adjani's involvement was enough to secure the necessary funding, and the film went into production in the summer of 1988.

Gaspard-Moreau prepared a new edition of the novel with an afterword by Chabrol to tie in with the film's release. The film was a far greater critical and commercial success than the original novel had ever been and, aside from some minor changes, is a largely faithful adaptation, with the Saint-Louis setting impeccably realised by Chabrol. Predictably, Brunet hated it. Following a specially arranged screening at Gaumont's headquarters in Paris, he locked himself in a toilet cubicle and could be heard sobbing loudly for fifteen minutes. In addition to the narrative changes, he felt that Manfred Baumann had been portrayed as a somewhat comic and pathetic figure. It was the reaction of a naive young man from the provinces who too closely identified with the protagonist of his book. It was not a fictional character he was watching on screen, but a projection of himself. Eventually, it was Chabrol himself who persuaded Brunet to emerge from the cubicle. The two men went to a nearby café, and the director managed to convince him that he had not intended to ridicule his protagonist — only to humanise him somewhat. The cinema audience, he told Brunet, was not as sophisticated as his literary readership — they required a little sugar in their coffee.

Brunet was sufficiently placated to attend the premiere. In order to capitalise on the attendant publicity, his publishers put Brunet up in a hotel on Boulevard Saint-Germain for a month or so. He was subjected to numerous interviews and, under strict instructions from his publisher, he kept his reservations about the film to himself. This was to be the only significant period of his life that Brunet spent away from Saint-Louis. He appeared to revel in the attention. For the first time, people wanted to be in his company and to listen to what he had to say. And if he behaved eccentrically . . . well, he was a writer — it was only to be expected. What he did find hard to deal with, however, was the constant stream of questions about his next book. In Paris, he discovered, everyone had a project on the go, or more likely a whole slate of projects in various states of development. Brunet took to enigmatically deflecting such queries by saying that he preferred not to discuss his work before it was completed, a strategy which only served to increase speculation.

After the premiere, a small party of cast and crew went for a late supper at a restaurant in the Latin Quarter. Some members of the cast, who were all too aware of Brunet's reaction to the film, spent much of the evening earnestly questioning him about his book, one or two of them promising to join him sometime for lunch at the Restaurant de la Cloche. Brunet was, of course, quite flattered by their attentions.

In all, he spent about six weeks in Paris. He seemed to enjoy his flirtation with celebrity and the company of the other writers and actors he met through Chabrol. He telephoned his mother every day, however, and these conversations often left him feeling morose. She complained of missing him and told him that his absence left her drained of all energy. Both Chabrol and his editor at Gaspard-Moreau, Georges Pires, tried to persuade him to move to Paris, arguing that it would be more conducive to his writing. Brunet was tempted, but in the end his mother won out, and he returned home.

After his sojourn in the capital, Saint-Louis must have seemed drearier than ever. The royalties from the sales of his novel allowed him to give up his job at the insurance office and concentrate on producing a second novel, for which his publisher had now paid an advance. Georges Pires telephoned regularly for progress reports. At first, Brunet spoke enthusiastically about his new project, but deadline after deadline passed and eventually Pires lost patience, telling him simply to get in touch when he had something to show him. Having given up his job, Brunet's days and weeks lacked structure. He lacked the self-discipline to follow a regular work schedule. He stayed in bed into the afternoon and then wandered from bar to bar until it was time to return for dinner. Ironically, the Restaurant de la Cloche was now off-limits. Many of the regular customers had by then read his book and did not take kindly to the way they had been depicted. Nor, in general, did the people of Saint-Louis approve of the portrayal of their town as a nondescript backwater. Rather than making him a local celebrity, Brunet's novel had made him an outcast. The last two years of his life were uneventful. He occasionally managed a short burst of activity, but he was unable to sustain it. He never sent a single page to Georges Pires. Then, on 24 August 1992, he went to the railway station in Saint-Louis and threw himself in front of the 17.35 to Strasbourg.

His death merited a mere two sentences in *L'Alsace:*

> The novelist Raymond Brunet, 38, of Saint-Louis, yesterday threw himself under a train. He is survived by his mother, Marie.

He left no note. The desk in his father's study was entirely empty. Clearly, Brunet had prepared the way for his suicide by destroying his notebooks. As is often the case with such incidents, no one who knew him had any inkling of his state of mind. Raymond Brunet was not in the habit of unburdening himself, and even if he had been, it is hard to imagine to whom he would have spoken. Throughout his life, he found it impossible to form the kind of relationships, either passing or profound, which come naturally to most people. It would be futile to speculate on whether he suffered from a diagnosable mental condition — we shall never know. The tragedy is that, as the short period he spent in Paris proved, he was capable of happiness. Had he found the courage to leave Saint-Louis, his life might well have turned out differently. And we might have more than one Raymond Brunet novel to enjoy.

As it is, we have *The Disappearance of Adèle Bedeau.* It is not for a translator to offer a critique. Those who are making their first acquaintance with the novel deserve to do so unencumbered by the opinions of others. However, one thing is worth making clear — while there are many parallels between the novel and the life of Raymond Brunet, *The Disappearance of Adèle Bedeau* is a work of fiction. The Restaurant de la Cloche and Saint-Louis itself are exactly as they are described in the novel (and remarkably unchanged) and a few of the characters are clearly based upon real people. The events of the novel, however, are entirely

400

invented. Brunet became tetchy when interviewers suggested that his novel was autobiographical, construing this as a slight upon his powers as a writer. In the preface to his autobiographical novel *Pedigree*, Georges Simenon wrote that 'Everything is true while nothing is accurate'. It is as fitting a formulation for *The Disappearance of Adèle Bedeau*.

GMB, February 2014

ACKNOWLEDGEMENTS

I would like to express my deep gratitude to Victoria Evans for her support, encouragement and wise counsel throughout the writing of this novel.

Thanks also to David Archibald, Craig Hillsley, Sara Hunt, Sonia Hurel, and Thomas Stofer for invaluable editorial advice. I would also like to acknowledge the support of the Scottish Book Trust through its New Writers Awards scheme.

Finally, this book would not have been written without the unstinting patience, love and understanding of my girlfriend, Jen Cunnion. Thank you.

ABOUT THE AUTHOR

Graeme Macrae Burnet has established a reputation for smart and literary mystery writing with his highly praised novel, *His Bloody Project*, which was named a finalist for the Man Booker Award in 2016. He was born and brought up in Kilmarnock and has lived in Prague, Bordeaux, Porto, and London. He now lives in Glasgow, Scotland.

The employees of Thorndike Press hope you have enjoyed this Large Print book. All our Thorndike, Wheeler, and Kennebec Large Print titles are designed for easy reading, and all our books are made to last. Other Thorndike Press Large Print books are available at your library, through selected bookstores, or directly from us.

For information about titles, please call:
(800) 223-1244

or visit our website at:
gale.com/thorndike

To share your comments, please write:
Publisher
Thorndike Press
10 Water St., Suite 310
Waterville, ME 04901